Lesley Green is an Occupational Health Advisor, responsible for advising management and staff on health issues that could be affected by work. She trained at Guy's Hospital London, and spent three years as an officer in the Army. This is her first book.

LESLEY GREEN

HILDA ANNERSLEY HEADMISTRESS

Copyright © 2005 Lesley Green

The moral right of the author has been asserted.

Apart from any fair dealing for the purposes of research or private study,
or criticism or review, as permitted under the Copyright, Designs and Patents
Act 1988, this publication may only be reproduced, stored or transmitted, in
any form or by any means, with the prior permission in writing of the
publishers, or in the case of reprographic reproduction in accordance with
the terms of licences issued by the Copyright Licensing Agency. Enquiries concerning
reproduction outside those terms should be sent to the publishers.

Matador
9 De Montfort Mews
Leicester LE1 7FW, UK
Tel: (+44) 116 255 9311 / 9312
Email: books@troubador.co.uk
Web: www.troubador.co.uk/matador

ISBN 1 904744 91 5

Cover illustration: Andy Clarke

Typeset in 11pt Stempel Garamond by Troubador Publishing Ltd, Leicester, UK
Printed by The Cromwell Press, Trowbridge, Wilts, UK

Matador is an imprint of Troubador Publishing

For Rachael Pelter; for your encouragement, ideas and help. This couldn't have been written without you.

CONTENTS

Foreword ix

Acknowledgements xi

CHAPTER ONE	Echoes and Awakening	1
CHAPTER TWO	Meeting Bill	12
CHAPTER THREE	Worst Case Scenario	27
CHAPTER FOUR	The German	43
CHAPTER FIVE	Faith	58
CHAPTER SIX	The Severn Bore	71
CHAPTER SEVEN	Six Months On	88
CHAPTER EIGHT	A Troubled Child	97
CHAPTER NINE	Sybil	112
CHAPTER TEN	Christmas	122
CHAPTER ELEVEN	The Tyrol	135
CHAPTER TWELVE	Escape From Tyrol	148

CONTENTS

CHAPTER THIRTEEN	Family	163
CHAPTER FOURTEEN	Decision	173
CHAPTER FIFTEEN	The Telegram	187
CHAPTER SIXTEEN	Co-Heads	199
CHAPTER SEVENTEEN	The Return	209

FOREWORD

This book details the time, a little over a year, from when Hilda Annersley, Headmistress of the Chalet School, was first injured in a road accident until her return to the school having fully recovered. For those people that collect the series it is therefore fairly easy to place it. It runs alongside the books, *Gay From China at the Chalet School, Jo to the Rescue, Mystery at the Chalet School, Tom Tackles the Chalet School* and *Rosalie of the Chalet School.* There are occasional references to things happening in these books throughout the story.

For those that have not read the series, or have only read a few books, a little background might be in order. The Chalet School was founded and started by Madge Bettany on the banks of the Tiernsee, a lake in the Austrian Tyrol. The first pupil was her much younger sister, Joey. The series, starting with *The School at the Chalet*, traces the development of the school itself and of the Bettany family, following them through moving the school from Austria, to Guernsey, to Hereford and then an island off the Welsh coast and finally to Switzerland. During that time Madge Bettany marries Jem Russell, a doctor setting up a Sanatorium in the Austrian Alps and later Joey marries Jack Maynard, Jem's lieutenant. At the time of this book, the Chalet School is in Hereford, having had to leave both Austria and Guernsey due to the Nazi regime. The flight from Austria was particularly harrowing as Joey Bettany and Nell Wilson, Senior Mistress and friend to Hilda Annersley, had to escape with a number of pupils after an encounter with Nazi thugs in a nearby town. The school was then also ordered to leave.

Hilda Annersley joins the school in its third year, initially as English Mistress, but rapidly progresses to Senior Mistress and then Headmistress, a role she keeps for the remainder of the series. While a fairly significant character, she had only a small amount of background – some tantalising glimpses into her past. I have tried to use these glimpses and build a far more detailed picture. Details about her home life, age, education and even her motivation are sketchy and I have invented a number of items that seemed to fit.

Dating within the Chalet School is always difficult; some of the books were written out of sequence and the author revised and changed her characters ages and dates of significant events to suit the story. However, one episode she cannot change is the date of the start of WW2 and as Joey Maynard's triplets are born only two months later, they are used as a reference point. I have dated the start of my book to just before the Summer term in 1943, the book continues through until May 1944. While there may be some that disagree with my dates, I am at least as accurate as the author of the original series!

ACKNOWLEDGEMENTS

Firstly, Elinor Brent-Dyer, author of the Chalet School series. For a series of children's books to still have such popularity more than 35 years after her death – the author must have made them very special. Thank you for creating the world and people of the Chalet School, I sincerely hope that you would have liked my ideas on developing some of your characters.

Next, for the website The Chaletian, and in particular the Chaletian Bulletin Board. Devised by Liss Havilland, this board was the reason I began to write, it rekindled my love for the series and allowed me access to many like-minded fans. Also for Liss's expertise in setting up a website to promote the book. Thanks Liss!

Finally, the members of the board, for their encouragement and support, some gave particular help when I was writing the book, some just gave encouragement. Among them I'd like to thank Rachael, Jennie, KB and Lisa_T. There are a great many others who have also helped, too many to list.

CHAPTER ONE

ECHOES AND AWAKENING

There was a smell, petrol, strong, and sounds, shouting, some screams. It was impossible to detect more. Then the voice came to her from far away....

"Go to the police box in the next street," the voice had a soft Devonshire burr. "Ask for both ambulances and the police. There are some serious injuries," a pause, then the voice continued, "Ask for a priest too."

A different voice, female, "Can I help Constable? I'm a nurse."

"Yes ma'am, I'd appreciate it if you could look after this lady," his voice lowered, "A serious head injury ma'am, I don't think she'll live."

"Yes I can see that, have you seen the blood from her ear is watery?"

"No, I hadn't noticed that, what does it mean?"

"That this lady has a fractured skull, very serious. What about the others?"

"Some dead that I can see, the driver is, the conductress looks badly hurt too and an old man. The rest have various injuries but not life threatening. Except her."

"Well don't worry," the female voice continued grimly, "I'll take care of her, you look after the others."

The voices faded...

* * *

"How is she nurse?" a low, cultured voice.

"Stable sir, I thought she was rousing earlier but the 'Coma

Scale' is unchanged."

"Well continue the observations every fifteen minutes, and remember that even when deeply unconscious a body can sometimes still hear!"

"Yes doctor," the voice was long-suffering, "I am well aware of that!"

Footsteps moved the owner of the cultured voice over to the other side of the room. "You see the situation Sir James?"

A different voice, a known one, replied, "Perhaps you could give me an update?"

"I understand that you are standing as next of kin?"

"Yes, a hold over from when we were in Austria, the School is down as next of kin for most of the Staff, and as my wife is unwell..."

"Understood, well your friend had a severe head injury causing a fracture to the skull and a sub-dural haematoma..." he stopped as another voice suddenly spoke.

"Doctor!" The voice was exasperated, young and well known. "I need to know exactly what has happened to Hilda Annersley, and I need to be told in layman's language. I would not expect you to understand me if I were speaking Russian, nor do I think you should expect that I understand medical language without the training." A golden voice.

"Jo!" The male voice sounded both exasperated and embarrassed, "I know you are upset but..."

"No problem Sir James, I have a tendency to lecture! Mrs Maynard, put simply, Miss Annersley fractured her skull and badly bruised her brain due to the accident, and this caused severe bleeding within her skull. The skull is an almost closed box and there is nowhere for the blood to go."

"You mean it presses onto the brain?"

"Yes, with sometimes fatal results. In Miss Annersley's case she was lucky."

Sir James' voice: "You performed surgery?"

"Yes, burr holes—that is holes drilled into the skull Mrs Maynard, to relieve the pressure—you may have heard of it as 'trephining'? I believe it was sufficient but she will take some time to recover consciousness and a long time to return to her normal self."

"Will she make a full recovery?"

"That I cannot say. With head injuries, especially complicated by surgery, there are far too many variables. At the moment I cannot even say if she'll recover consciousness, although the signs are good."

"There was no spinal damage?"

"No Sir James, but as I'm sure you are aware damage to the brain itself can leave disabilities far more drastic than those from a severed spine."

"Oh Jem, not that for Hilda!"

"That's enough Joey; I think we should be going now. Many thanks Mr Roberts for allowing us access..."

* * *

"Dammit nurse I've got to see her, it'll only be for a few minutes." A new voice roused the patient in bed although not fully towards consciousness. The voice continued brokenly, "you don't understand, it was my idea we holiday together, and my idea we travel to Devon and Cornwall. If she were to die...."

"That's not going to happen, Miss Wilson," the voice was soft, understanding, "Miss Annersley is making good progress, we fully expect her to awaken in the next week or so and you are not yet fit to be out of bed yourself, it's only ten days since the accident, your leg needs more time to heal properly."

* * *

The voice was extremely irritating, "Open your eyes, Hilda, come on, open your eyes for me," she was very tired and the voice would not shut up! Eventually, to stop the noise she opened her eyes slightly but was unable to focus on anything.

The voice continued to give commands, "Good, now squeeze my hand," she felt her left hand being held. "Squeeze my hand, that's it, now talk to me Hilda, what's your name? Give me your full name."

The voice would not stop! The patient mumbled her name crossly, "Hilda, Mary, Annersley!" Now perhaps the voice would stop.

"Any luck, Jan?"

"Yes, doctor, she's definitely 'coming round', she's obeying commands and is able to repeat her name."

"Excellent, let's hope her progress continues, call me immediately she wakes."

* * *

Hilda Annersley slowly awoke, for some time she lay staring up at the ceiling, her brain slowly assimilating that she had regained consciousness. Eventually she moved her eyes to look at her surroundings. She was in a small, square room; there was a large window to one side with heavy blackout curtains and, on the opposite wall, an alcove. In front of her was a single door. The room had little furniture; she could see only her bed, a locker, a table and a chair. There were hospital screens stacked against the wall. It was night and the blackout curtains were drawn, electric lighting was bright and painful on her eyes.

Hilda noted that she was lying, almost flat, on her back in the bed. She looked down at herself and saw a plaster cast on her right arm and a transfusion running into her left. Moving her head slightly she was unable to stop an agonised groan escaping; she was aware of an all-consuming and severe pain in her head, far greater than anything she had ever experienced before. The pain seemed to affect her entire body; every movement seemed to cause additional shooting pains in her head and bouts of nausea. In addition she noted sharp pains in her right wrist and her chest. She also felt that her head was wrapped in cotton wool, almost as though she had 'stepped outside' her body!

A movement caught her eye and she glanced over towards the door. A young woman in a nurse's uniform was coming in, her eyes lit up as she saw her patient was awake. She moved toward the bed,

"You're awake finally," she smiled, "it's good to see you."

Hilda swallowed; her mouth feeling exceptionally dry and when she spoke it was barely above a whisper, "Where am I?"

"In hospital, Royal Devon and Exeter Hospital, you were in an accident. You have been in a coma for the past three weeks." The nurse's voice had a slight Cockney twang.

"Three weeks?" she whispered.

The nurse nodded, "Yes, it's April 29th today, your accident was on April 9th."

"I can't remember any accident."

"You hit your head in the accident; your memory could be affected. What's the last thing you can remember?"

Hilda's eyes closed slowly then re-opened. "I remember the last day of school," she said, haltingly.

The nurse looked concerned, "School? But how old were you? What year was that?" she appeared rather worried.

Hilda lifted an eyebrow, finding even that movement painful. "I was 38," she said dryly, "and it was 1943!"

The nurse looked puzzled for a moment then her brow cleared, "Oh of course! You're a school mistress aren't you?"

"Headmistress," the reply was firm. "But I don't understand," a puzzled note. "The last memory I have is April 1st, last day of term at school." A look of bewilderment on her face; "You say my accident was April 9th. Why can't I remember anything further?" Her voice showed some anxiety.

"Because you have had a severe head injury," a masculine voice answered. A man entered the room. "Good to see you are awake Miss Annersley," he continued. "I am Paul Roberts, your neurosurgeon; I operated on you just under three weeks ago." He came into the room and ran a practised eye over his patient before sitting in the chair by the side of the bed.

"Now," he continued, "as I said, you have had a severe head injury, you have also required brain surgery, your memory will be affected. You may never retrieve those missing days but that is a normal reaction, all right?"

Hilda nodded slightly, then hissed as the movement produced an escalation in both pain and nausea.

"Try to keep still for now, Miss Annersley, you will find it very painful otherwise." The doctor faced his patient before continuing, "I'm afraid there is nothing I can give you for the pain. Any drugs would mask symptoms relating to your head injury, so you will have to cope without analgesia."

She closed her eyes in acknowledgement, "What else?" she whispered.

"Other injuries? Nothing as serious, but you've broken your right wrist and a couple of ribs, you've also got extensive bruising." Mr Roberts paused then continued, "Your head injury is going to take a long time to heal, you will have to be patient."

Hilda smiled, "I'm a very patient person." Her eyes grew heavy and, within seconds, she had fallen asleep.

The next time Hilda awoke it was to discover that daylight was flickering in through the open window. Two nurses helped her wash and change and then she was allowed to sit a little more upright in the bed. Although her head still ached abominably, the detached feeling she had experienced before seemed to have eased.

"Are you feeling any better?" It was the nurse with the London accent. Miss Annersley looked across at her more closely; the nurse was only in her early twenties, a little below average height and slim. She had short blonde hair and deep blue eyes. She was very pretty with soft, friendly eyes but a no-nonsense chin.

"A little, I still feel very confused, and thirsty," the last with some surprise.

The nurse smiled, "We've removed the drip now so you're bound to feel that. I'll get you a drink first, then you can ask me any questions you like." She suited action to words.

Hilda drank almost two glasses of water without pausing for breath and then sank back on her pillows, "What's your name Nurse?"

"I'm Jan, Jan Wetherall."

"Tell me please about the accident," she whispered.

"I'm not sure of all the details but I understand you were in a bus, on a hill, when the steering failed and the bus ran into a wall and overturned. The driver and a couple of others were killed but otherwise you were the most seriously hurt. Your friends were injured too but not so badly..." She stopped as her patient gripped her arm tightly.

"My friends?" the voice was worried.

"Yes Miss Annersley, you were with three friends, I think they are also teachers, a Miss Wilson, a Miss Edwards and a Mademoiselle de Lachenais (this last pronounced with difficulty); wait a moment." She disappeared out of the room to return with a nursing log book. "Yes I thought so, your friends were all transferred here a few days after you, one of them even tried to get in to see you," she continued. "A very forceful attempt apparently."

Hilda smiled slightly, "That would be Miss Wilson," she said with authority.

"How did you know? You were deeply unconscious at the time, can you remember it?"

"No, but it's exactly what she would do." Her voice was faint but amused. "She's very determined!"

The nurse nodded and then continued, "She has requested to see you as soon as you are awake."

Hilda interrupted, "I would like to see her please." It was not a request.

The nurse looked worried, "You are not allowed visitors yet." She stopped seeing the concern in her patient's eyes, "I'll see what I can do."

* * *

Some time later the door opened to admit a nurse pushing a wheelchair, in the wheelchair sat Nell Wilson. Hilda could see lines of pain in her friend's face and that she had lost a lot of weight. Her left leg was encased in plaster and she had assorted cuts and bruises visible on her face and arms.

The nurse spoke quietly, "You can have just a few minutes."

For her part Miss Wilson was horrified at the sight of the Headmistress. Hilda Annersley was as white as her sheets except around her eyes, which were still purple and swollen with bruising. She was very thin and frail-looking, an appearance exacerbated by the plaster cast on her right wrist and the severe bruising on both arms. A large bandage covered her head and her voice, normally low and rich, was faint and croaking. As she moved or spoke waves of pain and nausea caused her to wince and stop, so her movements and speech seemed disjointed.

Miss Wilson was pushed toward the left side of Hilda's bed; once she was positioned she grasped her friend's hand, "Hilda, I'm so glad to see you."

Hilda looked across at her visitor and was astounded to see that she had tears running down her face. "Nell, you're crying!" Her voice was full of wonder, " I don't think I've ever seen you cry before!"

Nell Wilson brushed the tears from her eyes impatiently. "Of course I'm crying! I thought you were dead! Until yesterday we didn't even know if you were going to recover consciousness!" She took a shuddering breath then continued. "Hilda, I am so sorry. All of this is my fault!"

Hilda Annersley smiled slightly, "Your fault Nell?" her eyes closed then re-opened very slowly. "Hardly! Unless you're saying that you were responsible for the failure of the steering on that bus !"

"No, but it was my idea that you came with me to visit Cornwall, because you needed a break! Hell, Jack Maynard practically forced you to take a break!" She laughed scornfully, "And I chose our route." She stopped as Hilda raised a hand.

"I have absolutely no memory of any of this, Nell, and I'm told that I may never recover that memory. But you are being ridiculous." Hilda stopped as a wave of pain and sickness swept across her, then continued, "It was an accident, you have no reason to feel guilty. I shall recover, in time."

"I hope so," Miss Wilson paused, "I never realised how much you meant to me, until I thought I was going to lose you. I know we've been friends for a long time, and that these past three or four years we've been especially close—what with the war, and Con Stewart getting married and all." She stopped for a moment before continuing.

"The night we were transferred over to this hospital, you spent hovering between life and death. I know that both Jem Russell and Jack Maynard thought so, they stayed overnight, waiting. Dollie was too ill to be told—she's still weak—but Jeanne and I stayed awake all night. When Jem came in at 6am to say you'd survived the night..."

She swallowed hard then continued. "I know you have family, Hilda, but I don't, not close anyway. You are the nearest thing I have to a family and it took seeing you almost die for me to appreciate that." Nell Wilson flushed slightly as she admitted her innermost thoughts. "Don't worry," she smiled. "I don't expect you to feel the same way!"

Hilda paused as a wave of nausea hit, she concentrated, since regaining consciousness she was aware that her thought processes were muddled, but one thing, above all else was clear, the feelings she had for the woman by her side. She struggled to put it into words, "Yes, I have family, Nell," she began quietly, "but my brothers are both a great deal older than I; we have never been very close. I have cousins too, but again we have lost touch." She grasped Nell's hand tightly before continuing. "I care a great deal more for you. When the nurse told me that friends of mine had also been involved in the accident I immediately thought of you. And I needed to see you straight away." She took a breath before continuing quietly.

"You used to have a sister didn't you, Nell?"

"Yes, she died."

"I've never had a sister," she looked over at her friend, "but I've always wanted one. We can be family to each other, if you'd like." Hilda smiled shyly and Nell Wilson nodded in agreement, further tears running down her cheeks.

Both women were silent for a time; Hilda tightened her grip on Nell's hand as another bout of pain swept over her. Once the pain in her head had receded she turned to her Senior Mistress.

"How badly were you injured, Nell?"

Miss Wilson indicated her left leg ruefully, "I broke this one again! Same one I injured in the Tyrol. I also had numerous cuts and bruises. Luckily I didn't lose consciousness at the time of the accident, so was able to help the emergency services with identification. Both Dollie and Jeanne were knocked out for a short time, and you, of course, were out for nearly three weeks!"

"So I've been told!" Hilda's voice was quietly amused. "Being able to see all that happened after the accident can't have been p-pleasant," she continued.

Nell shook her head, "Not really, I was frantically trying to find out what had happened to you, Jeanne and Dollie and then, just to really make me feel good, I was being asked by the ambulance people if you were Catholic as they felt that, if so, you needed the Last Rites!"

Hilda Annersley glanced over at her friend in mock seriousness, "I hope you told them the truth? I'd have had trouble explaining things to my father if I'd reached Heaven as a Roman Catholic!"

Nell laughed, the first time she had seemed happy since entering the room. "You mean an Anglican Bishop would not have understood?" she smiled. "Don't worry, I wouldn't have done that to you. Anyway you were rushed off first—brought directly to this hospital as the neurosurgeon was here. The rest of us were originally taken to the local hospital and they transferred us over here a couple of days later."

"What happened to your hair?" Miss Annersley was having difficulty now keeping her eyes open.

Miss Wilson reached up to her head, her long thick hair, almost white since her adventures in Spartz during the Anschluss, had been cropped. "They had to cut it, I was bleeding badly from some cuts to the head and they couldn't find them. Luckily my hair grows quickly!"

Nell then informed Miss Annersley of the condition of the other two victims including their injuries and current condition. "Jeanne is getting on fine, she sends her love by the way, she has broken an arm and a bone in her foot but they are healing well.

She's a little worried about whether she'll regain all her strength but says it'll be a while before she can climb in the Alps anyway!" she smiled, and then continued. "Dollie's had a bad time, she had a compound fracture to her leg and there's always the possibility that bone infection will set in. They operated on her the day after you but they think she'll make a full recovery. They've got some of that new drug Penicillin, it's supposed to make infection a thing of the past." She stopped there, Hilda Annersley's eyes had closed and she appeared to be asleep.

The nurse touched her arm, "She will be sleeping a lot for the next few weeks, Miss Wilson. You'd better come away." The chair was quietly wheeled to the door.

A soft voice stopped her. "Nell," Miss Annersley's eyes remained closed but her voice carried, "you're not still blaming yourself are you?"

Nell turned, her eyes dark, "Oh Hilda, it's not that simple. I have never felt so helpless as when I saw you lying there in the road. Not even in Spartz that day, at least then I could do something. But there was nothing I could do for you, all I could do was pray."

"Well your prayers obviously helped—I survived didn't I? You just continue to remember me in your prayers. Our God does not blame you," the blue-grey eyes opened again and looked directly at her friend, "and neither do I."

CHAPTER TWO

MEETING BILL

"These are the last three, Hilda, Happy Birthday and God Bless. Thinking of you. Madge." The white haired woman picked up the final two cards.

"There's a telegram from India, Hilda, *Many Happy Returns of the Day! I'm sure you'd rather be celebrating elsewhere but never mind, Dick and I will not be back in England for some months yet—you are sure to be fit by then and we'll be able to treat you. Love Mollie, Dick and Second Twins.*"

"And this card's from Joey," Nell Wilson, still thin but looking far better than two weeks before, picked up the last card to read to Hilda Annersley. "*Hilda, glad to hear you're still improving—slow but sure! Don't worry about the School; we'll still be here when you get back! Many happy returns of the day, tell Bill not to eat all the cake! Have enclosed latest photo of Steve—isn't he bonny? Will be along to see you at Half Term. Love Joey.*"

Miss Annersley looked at the photograph, "He looks like Jack," she observed quietly; she was still having difficulty speaking, but had admitted that the pain and nausea were less of a problem if she kept still.

Miss Wilson looked down at her friend; Hilda was still on strict bed rest and allowed to sit up only for very short periods. However she did appear to be sleeping less and Nell took that for a good sign. Between them Nell and Jeanne de Lachenais had visited their Head each day, although only able to stay for a few minutes they had both thought they had seen minute improvements in her condition: however there had been some shocks.

Ten days before Hilda had been seized with an acute attack

of pain and sickness while Nell was in the room. In addition, while being shepherded out, Nell had seen that the bandage covering Hilda's head had suddenly become stained with blood. Nell swallowed as she thought back to that day; she had genuinely thought that her friend had suffered a fatal haemorrhage. It wasn't until a number of hours later that one of the nurses had reported that the blood had mainly come from the surgical wound, not because of further brain trauma.

Miss Wilson had also had a chance to speak to Jem Russell and found out exactly how precarious Hilda's hold on life had been just after her surgery. And she knew that it would be a long time before Hilda could even consider returning to her normal life.

In appearance there had been little change to the Head; the bruises around Hilda's eyes had slowly faded; however the swelling remained and Nell had noticed that Hilda could still not keep her eyes open for long. Because of the continual nausea an infusion had been restarted and, as her other hand was still encased in a plaster, Hilda was unable to do very much to help herself. In addition, she had been banned from attempting to read anything—including the numerous cards and letters received from the school.

Nell had enlisted the help of one of Hilda's nurses with regard to the post from the School, and ensured that herself or Jeanne saw all post before being passed on. They did not want any hint of difficulties to reach Hilda. Joey had sent another letter—this one to Nell—practically begging both Nell and Jeanne to return.

Nell recalled herself to the present as one of the nurses appeared to inform her that the visit was over. "Hilda," she said softly while slowly standing and clutching her stick, "I'll not be seeing you for a while, tomorrow I'm returning to the school."

Hilda Annersley looked round, frowning, "I-I-isn't that rather sudden?"

Nell laughed, "Oh no, it's been planned for over a week now. I think they need the beds!"

"Are you sure you're fit enough? You started walking only a

few days ago. And your leg is still in plaster."

"I'm fine! My leg has almost completely healed and I need the exercise." Miss Wilson's voice had a jovial quality to it. "I'll not be able to see you until half term at the earliest."

Miss Annersley nodded slightly, "I understand," she whispered, "you just take care Nell, I would not want you to go back too soon and hurt yourself."

"I'll be fine, and Jeanne should be fit in a few weeks, then it'll only be Dollie and yourself." She bent to kiss her friend's cheek, "Now you get well, and obey your nurses!" She left quickly to avoid any more questions.

Hilda Annersley watched her leave, aware that something was wrong; she had the strangest feeling that her closest friend had just lied to her.

* * *

The nurse with the London accent re-entered the room after seeing Miss Wilson out. She re-arranged her patient's pillows and placed some more of the cards on the bedside locker and table.

"You'll miss your friend now she's going, won't you?"

"Yes, I have relied on her visits these last two weeks," Hilda answered absently.

"Can I have a look at your cards, Miss Annersley?" the nurse asked.

Hilda looked round, "I beg your pardon, Jan, what did you say?"

"I said, can I look at your cards?"

There was a moment's silence when it seemed that the woman in the bed was having an internal debate about something, "Yes, of course you may, Jan."

Jan looked through all of the more recent birthday cards.

"That's a lovely-looking baby, and your friend Joey sounds fun. Is this 'Bill' another friend of yours?" the nurse asked innocently.

Miss Annersley smiled faintly. "Bill is the School name for

Miss Wilson, strictly behind her back of course. Joey Maynard is an ex-pupil of the School and therefore uses the name."

"Oh I see," Jan Wetherall found this amusing, "Doesn't Miss Wilson mind?"

"I believe she is used to it by now, it was her nickname while she was studying for her degree as well."

"What about you? Has the School got a name for you?"

"I'm known as 'The Abbess', although the School is not aware that I know it!"

"How appropriate," the nurse laughed. "You and Miss Wilson are great friends," she continued, "have you known each other long?"

Miss Annersley considered, "It'll be ten years this autumn," she whispered. "She was already at the school when I started. We became friendly following an incident with her form." Hilda settled back in the bed and slowly drifted into sleep, her mind returning to her first term at the Chalet School.

* * *

"In addition to looking at the story itself, remember that Charles Dickens was writing his novels for two purposes, firstly as an entertainment, but also as a way of ensuring that his social commentary reached as wide an audience as possible.

"With regard to Shakespeare, however, he was writing as entertainment only, his only concerns being that, firstly he made enough money, and secondly he did not upset the authorities."

"Miss Annersley?" Bette Rincini, the Head Girl, raised her hand, "The novels of Charles Dickens are easier to read than Shakespeare's plays, but even they have difficult passages and language. There has been some suggestion that the novels and plays should be updated, to allow people today to read them more easily. What do you think?"

"In my opinion, you have to read any story while remembering the context and the time in which it was written," replied the mistress. "Charles Dickens was writing for a reasonably well educated audience—they had to be able to read for example,

William Shakespeare however, although he was educated, knew his audience was not. He was writing for the London mobs of the sixteenth century, not for girls of the early twentieth. Some of his work therefore may appear to be anachronistic, certainly his language may. Would you consider that his work should be 'updated' to allow it to sound modern?"

The Sixth Form all shook their heads, Bette commenting, "It would be an insult!"

Miss Annersley smiled, "I believe so, and the sentiment applies for any author, changing the language or references may well destroy the work itself. Now, with regard to Dickens, I'm afraid any more information about early Victorian life will have to wait until your next lesson with Miss Carthew. I am more interested in the characters themselves. If we move to the character of Fagin and ...."

* * *

The Sixth Form listened intently; the new English mistress had a beautiful speaking voice and a way of phrasing sentences that spoke of a great love of her subject. Grizel Cochrane, Games Prefect of the Chalet School, thought that the school was very lucky to have Miss Annersley to replace their beloved Madame. Grizel herself was no English scholar, but she had discussed the new mistress at length with Jo Bettany and had found Jo to be extremely impressed and enthusiastic.

The new mistress was in her late twenties, a very calm and even-tempered person; tall and slim with brown wavy hair and piercing blue-grey eyes. In the first three weeks of term she had impressed all the girls with her unconscious air of quiet dignity. On thinking back to her own Middle years and the number of quick and naughty girls in the Fourth Form, Grizel did wonder just how much control the English mistress could exert should there be a bad outbreak. She was about to find out!

Grizel resumed concentrating on Miss Annersley's description of the main characters in their set book. A sudden escalation of noise from the floor above broke through to the quiet classroom. Miss Annersley stopped speaking and listened to the noise.

"Which classroom is above this?" she asked softly.

"That would be the Geography Room, Miss Annersley," Rosalie Dene replied promptly. "I believe the Fourth have a lesson there with Miss Wilson at this time." Rosalie was well known among her classmates for being able to carry numerous timetables in her head!

Luigia di Ferrara, a quiet Italian, added, "I noticed Miss Wilson going past a few minutes ago—I assumed that she was answering the telephone."

"I see," Miss Annersley thought for a moment, during which time the noise level from the classroom above rose considerably. "*That* cannot be allowed to continue," she said with determination. "Continue working your way through this exercise girls and finish it off during prep. I must deal with the Fourth Form." She gave the Sixth a quick smile before heading out of the classroom.

In the Geography Room a minor riot appeared to be in progress. The Fourth Form was the largest form in the school and almost all the girls appeared to be taking part. Four or five girls were standing beside the Mistresses desk wrestling with one of the large globes, others were indulging in a shouting match, while, in one corner, two girls were drawing pictures on the blackboard. Miss Annersley entered the classroom unseen and stood grimly surveying all within. She walked up to the Mistresses desk just as one of the globes fell onto the floor and shattered. There was a sudden silence as all girls looked to the source of the noise and realised that the English Mistress was in their midst.

Miss Annersley said nothing at first; she slowly walked up and down the rows of desks noting the shattered globe, disrupted papers and impudent air to the Fourth Formers. "Everyone return to her desk, immediately!" she ordered.

The Fourth jumped, Miss Annersley's voice; while still deep and low, was as cold as ice. They hurried to obey, some of them attempting to sit down. "Evadne Lannis and Signa Johansen stand up! I did not give anyone permission to sit!" Evadne and Signa both leapt to their feet, colouring furiously.

"Had I been asked," Miss Annersley began quietly, "I would have said that the Chalet School had suddenly obtained a Kindergarten and that all the children in here were, at most, five years old!" The English Mistress moved to the front of the classroom, stepping over the broken globe as she did so. She faced the class in silence; her blue-grey eyes suddenly a flinty grey.

"Giovanna Donati, you are Form Prefect I believe? Explain this!"

Giovanna's head had risen on hearing her name however on catching the mistress's eye she lowered her gaze once more. "M-Miss Wilson had left us work to do that included having to check positions of particular islands on the globe," she faltered.

"I see; did she also leave instructions that you were to damage equipment and disrupt my lesson?"

"No-o-o."

"Then you obviously considered it to be an unwritten instruction?" Miss Annersley's tone was faintly ironic.

Suzanne Mercier suddenly spoke. "It was my fault Miss Annersley, I argued with Evvy—I mean Evadne—about the location of the Solomon Islands, then everyone else got involved and..." she trailed off under the gaze of those steely eyes.

"Then I am to believe that no-one else in this classroom has a mind of their own, Suzanne? That seems to be a somewhat arrogant suggestion."

Miss Annersley looked again at Giovanna as the bell for end of morning lessons sounded. The Fourth looked uneasily at each other but did not dare move.

"What were Miss Wilson's instructions, Giovanna, and how long ago did she leave you?"

"She wrote her questions on the board, Miss Annersley, she went to answer a call about 15 minutes ago."

Miss Annersley looked over at the board, noting that the questions had been half erased and some caricatures drawn. "Who is responsible for the defacement of the blackboard?" she asked. Two girls raised their hands fearfully, Miss Annersley noted their names, "and the breaking of the globe?" Five hands were raised. "Well I'm afraid that all of you will have to report your crimes to Miss Wilson, I'm sure she will be angry with you. As to the reason for my being here..." she paused to look around the classroom before continuing.

"I have only been at the Chalet School for a few weeks, but I have been impressed by how much the girls here are trusted, in my experience this does not occur in most schools. There is a great deal of reliance on the girls' own sense of honour and decency, and, in the main, this trust is reciprocated. Then I come to this form."

Miss Annersley paused again and looked around at the Fourth.

"And it seems that here the authorities are sadly mistaken in trusting the girls. It seems that children of 13 or 14 cannot be trusted even if left for only a few minutes and with sufficient work. Miss Wilson, it seems, thought that you were honourable people and you have repaid that mistake by damaging equipment and defacing school property."

Miss Annersley leant forwards over the desk and continued, "In short, this form is not trustworthy, and does not appear to have any honour." She looked around at the girls; fully half of them seemed to be quietly crying, while the rest were darkly red, some biting their lips. As she had ended her sentence about the girls having no honour a number of the girls had visibly winced.

The beautiful voice continued remorselessly. "Perhaps the Chalet School authorities are wrong about all girls, or it may be that only this Form harbours those who cannot be trusted. Time will tell. For the present, those of you responsible for breaking the globe and defacing the blackboard must confess to Miss Wilson. I'm sure she will supply a suitable punishment. For the generalised break down in order, disruption of my lesson and obvious lack of honour—this form will revert to Junior status for the next week. That means that you will keep Junior hours, including bedtime, sit at the Junior table for meals, and be supervised by a mistress or Prefect at all times. It will depend on your behaviour as to whether I will recommend to Mademoiselle that you retain Junior status for the rest of the term.

"Now, you are very late for your meal, (the bell for Mittagessen had rung during her speech) I suggest you hurry along to the Speisesaal and apologise to Mademoiselle." She dismissed them.

Miss Wilson watched in silence as the Fourth Form crept out of the Geography Room and passed by her on their way to the Splasheries. The form moved in total silence, not even looking up and did not see her. The Science and Geography Mistress had been at the Chalet School for the last two terms, she was in her mid twenties with chestnut-brown hair and grey eyes. Standing perhaps an inch shorter than Miss Annersley, she was far more athletic in build. Once the Fourth Form had all disappeared she joined her colleague.

Miss Annersley looked up from the Mistresses desk. "Oh, Miss Wilson," she began, "I'm afraid these children have managed to break one of your globes."

"So I heard," Miss Wilson said. "I was just behind you when you descended on the class, I'm afraid I shamelessly stayed and listened." She smiled and then continued, "It appears that I will have to look to my laurels!"

The English mistress looked puzzled and Miss Wilson continued, "In the two terms I've been here, I have cultivated a reputation for sarcasm such that none of the girls would ever choose to be reprimanded by me." She paused to glance over at her colleague with dancing eyes, "However, if I were to ask any of the Fourth Form now, I think they would choose me rather than have to face you again!"

Miss Annersley smiled rather shyly. "My apologies Miss Wilson, I did not know it was a contest!"

"No contest, my dear! I'm delighted to discover that there are others with even more command of the English language than I, though that's hardly surprising considering you're the English Mistress!" She laughed then added, "And my name is Nell."

"I'm Hilda," Miss Annersley replied, "or Nan if you prefer, a nickname from my childhood."

"Well Hilda, I'll admit that I was surprised to discover just how good you were at dealing with an unruly group of Middles! You'll forgive me, but your entire demeanour does not immediately suggest it."

Miss Annersley nodded, "I appear to be too calm and mild mannered? Yes, others have remarked upon the same thing, in my previous post the Head even expressed concerns about whether I would be able to instil discipline! Her concerns evaporated the first time some young monkeys attempted to 'play up' the new mistress."

The two mistresses laughed companionably. "We'd best get along to Mittagessen," Nell Wilson said, smiling. "We don't want to miss the meal—the food is very good here!"

"Too good," returned her colleague, "if I don't start exercising more I'll be gaining weight! I'm going to have to find someone to show me the best places to walk."

"That's easy," Nell Wilson nodded. "I'll show you—after all, I am the Geography Mistress, I should be able to introduce you to the Tyrol." She smiled over at her companion. "I generally go out for a walk early morning—before the rising bell—I'll call for you."

* * *

Jan Wetherall entered the room noiselessly, closing the door behind her. Hilda Annersley was sitting up in bed, her head in her hands. There was a knock on the door and the nurse went to answer it. Outside stood the small Frenchwoman she knew as Mademoiselle de Lachenais. Since Miss Wilson's departure two weeks before, she had visited Miss Annersley every day, the last few days even managing to walk without using a crutch. The woman smiled as she recognised Hilda's nurse.

"Pardon nurse; is it not a good time to visit?"

Jan glanced back into the room. "I don't think so, Mademoiselle, Miss Annersley is in a great deal of pain at the moment. She wouldn't want people to see her."

Jeanne de Lachenais nodded understandingly, "then I will go keep my other friend company—Dollie, she is becoming very frustrated that she is still tied to her bed." She touched Jan on the arm. "You take care of Hilda, cherie, and I will return tomorrow perhaps."

Hilda looked up slowly as Jan pulled the door shut; although the bruising around her eyes had faded she appeared white and drawn. Pain from her head was currently reaching a crescendo and every movement was agony.

"Jan," the whisper was barely audible, "please, can you give me something for the pain?"

The nurse walked over to stand beside her patient, "I'm sorry Miss Annersley, I can't give you anything. It's too dangerous; any painkiller will mask symptoms from your head injury." She looked down sympathetically at the stricken woman, "I'll leave you alone, and you may find it easier to...."

She stopped as Hilda reached out to grasp her arm, "Don't go Jan, please, I need to concentrate on something, anything!" Her eyes closed as another wave of pain hit.

"Talk to me Jan, take my mind off of my head!" She stopped there and laughed softly, "That sentence doesn't make sense!" she observed.

Jan Wetherall smiled as she replied, "well you should know!" The nurse grabbed a chair and sat herself next to the bed. "What do you want me to talk about?" she said softly.

Hilda Annersley was silent for a while then, "have you always wanted to be a nurse?"

"Since I was five years old," Jan replied quietly, "though I nearly didn't make it."

"Why not?" Hilda lifted her head slightly to gaze enquiringly at the nurse. Jan noticed that she had tears running down her cheeks.

"I had to leave school at 14." Jan shrugged; in answer to her patient's startled look she elaborated. "My dad was a docker, worked at Surrey Docks—that's on the Thames', South East London—he was killed in an accident at work."

"That's terrible," Hilda's eyes darkened, remembering her

own mother dying when she was a similar age.

"Yeah well, I'm the oldest; I've got two younger brothers and a kid sister who was barely six months old at the time. Mum couldn't work, so I had to." The little nurse's matter-of-fact tones belied the pain in her eyes.

"Did you not have any family or other resources?" the quiet voice asked.

Jan Wetherall smiled ruefully, "I'm afraid my family is pure working class, Miss Annersley, we have no stocks or shares, no real savings. If a man's killed at work there are plenty of others to take his place, his family are just ignored by the owners. If I'd not worked, we'd have starved."

"I'm sorry nurse," Hilda lifted her head to look directly at Jan, "that must make you feel bitter towards those who have money."

"Like you, you mean, Miss Annersley?" Jan's voice was amused and she shook her head. "No, I'm not jealous of those with money. And I wouldn't swap my family for the entire Kingdom!"

Hilda nodded then tensed again as pain swept over her; Jan noticed the effects and stood up.

"Lie back now, ma'am, you'll feel better if you can relax—lie down and I'll arrange the pillows to support your head." Hilda obeyed and felt a slight easing of her pain. The nurse sat back in her chair and Hilda reached out to touch her arm.

"Did you find a post?"

"Oh yes, not that well paid—it was in a local bakery—but there were perks, including a lot of extra food for the kids. Then, after about two or three years I applied for a job at the local hospital—St Olave's—it was as a nurse helper."

"Is that when you started nurse training?" Hilda's voice suddenly stopped as another intense wave of pain hit. Without realising it she tightened her grip on Jan's forearm. The nurse bore the pain stoically.

When the wave had passed Jan continued, "I stayed at St Olave's for the next four years, learning all I could, I even managed to go to some lectures with the student nurses. But, no,

I haven't any formal nurse training, I just learnt as I went along."

She turned to look into her patient's eyes, her face suddenly very anxious. "Does that worry you, Miss Annersley?"

Hilda Annersley paused before replying, "I always judge by results, Jan, and as far as I'm concerned you are an excellent nurse." Another wave of pain interrupted her, once it had eased she continued: "The person I replaced as English Mistress at the Chalet School had no formal training, yet she was an inspired teacher. Sometimes a person is so good that training is not necessary."

"Why was she being replaced then?" Jan was intrigued.

Miss Annersley smiled. "She had just married." She glanced over at the nurse, and then added: "She is the founder and owner of the Chalet School!"

Jan laughed, "Your Boss then?"

Hilda nodded gingerly, still smiling, "Madge Russell never had a chance to obtain any professional qualifications, and I think she has done rather well. You are in good company." Her eyes closed as another wave of pain hit, her hands clenching convulsively. "How did you finish here, Jan?" Hilda's voice was weak but interested.

"Oh, that was Hitler's fault," Jan laughed. "During the Blitz, when he decided to bomb London rather than the Kent airfields. His bombers went for the docks and the house next to ours was hit."

"Your family were not hurt?"

"No, we were fine, but we had to be evacuated. Mr Roberts had been sent to St Olave's for three months, when he returned to Exeter he asked me to go along, to be his specialist nurse on the neurosurgery unit. My family joined me."

"I never thought I would feel gratitude toward Herr Hitler!" Hilda's tone was light.

* * *

The following day saw Jeanne De Lachenais visiting Miss

Annersley: Hilda had managed to sleep fairly well overnight and the pain from the day before had receded. She and the Frenchwoman spoke together for over an hour, Jeanne sympathising with the Head about the pain she was enduring.

"Cherie I do know a little about how it feels, oh not this recent effort, but remember three years ago when I had appendicitis? The pain then was incredible!"

"I'd forgotten about that Jeanne, you were away most of that term."

The Frenchwoman nodded. "Longer than on this occasion," she observed.. "Hilda, I am being discharged day after tomorrow. I will spend a few days convalescing before re-joining the school after half term."

Hilda nodded slowly. "I've been expecting it, Jeanne, ever since you began walking again. Well, as Dollie is still not able to get up, I will have to visit her instead."

She turned to speak to nurse Wetherall, swapping back from French to English with consummate ease. "Will that be possible, Jan?"

Jan shook her head. "Miss Annersley, I have no idea what you were talking about—you were speaking French remember?" she smiled.

"My apologies dear, we are mostly trilingual and use English, French or German indiscriminately." Hilda paused then added, "Not German at the moment of course!" She then repeated her idea in English.

"You are not really allowed out of bed yet, Miss Annersley," the nurse paused, thinking. "I'll clear it with Mr Roberts," she smiled, "as long as you are well, there should be no problem with you visiting for short periods. You'll have to go in a wheelchair of course."

Two days later, after waving goodbye to Jeanne de Lachenais, Hilda was wheeled out of her room for the first time in more than seven weeks. She was taken to a different floor and into a private room on the Orthopaedic ward. Dollie Edwards inhabited the only bed in the room that was, as far as Hilda could see, a mirror image of her own. Dollie was lying back in bed, her right leg encased in bandages and attached to a system of pulleys above the bed. Some heavy weights hung down the end of the bed pulling the leg remorselessly. Miss Edwards was reading a newspaper when Hilda entered, she looked up lethargically but, on seeing Hilda, her entire demeanour changed.

"Hilda, Hilda Annersley, is it really you?" the younger mistress cried delightedly. "But this is wonderful! It's so good to see you."

Hilda laughed. "It's good to see you too Dollie. How are you?"

"Oh, never mind me. More to the point, how are you? When Jeanne finally told me just how ill you'd been I was horrified. And I must say you do look as though you've been unwell!"

Hilda raised an eyebrow at this. "I see you have not gained any tact while being in here Dollie," she replied dryly.

Miss Edwards coloured slightly and replied defensively. "Well I'm sorry, Hilda, but my last memories of you are just before we got on that cursed bus. The difference is fairly significant!"

"My last memory of you is the last day of the Easter term!" returned the Head.

The two women spoke for some minutes before Hilda's speech started to falter. The nurse recognised the signs and immediately brought the visit to a close.

CHAPTER THREE

WORST CASE SCENARIO

Two weeks later, Hilda Annersley was roused from her reverie by a voice from the door. "Hello Hilda, surprised to see me?" Hilda was sitting in a chair near the large window, with its view out onto the city. She turned slowly; keeping her head as stable as possible, and a wide smile grew as she saw the owner of the voice.

"Dollie Edwards! And up walking no less! This is a surprise! Come in, come in do, it's wonderful to see you." She indicated the chair next to her and Miss Edwards walked into the room. She was using two crutches to walk and, even to Miss Annersley's unpractised eye, was obviously still in some pain from her leg, however she managed the short distance without difficulty.

"When I saw you three days ago there was no indication that you would be up and about so soon, Dollie." Miss Annersley smiled across at her junior mistress with some warmth.

"No, it was rather a shock for me too, Hilda!" Dollie sat in the chair with an air of relief; "My surgeon came on his rounds the day before yesterday and suddenly decided that I'd had enough traction. They had me up walking before I'd caught my breath!"

"You haven't walked all the way here from your room have you?"

"No, one of the nurses brought me down in a wheelchair — I've just walked from the lift." Miss Edwards smiled ruefully, "And believe me that's far enough for now! I couldn't believe how difficult I found it, or how painful!" She looked across at the Head, "How about you, Hilda? How are you getting on?"

Hilda Annersley shook her head very slightly. "I do not seem to be improving, Dollie. I must admit to becoming somewhat frustrated at my lack of progress," she stopped to look across at Miss Edwards with a raised eyebrow, "and before you say it, I've already had any number of people tell me I must be patient! Even I have some limits!"

"I wouldn't have dared say that, Hilda," Dollie Edwards smiled. "I know how annoying it was for me to keep hearing it!" She stopped to move her leg to a rather more comfortable position and then continued. "I will say though that, out of the four of us involved in the accident, it was perhaps a good thing that you were the one with the head injury. Can you imagine Nell, for instance, having to deal with all of this?" Dollie's lips were twitching.

Miss Annersley smiled. "I'm sure Nell would have managed," she paused before adding, "I'm not so sure about her language though!"

"Have you heard anything from her recently? How are things at the school?"

"I received a letter from her last week, the school has German measles! She was writing to explain why she was unable to get away for Half Term. She's in charge now—the substitute Madge employed had another offer apparently, so didn't stay the term."

"So I heard." Miss Edwards glanced across at her senior rather quickly, but didn't elaborate, Miss Annersley, leaning her head back on the head rest of her chair, did not notice the look.

"Well I don't think there is such a problem now as when the accident first occurred," Hilda continued, "with Nell in charge and Jeanne back I think they are managing."

"Yes, I know both Joey and Simone have helped out too, plus Mrs Redmond returning helped."

"And when do you hope to return, Dollie?" Hilda Annersley turned to look at Dollie Edwards once more, her blue-grey eyes warm.

"I'm hoping to be fit for next term, Hilda," Dollie replied quickly, "my surgeon says that, all being well, I can be discharged next week. I'll be going to my parents to convalesce—I think I'm likely to get spoilt!" She smiled and then looked across at Hilda. "What about you, Hilda? Any ideas on how long?"

Hilda shook her head ruefully, "I have no idea, Dollie, whenever I broach the subject I'm told it is too early to tell." Her eyes darkened dramatically as she said this, "I don't think, yet, that they know themselves!"

Miss Edwards stayed for another hour before the nurse from the orthopaedic ward appeared to escort her back to her own room. Nurse Wetherall, appearing some twenty minutes later, found Miss Annersley sat, staring out of the window, her face blank.

"Hello, Miss Annersley, how're you feeling?" The nurse had been away for two days.

There was no reply.

Jan walked up and placed her hand on her patient's shoulder, "Miss Annersley, are you OK?"

Hilda looked around. "I beg your pardon, Jan, I was thinking about something. What did you say to me?"

"I asked if you were OK, Miss Annersley," Jan began. "But I think I already know the answer to that. What's the matter?"

"I had a visit from my friend earlier," Hilda began, "she is being discharged next week."

"I see, and you're jealous?"

The pale woman smiled. "Perhaps, a little," she admitted softly.

"Nothin' wrong with that, you know," Jan grinned. "I'd be jealous too if everyone else had been allowed out and I was still stuck here!" She squatted down beside Hilda. "You do know that, compared to you, the rest of them got off pretty lightly, injury-wise?" she asked.

"Even Miss Edwards?"

"Yes, even her. Your injury is far worse and will take a lot longer to recover from," the nurse was adamant. She stood. "I think you could do with a drink," she smiled. "I'll be back soon."

Jan disappeared to return some minutes later with a cup of tea on a small tray. "There you go, Miss Annersley, try that, I make a good cup of Rosie though I say it myself," she smiled.

Hilda smiled back, a little confused, "Jan," she said, just as the nurse was walking over to straighten the curtains, Jan looked back at her patient, "I'm sorry Jan, but what did you just call my drink?"

Jan grinned. "A cup of Rosie, Miss Annersley," Hilda looked confused. "Rosie Lee, tea," Jan replied.

"A rhyme?" Hilda Annersley sounded even more puzzled now.

"Cockney rhyming slang, ma'am, have you never heard of it?" Jan sounded surprised.

Miss Annersley smiled, "Jan, I am renowned at the school for insisting that everyone use grammatically correct English and no slang, I'm afraid I have never heard of this rhyming slang."

"Oh, well it's a sort of language used by the cockney sellers in markets—a way of referring to things by using a rhyme," Jan explained with a smile. "It's also used by Londoners in general for very common words." She stopped there as something occurred to her. "Oh dear, I've just realised what you said, Miss Annersley."

Hilda looked over, puzzled.

Jan laughed, "If you insist on correct English all the time when you're working, you must be biting your tongue listening to me!"

Hilda Annersley laughed, a distinct twinkle in her eye. "Jan, I make it a rule, never to correct someone while they are looking after me!"

"That's alright then!" Jan grinned as she went to leave the room; Hilda's voice stopped her.

"Thank you, Jan."

"For the tea?"

"No, my dear, for making me laugh. I really was rather upset at Dollie's news, you've made me feel much better!"

* * *

Sir James Russell appeared at the door of Miss Annersley's room just after six pm. Hilda was sitting by the large bay windows with their view onto the city. She looked round slowly as her visitor appeared.

"Jem, how good to see you!" she said, reaching out a hand.

The doctor took her hand and shook it warmly. "Hilda, just a flying visit I'm afraid! Madge sends her love, I thought as I was in the neighbourhood I'd come see how you were getting on." His blue eyes took in her still frail appearance and pale complexion. "I asked your Mr Roberts for an update, he seems to think you're doing well."

"I was allowed out of bed, finally, two weeks ago," Hilda said quietly. "They removed the plaster from my hand at the same time. How is Josette?"

"Much better thanks!" Jem Russell's tone was soft as he thought of his younger daughter. "When I think of what could have happened." he paused and smiled at Miss Annersley. "We could have done with you being there to tell young Sybil the error of her ways!"

"From what I understand she has had enough people doing that!" Hilda reached out to touch the Doctor's arm, "Make sure she also knows that you forgive her, Jem."

Jem looked at Hilda for some moments before nodding abruptly.

The doctor stayed for only a short time before pleading prior commitments. Once he had left Hilda Annersley sat thinking for some time. She then asked a nurse if Mr Roberts was still in the hospital.

"Not now ma'am," the nurse replied apologetically.

"Oh, well could you leave a message that I should like to see him first thing tomorrow?"

The surgeon appeared just as Miss Annersley was being helped to her chair the following morning, the Head was still extremely unstable and having severe difficulties walking, relying on the strength of Nurse Wetherall to stop her falling. Mr Roberts sat in the second chair beside her.

"I understand you wished to speak to me Miss Annersley?"

Hilda nodded slowly. "You spoke to Jem Russell yesterday," she began. "Did you discuss my prognosis?"

"We did," he replied.

Hilda Annersley's eyes flashed. "Without first consulting me?" she said softly. "I was under the impression, given 'medical in confidence', that I should be given that information first!"

Mr Roberts looked slightly shamefaced, "Perhaps you should," he admitted, "but as Sir James is standing as your next-of-kin, and is a fellow doctor, I felt it was appropriate."

Hilda shook her head gingerly. "No Doctor, it was appropriate while I remained unconscious, but not now. In future I would appreciate being informed about anything appertaining to my condition before anyone else—even a good friend like Jem Russell—he has a tendency to keep information to himself where women are concerned, and I refuse to be treated like a child."

Hilda looked across at her surgeon. "Now, perhaps you can tell me exactly how my recovery is progressing?"

Mr Roberts smiled. "Of course, your progress has been slow but sure, the head wound has healed well as have the fractures. The problems you have had with walking and balance will slowly disappear as the internal bruising is reabsorbed..." he stopped as Hilda was shaking her head.

"Mr Roberts," Miss Annersley's voice was quiet but determined, "years of teaching have enabled me to recognise when someone is lying to me or attempting to prevaricate! It's more that ten weeks since the accident and two weeks since I was allowed to try walking. I've noticed no improvement in that time. My balance remains poor and my walking unsteady; in addition I find that I am unable to read, and find it difficult to discern more than one voice at a time. I cannot even listen to the radio." Hilda Annersley stopped there and swallowed before continuing. "Mr Roberts, I am not unintelligent; I appreciate that a head injury may have serious consequences. I would like your full opinion." She ended quietly.

Mr Roberts glanced over at his patient, trying to judge

exactly how much information should be imparted, he sighed. "Miss Annersley, I am extremely grateful that you were never one of my tutors. Very well, I'll give you exactly the information I gave Sir James. You are quite correct, head injuries can have serious consequences, and sometimes those consequences are permanent. Now in some ways you have been extremely fortunate, you have retained almost all your memory, all of your intellect and, to my definite knowledge, your teaching abilities! However all the problems you currently have could be permanent."

"You mean...."

"I mean that you may never be able to walk properly, and you will be unable to read or write." Mr Roberts continued grimly, "You may also find social activities will be severely curtailed as you will not be able to cope with having more than one or two people near you at any time."

He stopped there, noting the signs of distress in his patient's eyes. "I'm sorry to have to bring you this news," he finished softly.

Hilda Annersley smiled faintly, "I did ask for the truth," she said. "Tell me doctor, how certain are you that this will be my fate?"

"I'm not, not yet, but the longer you continue without improvement, the more likely it is that all, or part, of the scenario I gave you will be proven correct."

He stood up to leave but Hilda's voice stopped him. "What was Jem Russell's reaction to this news?"

"He said that it would be best if you were not told," the doctor smiled slightly. "You're correct, he is over-protective." He left the room.

Hilda sat staring out of the window in silence. Nurse Wetherall walked over to sit beside her. "Did you want to talk about it Miss Annersley?" she asked, "It sometimes help..." she broke off as another nurse entered the room.

"Miss Annersley? You have some visitors, a Lady Russell and Mrs Maynard. Shall I show them in?"

Nurse Wetherall was about to deny the visitors' access when

Hilda stopped her, "I should like to see them," she admitted quietly, "but you must say nothing to them of Mr Roberts' information." Her eyes were steely with determination.

Nurse Wetherall nodded reluctantly then signalled that the visitors could be admitted.

"Hilda, my love! Oh it is so good to see you!" Joey Maynard, tall, dark with a sensitive face and black eyes, rushed into the room to kneel beside Miss Annersley's chair.

"Joey, get off the floor do! Anyone would think you were a Middle still!" The laughing voice belonged to the second lady, smaller and older. Lady Russell had dark curls and eyes and she moved into the room at a far more sedate pace.

"Joey, Madge how wonderful to see you!" Miss Annersley's voice was still weak but held great warmth. "I didn't expect you until the holidays. How have you managed to get away from the School, Joey?"

"Jack was down here visiting a colleague and we hitched a ride." Joey explained succinctly, "I've got no classes today, oh thank you nurse (this last to the nurse who had brought in another chair), I've no classes and Josette is improving so we thought we'd take advantage and come visiting."

Lady Russell bent to kiss her friend's cheek "Jem suggested we come, I'm so sorry I couldn't come before Hilda," Madge sounded very apologetic, "but Josette has been quite bad."

"She's improving now though?" Hilda sounded worried.

"Oh yes, she'll be fine now. Luckily she wasn't involved in the German measles epidemic..." Madge stopped short and looked worried.

"Nell Wilson told me about it," Miss Annersley smiled, "when she wrote to explain why she couldn't get down to see me at half term. A great pity that Gay Lambert managed to contract it while visiting home!"

There was a quick exchange of glances between the sisters and then Joey replied, "Well it's over with now!"

Hilda Annersley was able to discern slight evasion in both sisters' replies, but not enough to seriously concern her. The rest of their visit continued with talk on other topics and a general progress report from Hilda. She did not mention her recent talk with Mr Roberts.

The women stayed for almost thirty minutes before Nurse Wetherall, seeing signs of strain in Hilda Annersley's face, suggested that they now leave. The nurse herself saw the two out.

"Excuse me nurse?" Mrs Maynard's beautiful voice was full of concern, "Please, tell us how Hilda Annersley's recovery is progressing!"

"She seems very low at the moment," observed Lady Russell worriedly, "is that normal for this stage in her recovery?" The nurse managed to placate the sisters' fears somewhat without breaking Miss Annersley's confidence and was able to return to her patient. On her return she saw that Miss Annersley was staring out of the window, her face impassive.

"Why didn't you tell them? They're good friends of yours, they appear to be good people, yet you didn't say anything about the news you'd just been given!"

Her face still, Hilda Annersley looked up at the nurse, "I couldn't burden them, they have had a number of difficulties because of the accident and my absence—more I think, than they've admitted to me. Besides, Madge Russell is expecting an addition to her family soon, and her four year old daughter was seriously burnt in April, she should not be upset and Joey," Hilda paused for a moment, "Joey has a small baby and she is probably the most empathic person I know, but she is not emotionally strong. She has only superficially recovered from thinking her husband was dead last November. I cannot burden either of them."

"And your friend Miss Wilson is running the School, in your place, so you'll not contact her." Jan continued as she came to sit beside her patient, "So tell me, who can Hilda Annersley speak to? Or does she think she can deal with this on her own—and before you answer remember that nurses are also pretty good at recognising lies!"

Miss Annersley half smiled at this though her eyes remained dark, she turned to look out of the window again, seemingly lost in thought, then she suddenly asked, "Do you know what my two greatest hobbies are, Jan, the ones that were on my admission form to Oxford?"

Nurse Wetherall shook her head.

"Reading and walking. And I am an English graduate, and a Headmistress," Hilda replied, her voice shaking slightly. She continued. "So if this news is proven correct, then that's my entire life destroyed!" On the last word her voice broke and silent tears began to run down her face.

Jan Wetherall swiftly pulled the screens around, shielding her patient from outside eyes. She then sat next to Hilda and placed an arm around her shoulders. Hilda turned her head, burying her face into the nurse's shoulder and continued her silent sobs while Jan held her.

Hilda continued sobbing gently for some minutes: eventually the sobs ceased and she raised her head. "I'm sorry nurse that was unforgivable of me."

The nurse shook her head. "You have done nothing that needs forgiving," she said gently. "Miss Annersley, Hilda, you have just been given possibly the worst news imaginable. Anyone would react; you are only human after all."

She withdrew to allow her charge to 'tidy' herself. Once she had replaced a few items in the bathroom she returned. Miss Annersley was looking a little more like her old self, although with far greater swelling around the eyes.

"Feeling better? Good, but I expect you are tired now and your head is aching. I think the best thing would be if you return to bed for a few hours or so.... What's wrong?" For, at her words, Miss Annersley had started to chuckle softly.

"I've lost count of the number of times I've said those very words, normally to young 'sinners' sent to my study for me to administer Justice!" Hilda was half laughing, half crying now, "I *never* expected that someone would be saying them to me!"

Jan smiled. "Well, next time you'll know exactly how they're feeling," she noted that Miss Annersley's eyes were almost shut due to the pain from her head. Helping her into bed, the nurse then closed the heavy blackout curtains, darkening the room immediately. "Miss Annersley?" she called softly, not wishing to wake her patient if she were already sleeping. Hilda's eyes opened slightly. "I know that, at present, things seem very black, but however terrible they appear you shouldn't lose hope. There are always people who are willing to help and you may still recover."

"I know that, my dear."

"One more thing, when I was only a baby I remember my gran repeating a phrase to me. She said it was something to use when the entire world was against you." The nurse frowned, trying to remember. "Though He slay me, yet will I trust Him." She smiled slightly, "She said it was from the Bible and had always helped her."

Miss Annersley's eyes brightened, "You had a very wise grandmother," she said softly. "Thank you for that." Her eyes slowly closed and she slept.

* * *

The following morning Miss Annersley was visited by both Nurse Wetherall and Mr Roberts arriving as she was finishing breakfast. Miss Annersley was surprised to see them so early; Mr Roberts generally didn't make his rounds until mid-morning.

"Good morning, Miss Annersley," the doctor smiled. "Jan and I have a proposition for you." He sat down next to her, Jan Wetherall beside him.

"I appreciate that the information I gave you yesterday was devastating," he began, "however we believe that a new type of regime may be the answer."

"A new regime?" Hilda seemed to have regained her customary calm. However Jan could hear a slight tremor in her patient's voice and see dark circles beneath her eyes.

"There are some new, exciting developments in the science of rehabilitation for head injuries," Mr Roberts began. "It is thought that a great deal of the problem is due to the brain 'forgetting' some of its more basic functions."

"You said yourself, doctor, that my memory was hardly affected." Miss Annersley's voice was without inflexion.

"Not your memory, Miss Annersley, your brain's memory," Jan attempted to explain.

Hilda raised one eyebrow at both of them but said nothing.

Paul Roberts sighed. "We're explaining this badly, Miss Annersley, suffice to say, your brain has, itself learnt any number of skills during your lifetime. These skills include walking and reading among others. Your head injury and the surgery have, between them, destroyed some of the links in your brain, but the theory is that you can forge new links."

Their patient looked interested despite herself. "How would I do that?"

"You would have to re-learn these skills, and you would have to do so while fighting your body's own certainty that you could not!" The doctor paused a moment before continuing. "I'll not lie to you, Miss Annersley, this will not be pleasant. You will literally have to fight against your own instincts. I don't think that many would have the strength of character to be able to do this."

"But you believe I have?"

The doctor nodded. "Yes, with help, and Jan here will be responsible for encouraging you!"

"More than that, Miss Annersley," cut in the nurse, "I will be nagging you. I've always wanted to be a sergeant-major!"

* * *

Hilda Annersley walked slowly but with intense concentration, her eyes fixed on the opposite wall. She was aware that Nurse Wetherall was walking beside her but did not wish to ask for help. She could hear the nurse's stream of encouragement as she walked.

"That's it, keep going you're almost there. Don't stop now!"

Hilda suddenly experienced a fresh wave of nausea, severe enough to panic her.

"I-I-I feel sick!"

"Oh no you don't!" Jan's reply was swift and irreverent; "I've already cleaned this floor today." Her feigned indignation was enough to divert Hilda from her feelings and allow her to continue walking.

"Just a few more steps, keep going, keep..."

Hilda reached the wall and, in the same movement, Jan Wetherall placed a supporting arm around her and guided her to a waiting chair. Hilda collapsed into the chair, breathing heavily and trembling. Jan pressed a glass of water into her hands with instructions to sip slowly and breathe deep.

It was some minutes before Miss Annersley could speak. "Tell me I'm improving, nurse," she gasped. "I would hate to be going through all of this for no result!"

"You are improving Miss Annersley;" the nurse's voice was warmly encouraging. "Even Mr Roberts thinks so. When we started doing this ten days ago you could barely manage to walk five steps on your own, now you've just managed the length of the room—more than twenty steps."

"Some of the rambles and walks at the Chalet School may be five miles or more," came the dry reply.

Jan sighed, "Look," she said impatiently. "You were told this would take time, you are not going to be fit for a long while. If you keep comparing your condition now to what it was before the accident you're just gonna get more depressed. And it may delay your recovery even further."

Hilda Annersley was silent for some moments, then inclined her head toward the nurse. "Point taken, Jan," she said softly. "Alright, when do I next try this?"

"I think we'll stick to twice daily for now, ma'am. We've also got to tackle your reading sometime this morning."

"Ah yes," and now Miss Annersley was genuinely amused. "You must teach the English Mistress how to read!"

Jan smiled. "You already know how to read—your brain just needs convincing of the fact!"

Later that day the Matron of the hospital visited Miss Annersley: at the time Hilda was struggling to read through the front page of an old newspaper. Listening to the School Mistress laboriously trying to decipher simple words was rather a shock. After struggling for some minutes with one particular word Miss Annersley gave up and sat back in her chair.

"Spell the word out for me, Jan," she requested.

"G-R-O-T-E-S-Q-U-E," recited the nurse.

"Grotesque," returned Hilda with a mixture of satisfaction and annoyance. "It seems that my lack of ability to recognise words is restricted to vision and doesn't include hearing. That seems somewhat ridiculous!"

"Perhaps ma'am but I've come across even stranger things following brain surgery. Anyway, this is improving too; you managed most of the paragraph. Would different reading material help do you think? I have a *Complete Works of Shakespeare* at home somewhere. It would be more familiar."

Hilda Annersley smiled. "Too familiar, my abilities would increase dramatically! I know most of Shakespeare's plays by heart! No, we'd best continue with works I haven't read before. Maybe an up-to-date copy of *The Times*, that will at least keep me informed about the War!"

Jan nodded and left the room.

The Matron came up to shake Miss Annersley's hand. "Good day, Miss Annersley, are your lessons progressing well?"

Hilda smiled at the Matron, having a great deal of respect for the senior nurse of the hospital. The Matron was a woman of average height, in her early sixties. Immaculate in her uniform, she ruled the hospital with a rod of iron, yet was well respected and liked by all her staff and, Hilda could tell, by all the doctors. She reminded Hilda of Matey, back at the school.

"Good day Matron, my lessons are, I'm afraid, progressing very slowly." Hilda smiled ruefully, "Though I'm sure that Nurse Wetherall would consider I was making good progress."

"Nurse Wetherall is an accomplished nurse," replied the Matron, "it is a great pity that she does not have any formal training."

Hilda's face darkened slightly. "I understood that that was not a problem in her current post—it was decided that her previous experience and knowledge were enough for her to be accorded the title and privileges of nurse."

"They are, she is more than qualified to perform her current role. No, I'm thinking of the future." The older woman came to sit beside Hilda, who was sitting in her normal spot next to the large window.

"I should explain," she began. "I will be retiring next May and my successor will be the woman who is currently the Sister of this floor."

Hilda nodded; she had met Sister Davidson many times and considered her a worthy successor.

"That will, of course, leave the Sister post vacant. Now, if nurse Wetherall had received formal training, I would have no hesitation recommending her for the post. However, the hospital board will object, and block her appointment because of her, unusual, method of entry. They do not mean to be obstructive, and they do recognise that Nurse Wetherall has the skills and experience to do well. But she never achieved any academic success, and that will tell against her in the future."

"Jan is not unintelligent," began Miss Annersley. "If it's just passing some exams that's required could she not study for them?"

"She is, she currently attends evening classes, in fact she has already obtained passes in three subjects but the tutor this year is appalling, she will never learn enough to pass her exams." The Matron glanced over at Miss Annersley before continuing. "At a recent case conference your own case was discussed, Miss Annersley. Mr Roberts mentioned that your teaching skills were intact."

Hilda laughed. "I'm not fit to take classes, Matron!" she protested. "I cannot even cope with having more than two people in the room and my reading has only barely passed Kindergarten level!"

"It would only be one person, Miss Annersley," replied the older woman. "And you said only a few minutes ago that you do not need to be able to read to know Shakespeare. I should imagine that also applies for a large number of other pieces of Classical Literature." She looked across at the patient.

Miss Annersley nodded, "True," she said, "I will have to think about this, Matron."

* * *

"You're not considering this out of some obscure guilt or something are you?" Mr Roberts looked worried. "You are a private patient here, Miss Annersley, it's not as though you are not already contributing to the hospital coffers!"

Hilda Annersley shook her head, smiling, "No, doctor, my only concern is helping Nurse Wetherall achieve her full potential. If it means that I give her some private tuition, well, it's not as though I don't have the time, is it?"

The surgeon smiled, "Well I have no objection, I would not expect you to teach for too long at a time, but I think I can rely on Jan herself to ensure that! In fact it will probably be of help in your own rehabilitation. Have you mentioned it to her yet?"

"Not yet, I'll speak to her tomorrow."

CHAPTER FOUR

THE GERMAN

Hilda Annersley and Jan Wetherall settled down for the morning's lessons. Although greatly improved, Miss Annersley was careful to read for only five minutes at a time.

On this occasion they were studying *Macbeth*, a particular favourite of Hilda's…

"The character of Lady Macbeth is shown in her first speech, when she first hears the news that her husband has been made Thane of Cawdor, and also hears about the prophecies of the three witches." Hilda's voice was soft but had not yet regained its rich qualities. "So how would you describe that character—using just that speech as reference?"

Jan Wetherall thought for a moment. "She's quick, she immediately sees the potential of Macbeth's promotion, and she doesn't think twice about the next step. She'll happily consider killing the king."

Hilda nodded. "And her thoughts on her husband?"

"She thinks he's weak, doesn't believe he'll have the strength to complete the task."

"What part of the speech tells you that?"

"The part 'Yet do I fear thy nature; It is too full o'th'milk of human kindness,'" Jan quoted.

Hilda continued, "….'to catch the nearest way. Thou wouldst be great; Art not without ambition, but without the illness should attend it.' Correct, she recognises that Macbeth has the same ambitions but doubts his commitment. Once the deed is done though, what occurs?"

"Their positions change, Macbeth becomes a cold-blooded monster while Lady Macbeth goes mad."

"Excellent, now find evidence within the play of when these changes in character occur. Look at different scenes including the murder scene, the discovery of the body and later, to trace when these characters change. What reasons can you think of for the dramatic changes in their characters? In addition how 'true to life' did William Shakespeare make his characters—do you feel they are believable?"

There was silence in the room as Jan bent her head to the book, researching the evidence required to answer Miss Annersley's questions. While her pupil worked Hilda rose slowly and walked over to the window. She stood looking out for some minutes before Jan's voice called her. Miss Annersley looked over sharply then gasped as she felt the room start to spin. Jan was by her in seconds, helping her over to her chair.

"Are you all right?" The nurse sounded worried.

"I'm fine," Hilda smiled. "I've just got to try to remember not to move so fast!"

"These fainting spells are becoming a real nuisance," Jan observed. "The only good thing is that Mr Roberts is convinced that they'll clear up as time goes on."

"I think they have appeared to be more frequent only because I'm moving about more," replied her patient. "And it occurs only if I'm too quick in twisting my head around. Now, why did you call me?"

Jan asked a few questions related to the assignment she had been given and Miss Annersley answered them. Jan continued to work for the next hour or so until, with an eye on her patient, she announced that the lesson was at an end and that Miss Annersley should rest. Miss Annersley attempted to protest but found her views ignored as the nurse quietly put her books to one side and helped Hilda over to the bed.

She looked up at the nurse with an expression of exasperation on her face. "Nurse, I am considerably older than you; I have excellent professional qualifications and a demanding post. I have the respect of my peers and I'm even tutoring you at present! So can you please tell me why I always feel like a child whenever I'm speaking to you?"

Jan Wetherall's face was impassive as she replied, "Oh that will be the Nurse's Charter ma'am—the ability totally to ignore the status of anyone who's currently her patient. It is allied to the skill to ensure that even a High Court Judge will feel like a five year old. You have to be able to show these skills before you're even considered for training as a nurse." Jan's face remained expressionless for some moments before splitting into a wide grin.

Hilda looked at her and then laughingly admitted defeat.

* * *

"Dammit Dave! I don't care that you're Head of Surgery, I'm the Neurosurgeon and I will not allow you to place one of my patients at risk!"

"She'll not be at risk Paul, I told you, we'll look after her as though she were the Queen herself. But we need her! A man's life is at stake."

"I don't care! Hilda Annersley is not going to be exposed to danger!"

The argument disturbed Miss Annersley, as it was occurring directly outside her room. She was sitting in her usual spot facing the large windows with a view out onto the city. Until the sound of raised voices she had been quietly dozing but now motioned to her nurse.

"What's happening Jan?"

Nurse Wetherall shook her head. "I don't know ma'am, that's Mr Connor; he's the Senior Surgeon, arguing with our Mr Roberts. They are normally close friends."

"Well they're obviously not very friendly at present. Help me up please."

The arguing surgeons were suddenly silenced by the arrival at the door of Hilda Annersley. "Gentlemen, may I suggest that any disagreement you have will be better resolved inside, rather than in the corridor?"

The two men looked somewhat sheepish and followed Hilda into the room, grabbing chairs on the way. Hilda sat in her normal seat facing the two doctors.

"Dave, this is Miss Hilda Annersley, my patient," Mr Roberts placed strong emphasis on the word 'my'. "Miss Annersley this is Mr David Connor, our Head Surgeon."

"Good morning Mr Connor." Miss Annersley's voice was soft and contained. "Am I to take it that your disagreement in some way refers to me?"

The two looked at each other, then Mr Connor replied, "Yes it does. I understand, Miss Annersley, that you speak German?"

Hilda looked from one to the other. "Yes," she admitted warily, aware that being a German speaker was not likely to make one popular in war-time Britain.

"Is it fluent? I mean can you speak and understand as a native?"

Miss Annersley looked questioningly at the doctor. "I speak colloquial German Doctor; the only accent I have is a slight Austrian one. There is nothing in my speech to indicate that German is not my first language. May I ask why you wish to know this?"

"Certainly, I have a patient in casualty at this minute. If he does not have surgery on his leg within the next few hours he will definitely lose the leg and may lose his life." Mr Connor paused to look across at Miss Annersley. "He is a German POW; he was shot down some time ago and captured on Dartmoor. Instead of informing the authorities immediately the local police just took him to the prison. He had been wounded when shot down and his leg was not treated properly. By the time the military caught up, the leg wound had become seriously infected. He speaks no English and we can't make him understand what we want to do. The War Office have said they can send a German speaker down to us but he'll not arrive until tomorrow—that may well be too late."

"You want me to speak to him?" Hilda Annersley's voice showed no emotion.

The doctor nodded, "I would be very grateful ma'am...."

Suddenly Mr Roberts interrupted. "Tell her the entire story first, Dave!"

"What my colleague is referring to is that this young Jerry has managed to slip away from his RMP guards and has barricaded himself in a store room. While he could be retrieved if I allowed the soldiers to go after him I'm not likely to have a live patient afterwards." The Head Surgeon looked grim at this revelation.

Mr Roberts looked angrily at his colleague before facing Hilda. "Miss Annersley, you yourself are still recovering. I know you are improving but it will be some months before you are well. An episode like this could seriously retard your recovery."

"Are you saying that you will not allow me to do this Doctor?" The question was mild but both doctors heard the steel beneath it.

Mr Roberts smiled, "I cannot say that, you are, after all, over 21! But I seriously advise against it."

"Doctor, if you were asked to risk your life to save another, would you do it?" The doctor remained silent, but his answer was obvious. Miss Annersley continued, "Then please allow me the same privilege."

A short time later saw Miss Annersley being wheeled down the corridors of the hospital towards the Casualty Department. The accident and emergency department of the Royal Devon and Exeter resembled an armed camp. There were a large number of heavily-armed soldiers guarding all the exits and a huge space had been cleared before a small storeroom.

A large, florid-faced sergeant, with RMP on his uniform, came up to the group and saluted to Mr Connor.

"You have a German speaker, sir?" The voice was deep and hoarse. Mr Connor indicated Miss Annersley and she looked up at the big sergeant. His entire demeanour exuded competence.

"Good to meet you ma'am, hope you know more German than me! I've not been able to get him to understand anything."

"You speak German, sergeant?"

"Only a small amount, ma'am." His Hampshire accent was apparent. "Learnt during the last War. Mainly it's just swear words—and that's all he seems to be using at the moment!"

"Is he dangerous, sergeant?" Nurse Wetherall was standing behind the wheelchair but her protective stance was obvious to all.

"He's a Jerry, nurse, and we're at war," the sergeant shrugged. "He has no weaponry with him, but I don't know what instruments may be in that cupboard."

Jan turned to the two doctors. "You cannot allow Miss Annersley into danger," she stated.

Hilda smiled, "Jan, I'm going to stay here." She turned back to the sergeant. "Have you a loud speaker or similar?"

The sergeant brought a bullhorn and motioned the small group to the front of the barricade. The first attempt at communication was rather unsuccessful. It is true that Hilda Annersley's first German sentences were greeted with a flood of words in reply but, on being asked about them, the pale woman smilingly shook her head.

"I believe the sergeant is more qualified to reply to his current conversation," she said softly. "As a lady I should not even admit knowing such words exist!" Her eyes danced as she glanced at her companions. "Let me try again."

Her next attempt seemed to be more successful. Conversation between the German soldier and the woman continued for some minutes. Then Miss Annersley sighed and turned to the waiting men. "He doesn't believe me, and he thinks the Military Police have brought him here for experimentation. He says he would rather die."

"But that's ridiculous," Mr Connor exclaimed. "How can he possibly think that?"

"Because in his country he knows that is exactly what happens." Hilda's voice was quiet and contained. The people surrounding her all looked shocked and Miss Annersley continued. "Believe me gentlemen, nurse, I lived in Austria between 1933 and 1938, and while the majority of Austrians I associated with were normal decent people, I saw evidence of the cancer that is Nazism infecting even the smallest towns nearby. This soldier will have grown up with Hitler and the Nazi ideals since 1933, possibly longer." She sighed and her eyes showed pain.

"Had I, and the rest of the school authorities recognised this sooner, a number of beloved people might still be alive today."

The two doctors glanced at each other before Mr Roberts spoke. "Is there any way he can be persuaded, Miss Annersley?"

"Perhaps," her reply was uncertain, "but I'll have to speak to him again." She turned again and began speaking the guttural phrases to the enemy soldier. After some time she relaxed somewhat and spoke again to the waiting audience.

"He's not sure, but seems prepared to trust me. He will come out if I can be waiting for him. He wants there to be someone who can speak his language nearby."

There were some minutes of furious negotiation between Hilda, the two doctors, Nurse Wetherall and the RMP sergeant. Eventually it was agreed that Miss Annersley would remain close by, but only once the airman had been thoroughly searched.

The airman slowly emerged from the storeroom, he was very young, perhaps nineteen years old, over six feet tall and dressed in a Luftwaffe uniform. He was limping badly and his left leg had a heavy bandage upon the knee, there was fresh blood on the bandage. The boy held both hands up above his head and looked around anxiously at the numerous rifles trained on him. Two soldiers went forwards and searched him, reporting back to the sergeant. The German spoke and all eyes went to Miss Annersley.

"He asks if he may shake my hand," she reported. She looked over at the sergeant. "I have no objection."

The sergeant nodded assent and the German limped forward to the figure in the wheelchair. He stopped just in front of the wheelchair and reached out his right hand, Hilda Annersley placed her hand in his. As soon as the airman held her hand he pulled, hard, Hilda was propelled out of the chair and spun around! She could hear the shouts of the soldiers and medical staff but could do nothing as the German was immensely strong! Still holding her right hand he swung his right arm across her waist, holding her in front of him like a shield. She started to struggle but stopped instantly when the airman retrieved a metal scalpel from within the bandages on his leg and held it to her throat!

There was a deathly silence, all sound within the department ceased. The German said a few curt sentences and Hilda Annersley translated. "H-h-he says that you should pull back." Her voice was breathless and quiet, she swallowed, then continued: "He says if you try to stop him, he will kill me."

Another short command from her captor. "He wants all the soldiers here in front of him, he doesn't trust those behind him." Hilda's voice became fainter as the German pressed the scalpel harder against her throat.

The surrounding men could do nothing but watch as the airman and his prisoner continued to speak in German.

"You lied to me, Fraulein!" the airman's voice was low and angry. "Did you think me stupid? You are not a patient here, you are in charge. Well your men will not fire on a woman officer!"

"I am a patient, I was hurt in a traffic accident in April." Miss Annersley swallowed again as she felt the scalpel press against her neck. "You are mistaken, these people do not want to harm you. Why do you think they bothered to ask you to surrender? If they had wanted you dead they would have allowed the soldiers to take over."

"If you are a patient why are you here?"

"I was the only one in the hospital who could speak German," Hilda Annersley said quietly.

All the time he was talking the German airman was slowly dragging his captive back to the storeroom.

"Still in hospital three months later, where are your wounds then?" The young man's voice was scornful. "I see nothing but this flimsy bandage on your head, as if that will convince me that you have been seriously hurt." As he said this he reached up to swiftly remove the bandage,. In doing so he caused Hilda's head to twist around sharply and she felt her senses slip...

The first thing Miss Annersley noted on waking was that she was lying on the floor, although her head rested on something soft. Looking around she was surprised to see her head was on

Jan Wetherall's lap, the nurse was seated beside her. They were both in a small storeroom; there was no sign of the airman.

"We're in the inner storage area," the nurse explained. "The Jerry is just outside, and he has the key to the outer door. Are you feeling OK, Miss Annersley?" Jan's voice was quiet.

"I think so," replied her patient, slowly sitting up. "What happened, and why are you here?"

"He didn't expect you to lose consciousness, I think he thought you were faking it."

"He did."

"Well, when you went limp it scared him, he picked you up and backed into the storeroom. We were all shouting at him but, without you, couldn't understand each other." Jan smiled slightly. "Then as he was about to disappear I ran forward saying 'Let me help' or something, and he seemed to understand. He beckoned me to come in saying 'Come with me'. The nurse looked over at Miss Annersley, "I thought he didn't know any English?"

"He doesn't, but some English and German words are very similar. In German the word 'help' is 'hilfe'; he probably recognised it. And 'Komm mit mir' means 'Come with me'." Hilda looked over at her nurse; "You shouldn't have placed yourself in danger, Jan."

"I wasn't going to allow him to kidnap you without doing something!" Jan Wetherall's voice was full of indignation.

Hilda Annersley smiled. "When this is over, I must introduce you to Joey Maynard! I think you have a great deal in common!"

"I'll settle for this just being over," the nurse's voice was wistful.

"How long was I unconscious?"

"Only a few minutes or so. The German laid you on the floor in here and then yelled at me while pointing at you! I gathered he wanted me to look after you and we've been here ever since."

"Have the people outside tried to contact us?" Miss Annersley asked.

"I've heard the bull horn being used a few times but, through that door, it's difficult to hear properly. He hasn't come back in yet, but I've heard him pacing up and down outside." She looked around at the well-laden shelves. "You know, he probably got that scalpel from one of these shelves, I'm sure if I look hard enough I'll be able to find something equally nasty."

Hilda Annersley shook her head. "No, Jan, you are committed to saving lives. Do you really think you could take one so easily?" Although her voice had not yet regained its full strength there were sufficient echoes to reach inside the nurse who blushed slightly.

"We are at War," she protested quietly. "He's the Enemy!"

"He's a young boy, in a foreign country, he's lost, injured and frightened," Hilda Annersley persuaded.

"That 'young boy' held a knife to your throat, you're still bleeding from the wound now!" returned the nurse.

Hilda reached up to touch a small trickle of blood running down her neck. Jan retrieved a small swab from the shelves above her, she placed it onto the wound and taped it securely.

"Even so, Jan. Whatever his deeds, you are not a murderer. This will be resolved, you just need to have faith."

Jan looked with affection at the older woman. "I think you have enough of that for both of us," she said quietly. "When this is over you must tell me how you manage to stay so calm."

"You appear to be perfectly calm yourself."

The nurse laughed, "That's because I'm good at masking my true feelings, you have to if you nurse. Inside I'm anything but calm!"

"Does a nurse never show their real feelings then?" Hilda asked, deciding to continue the conversation as a way of relieving emotion for both of them.

"Sometimes, if their patient is seriously ill," Jan replied softly, "if you ever see that your nurse is very worried about you, that's a time to start being worried yourself. Most of the time it means that the patient may be dying."

Miss Annersley considered. "I never saw that you were that worried about me," she said.

"You were unconscious at the time," the reply was quick. "But there were a number of days when we thought we were going…" She stopped as the door to the inner storeroom opened and their captor came in.

The airman entered the room, he was still holding the scalpel in his left hand but was limping more—it seemed that the condition of his wound was deteriorating, as though his earlier actions had damaged his leg further. He walked up to where Miss Annersley sat on the floor and addressed a few remarks to her.

"What did he say?" Jan was curious.

Hilda smiled. "He apologised to me, said he didn't realise I was a genuine patient until he saw my scars! Apparently his father sustained a similar wound during the Great War, he recognised it."

Hilda reached up to her head, realising that, for the first time in three months, her head wound was on show. At the time of the accident and surgery her head had been shaved, and her hair had continued to be cropped very short ever since. Hilda had seen in a mirror that the evidence of brain surgery was very obvious although, luckily, it would disappear once her hair was allowed to grow again.

The German addressed a few more sentences to Miss Annersley and she and the airman spoke for some minutes.

"Well?" Jan Wetherall said impatiently.

"He wants to surrender, but is scared that, after his attempt at kidnapping, the soldiers will not allow him to survive. I've said that we can help."

"What can we do?"

"You will have to go out there and explain to Mr Connor and that sergeant. Once you've done that let me know and he'll surrender."

Jan pursed her lips, "But what about you?"

"I'll come out when he surrenders," Hilda paused then, seeing Jan was about to protest, "it has to be that way Jan, no-one else can translate."

"Well OK, but he'd better look after you!" She glared at the airman as she said this, the airman smiled slightly and addressed another few sentences to Hilda.

"What did he say?"

Hilda smiled, "He said that he had heard that the British Tommy was a lion, but hadn't realised that some British women were lionesses."

"Hmph," Jan didn't sound displeased. "You just tell him that if he hurts you I'll ensure both his legs are amputated!"

Miss Annersley was still smiling as the nurse passed through the door and back into the casualty department. After locking the door after the nurse the German returned to his remaining hostage; Miss Annersley's smile faded and she watched in some trepidation as the airman sat beside her. The German, seeing her glance at the scalpel in his left hand, placed it in his breast pocket.

"Forgive me, Fraulein, I do not wish to frighten you," he said. "I wanted only to talk; I have been a prisoner for the past ten days, it is good to hear language I understand."

"If you have been a prisoner for ten days then you must know exactly how I'm feeling," Hilda observed quietly. She watched as the young man lowered his gaze in embarrassment.

"I'm sorry, I didn't mean to hurt you but I was so afraid." The airman stared at the floor for a long time before continuing. "There is a detention camp, near where I live in Hannover. It's been there for many years, it's not even considered a particularly bad place. My best friend during school was training to be a doctor, he told me of a visit there." The German looked up at Miss Annersley. "He said he saw Jews, people, being operated on without anaesthetic, and others being dissected, they had been gassed. He told me all of this the night before he killed himself."

"I'm sorry." Miss Annersley's voice was full of compassion.

"When I saw I was being brought here, all I could think about was what Hans had told me. He said that from the outside the building they were taken to looked just like a hospital, just like this hospital. It was only once they were inside that the horror showed. I thought this place was like Belsen, and I decided I would not submit."

He looked up at his hostage and gave a half-smile. "Instead I terrorise someone who only wanted to help!"

Hilda shook her head slowly. "It doesn't matter," she said. "I can understand why you acted as you did, and I'll ensure that the authorities know as well."

There was silence while the German regained control of himself.

"What is your name, Fraulein?" he asked, once he was composed once more.

Hilda told him and the airman's face split into a shy grin. "My little sister is also named Hilda," he explained. "She is six years old. My name is Wilhelm, Wilhelm Grauss." He paused for a moment and then reached out his right hand.

Hilda Annersley hesitated before she reached forward and grasped the hand.

A noise from the open door to the inner storeroom announced that the loud speaker was being used. Jan Wetherall's voice, magnified, informed Hilda that the German was to be allowed to surrender.

On being told of the offer the airman smiled and, wincing with the pain from his leg, stood up. He then reached down and lifted his hostage to her feet before, rather shame-facedly, presenting her with the scalpel. Miss Annersley, unsure exactly what to do with it, placed it in her dressing gown pocket! Opening the outer door the enemy airman then escorted his prisoner outside where there were both soldiers and doctors waiting.

* * *

The following day found Hilda restricted to her bed by doctor's orders; the ordeal of the previous day had, surprisingly, not caused as many problems as Mr Roberts had feared. Perhaps the most serious was that her right wrist, broken in the original accident, had been badly strained when the German airman had dragged her from the wheelchair. The wrist was now heavily bandaged. Hilda had been left with a severe escalation of her headache but this had eased somewhat overnight and the only other visible evidence was a small dressing covering her neck where the doctor had placed a few stitches.

Mr Roberts was of the opinion that by losing consciousness, Hilda had reduced the impact of the ordeal and caused it to have far less effect. Regardless, he was aware that his admiration of his patient had increased dramatically. Jan Wetherall had wasted no time repeating her observations about just how calm her patient had been. She had also emphasised that Miss Annersley had not wanted her abductor hurt.

Miss Annersley had spoken to both Mr Roberts and Nurse Wetherall earlier that morning, requesting that details of the ordeal be kept confidential. She did not want any information reaching her friends and colleagues, especially at the Chalet School, as the details would be certain to cause concern. The doctor and nurse had agreed, with one exception, that the War Office must be made aware of exactly what had occurred.

Mr Connor appeared halfway through the morning to check on her progress — and to apologise profusely once more!

"How is the airman?" Miss Annersley asked.

"He has done well, I think we have managed to save his leg," Mr Connor was mildly triumphant. "The translator from the War Office arrived this morning, so we at least know what he's trying to say!" The surgeon glanced over at the figure in the bed. "The German has requested to see you again."

Hilda nodded. "I would like that," she said.

"Are you sure?" The doctor sounded surprised.

Hilda Annersley smiled, "Provided you can guarantee he has had no access to scalpels this time, doctor!"

* * *

A few days later an official delegation from the War Office arrived to investigate the affair. As they needed to speak to both doctors, Nurse Wetherall and Miss Annersley, the meeting was held in Miss Annersley's room.

"And you're sure you do not wish to press charges, Miss

Annersley? This would be construed as a civil not a military matter, it would come under criminal law." The taller of the two men asked.

Hilda shook her head. "No, I do not wish to press charges, I was only slightly hurt and that will clear up soon. The boy thought he had good reason to act as he did."

The shorter man, a Lieutenant Colonel, nodded, "Well we are grateful to you all," he turned to include Jan and the two doctors, "we must, however mention that details of this affair will be classed as Secret, we will be asking all of you to sign the Official Secrets Act and request that it not be discussed with anyone else."

CHAPTER FIVE

FAITH

"Excuse me Nurse, is this the way to Hilda Annersley's room?"

Jan Wetherall looked round at the visitor, she saw a woman in her thirties, of average height and with brown hair and eyes. She did not recognise her as one of the many visitors Miss Annersley had received over the past four months.

"It is ma'am, but I'm afraid Miss Annersley is with the vicar at present," the nurse replied. "They should be finished in about ten minutes or so. If you'd like to take a seat in the waiting room I'll come and get you when she's free."

"Thank you Nurse."

Hilda Annersley and the hospital chaplain, the Reverend Mercer, had finished the Holy Communion service and were quietly discussing parts of the Bible when Jan Wetherall knocked and entered.

"Oh, sorry Miss Annersley, I thought you were finished."

"We are Nurse." Rev Mercer got to his feet. "We were just idly chatting!" He turned to his companion and held out his hand. "Goodbye Miss Annersley, I am on leave for the next two weeks so my colleague Rev Walker will be taking my place. I am sure he will find you as stimulating a conversationalist as I have, especially as he specialises in Theology. He is something of a traditionalist however, so speaking to you may well open him to new ideas!"

"Goodbye Father." Hilda shook the priest's hand warmly.

Once Rev Mercer had left Hilda turned to the nurse. "Did you want to speak to me Jan?"

"Yes, you have a visitor, a Mrs Randolph, she says she thinks you are her cousin!"

Hilda Annersley raised an eyebrow at this and Jan continued defensively. "Well that's what she said!"

"Interesting, I don't think I know anyone named Randolph. Well show her in please."

A few minutes later the nurse brought back the visitor. Mrs Randolph took one look at the patient and exclaimed, "Hilda Annersley, I thought it was you!"

"Helen? Helen Mordaunt? But it's years since I last saw you!"

The visitor laughed. "Not Mordaunt, I've been married almost thirteen years, the name is Randolph now!" The two women embraced.

Hilda turned to the waiting nurse. "Jan, this is a cousin of mine, well second cousin, our fathers were cousins, she and her brother were very good friends of mine when we were children." She turned to her cousin. "But it must be fifteen years since we last saw one another."

Mrs Randolph nodded. "Yes, at your father's funeral. We've lost touch since, it's wonderful to see you again!"

"Helen, how on earth did you find me? I had no idea how to get in touch all those years ago and the last address I had for you was returned as incorrect."

"I managed to lose the vast majority of my correspondence and letters during a move some years ago. You know how life takes over, there just never seemed time to hunt things down. I found you today through the largest stroke of luck! I'll show you." Mrs Randolph rummaged through her bag and brought out a crumpled sheet of newspaper. "I've been on holiday here in Exeter, helping an old friend with a house move. While I was wrapping some of her china I came across this report in a local paper..." She presented Miss Annersley with the newspaper, Hilda took it looking slightly embarrassed.

The nurse's voice cut across softly. "Mrs Randolph, Miss Annersley is not allowed to read at present."

Helen Randolph nodded, "Oh, of course, I'll read it to you, here it is....

Three Die In Horrific Bus Smash.

Three people were killed when the steering on a bus failed while the bus was coming down a hill near the centre of town yesterday. The three dead included the driver, the conductress and a male pedestrian. There were also many injured, most of them were taken to the local hospital St Arven's, although the most seriously injured, a Miss Hilda Annersley, a school mistress, was taken immediately to The Royal Devon and Exeter Hospital.

Now 'Annersley' is not a common name, so I immediately thought of you, especially as it said you were a schoolmistress. I phoned the hospital yesterday with a view to finding a contact address, I had no idea I would find you were still a patient four months later!"

"I had no idea the accident had been reported in any newspaper," Hilda Annersley said. "I wonder how they discovered my name!"

"Oh journalists have an absolute talent for finding out things," returned Mrs Randolph, "the point is it allowed me to find you!"

Miss Annersley smiled. "You are quite right Helen, now, tell me about yourself, you are married, do you have any children?"

"One, a young girl, Nell." Mrs Randolph smiled, "She's eleven—she's away with friends otherwise I would have brought her along to introduce you. We have a house near Chepstow. My brother Edgar is in the RAF, quite a 'high flyer' apparently." She laughed at the pun. "He's in Canada—some training mission or other, he's married too, has a daughter aged six."

"And your husband?" Hilda's voice was quietly interested.

"An old friend of Edgar's, Andrew, also in the RAF, he's a Squadron Leader, out in Italy somewhere." Her face immediately grew concerned. She then shook herself and smiled at her cousin, "And what about you?"

Jan Wetherall quietly left the room, leaving the two cousins to their news.

* * *

"Jem, how good to see you again, it must be six weeks since you were last here!" Hilda Annersley, standing beside the large bay windows walked over to greet her visitor.

Sir James Russell smiled warmly as he came into the room, "Hilda, you are looking so much better than the last time I was here."

The pair sat down, Miss Annersley looked across at the doctor. "Well, Jem, have you spoken to Mr Roberts this time?"

Jem smiled ruefully. "I tried Hilda, he said that I should ask you for any updates! It seems that you have convinced him that you are the only person entitled to know your own medical condition." Jem shook his head, "It came as rather a shock!"

Hilda Annersley looked over at him with a smile. "Jem, I will not be treated as a child, you should know that!"

"No, I understand," Jem Russell looked his friend directly in the eyes before continuing. "Hilda, I told no-one about the possible consequences six weeks ago, not Madge, Joey, Nell, not even Jack Maynard. I'm sorry I advised Roberts not to tell you, I didn't think you should be told because I thought you would find the news too overwhelming—you proved me wrong!"

"It's forgiven Jem," Hilda said softly, "now, update me, how are Madge and Josette?"

When Mr Roberts appeared some ten minutes later it was to find the two deeply embroiled in a story about Sir James' young sister-in-law. She seemed to have an original way of despatching burglars!

"Hello Sir James." Mr Roberts shook hands with his fellow doctor. "I imagine you would like a progress report?" he smiled at Miss Annersley as he said this. "With your permission, Ma'am?"

Hilda smiled her consent.

After filling Sir James in about the progress his patient had made over the last six weeks the young neurosurgeon went on to tell both his listeners of future plans.

"As far as I'm concerned there are no contraindications to

Miss Annersley being discharged by the end of the month," he concluded. "There are, however, some restrictions."

"Restrictions?"

"Yes," the surgeon looked at his audience. "Firstly, convalescence, this is going to take a long time, I do not expect to be able to give you the all clear to return to work before Easter next year!"

Hilda's face had paled considerably at that news. "But why so long doctor?"

Mr Roberts looked over at his patient, "It's going to take all your efforts to ensure you are fit to return then," he said gently. "Now, secondly, where you should spend your convalescence. At least until Christmas I don't want you staying anywhere that has children or otherwise loud households. You will not be able to cope with the noise. You need to find a place that's quiet, preferably with experienced nurses who can continue the work my specialist nurse here has started."

"What about the Sanatorium, doctor?" Jem's deep voice spoke. "We can ensure that Hilda does not come in contact with any infectious disease, and provide the nursing cover."

Mr Roberts thought, "That would be suitable Sir James, except, aren't you closely associated with the school?"

"Well of course!"

The surgeon shook his head. "In that case no," he turned to Hilda Annersley. "You need a complete break from that school of yours, it will retard your recovery if, every time there's a problem at the school, your advice is sought—and it would happen if you were living next door!"

"What do you suggest then doctor?" Hilda's voice was soft.

"I would recommend a nursing home," the doctor began, "if I didn't already know that all such places have been commandeered by the military. You need something similar, or a private house, so long as you are quiet and looked after—you will need to employ a nurse, at least for the first few months." The doctor got up to leave, "Think about it and let me know." he said. "Because your discharge from hospital is dependent on your having a suitable place for convalescence." He smiled in way of farewell and left the room.

Miss Annersley and Sir James looked at each other. "It never occurred to me that the San would not be suitable, and neither the Round House nor Plas Gwyn can be considered quiet, Hilda." Jem said. "We'll have a new baby within the next month or so, and Joey's four are hardly restful."

"No," agreed his friend. "In any case, being so close to the School, I don't think either will be suitable."

"What about relations?"

Hilda smiled. "I have two brothers but I've not seen either of them for years, Simon is a widower, lives mainly at his club in London. John has a large house in Buckinghamshire, he would have room but..." she stopped to glance over at the doctor. "It would not be a restful visit. My eldest brother is of the opinion that women should not work, he feels that they do not have the brains for it!" Hilda's eyes danced as she continued, "Plus he has never forgiven me for obtaining both a First from Oxford and an MA—he didn't achieve either!"

"Probably not the best place to convalesce then." Jem said with amusement.

* * *

The following day, a decision about her convalescence still unresolved, Hilda had another visit from her cousin. Helen Randolph was as sweet and friendly as ever and had been to visit Hilda on three previous occasions. Although they had not seen one another for so long they immediately fell back into an easy friendship. Helen Randolph was no intellectual but she was an educated woman and led a busy life in her village. She also had a wicked sense of humour and delighted in reminding the calm and dignified headmistress about childhood transgressions, or more exactly, delighted in telling Jan Wetherall about said transgressions while the embarrassed Miss Annersley protested!

As the nurse was showing Mrs Randolph out she mentioned that Miss Annersley was hoping to be discharged soon but that there were some difficulties. Helen Randolph made enquiries and then quickly returned to Hilda's room.

"Hilda, the nurse says you are having problems finding somewhere to convalesce," she began. "You may come to me if you wish."

Miss Annersley looked up in surprise. "Are you sure Helen? After all we've not seen each other for fifteen years, it seems rather a cheek."

"Nonsense," returned her cousin, "it's the least I can do, I'll be glad to help. The house always seems too big for me with both Andrew and Nell away. I'd enjoy the company. I assume you'll be employing a nurse?"

"Yes, Mr Roberts has recommended that I have a nurse with me, at least until Christmas."

"Well there'll be plenty of room for her too, I'll look forward to it." She waved goodbye and disappeared.

Later that day Hilda was able to inform Mr Roberts of the arrangements and confirm with him that she would be discharged at the end of the month.

"There is one more thing, doctor," Hilda said as Mr Roberts prepared to leave, she turned to the nurse. "I should like to speak in private please nurse." Jan nodded and slipped out of the room.

"What is it Miss Annersley?"

"You are aware of the tutoring I have been performing with Nurse Wetherall?"

"Of course."

"She has made excellent progress, I have been tutoring her in English and Religious Studies—she will need to pass both subjects if she has a chance of achieving her Matric next year."

"Yes, I know, she's worked hard since being transferred here."

"I believe she can pass these subjects, but only if she continues to have tutoring—and I'm told that her evening classes teacher is poor."

"He's incompetent."

Hilda nodded. "In that case, could you give your specialist nurse a three month leave of absence, and I'll employ her for that time?"

Mr Roberts stared over at his patient for some time. "And you'll continue the tutoring?"

"Of course, it's not a completely selfless act doctor, after all I'll have my specialist nurse over-seeing the first part of my convalescence."

"And if she passes these exams she'll get promotion?"

"I believe that's the plan. She'll still be attached to the neuro-surgical department, but with a full supervisory role—she will be able to train others in your methods."

The doctor nodded, "Yes, we would all benefit. Very well Miss Annersley, Jan may have a three month unpaid leave of absence, starting the day of your discharge."

* * *

"But are you sure you want me, Miss Annersley?" Nurse Wetherall looked rather stunned. "I've never been asked to special a lady's convalescence before."

Hilda Annersley's eyebrow rose at the term lady. "Jan, you've looked after me for the past four and a half months, what is so different about continuing once I've been discharged?"

"Well, you'll be in a fine house, with grand friends, and there'll be servants and stuff," the nurse shrugged. "I'm not part of that life, ma'am, I wouldn't fit in, even for just a few months."

Hilda stared at the nurse for some seconds before understanding dawned. "Why I do believe your class prejudices are showing, Jan," she smiled gently. "Listen child, I would not have asked for you if I did not believe you were the best. As I told you once before, I don't care about a person's background, I judge by results. It is in no small measure due to your efforts that I will be walking out of here soon." She paused and then added laughingly, "Besides, only yesterday you were laughing hysterically, along with my cousin, at some ridiculous episode in my childhood. It didn't seem then that you had any difficulty 'fitting in'!"

The nurse smiled, "Well Mrs Randolph is very funny! OK

Miss Annersley, if you're sure, then I accept. Thanks!"

※ ※ ※

Nell Wilson arrived at the hospital late one morning. After receiving permission to visit Hilda she walked carefully down the long corridor to her friend's room. As she entered the room she became aware that Hilda was not alone. A young vicar, not Father Mercer whom she had met some weeks previously, was talking with her friend. Nell apologised and would have left the room but Hilda signalled for her to remain.

"Nell, I didn't expect you so soon, I will not be long." Hilda smiled. "Father Walker, this is Nell Wilson, another schoolmistress and a very close friend. She is currently taking my place as Head while I remain 'hors de combat'."

The young man turned to greet Nell, "I am pleased to meet you Miss Wilson," he said shaking her hand. "I have always admired schoolmasters and mistresses, after all they are responsible for the correct moulding of our young." He smiled thinly.

"I would term it rather differently," Nell began.

But the clergyman continued. "Won't you join us? We have been discussing the development of the Protestant Church in England and on the Continent."

Nell looked slightly discomforted. "That may not be appropriate Father," she smiled. "I'm of the Roman Catholic faith." Her smile faded at the complete change in expression that suddenly overtook the priest.

"I see," he said, dropping her hand and, with some venom, he turned to speak to Miss Annersley. Although he lowered his voice Nell Wilson had very acute hearing...

"Forgive me my dear Miss Annersley, but is it wise for you to be consorting with someone about whose loyalty you can never be fully certain?"

Hilda's eyebrows rose at this remark. "I beg your pardon, Father but exactly what do you mean?" Her tone was icy.

The vicar waved an insolent hand in Nell's direction. "A Papist, madam. You have a position in society to uphold—you are headmistress of a prestigious school—but you cannot possibly countenance having as your deputy one who holds two conflicting allegiances. Especially as one of them is to Rome."

Miss Wilson's face darkened dramatically and she stepped forwards intending to rebuke the man, however Hilda Annersley was quicker. Standing up and facing the priest she looked, despite her surroundings, dressing gown and pallor, as stately as always.

"Sir, you forget yourself!" Her voice, while still with a slight harshness within it now also held suppressed rage. "This country is currently fighting a war against bigotry, I did not expect to find it within these walls."

The priest stepped back from her anger and tried to rally. "Now ma'am, I am far more learned in these things than you..."

"I doubt that," Miss Annersley interrupted. "I am the daughter of a bishop and I have been teaching Scripture classes since I was ten years old. There is no 'One True Way', Sir, and it is exceptionally arrogant of you to believe otherwise. I would suggest you study your books again because you are obviously in need of a refresher course in theology. I question how you managed to qualify in the first place and I will be writing to your bishop to acquaint him of my concerns."

The priest took one look at her face then gathered up his belongings and fled.

There was silence in the room, then Hilda sagged noticeably before sitting back in her chair, she looked up as Nell Wilson knelt beside her. "Nell, I'm so sorry, I had no idea he held such terrible views."

Nell smiled. "It's not important," she said softly. "I will accept idiots like him if I can also have friends like you."

Hilda Annersley smiled. "Our different faiths have never been a barrier to friendship Nell, and that's how it should be. I would hope that one benefit from this war would be that more people see that," she sighed, "but I am very afraid that it will take the human race a long time to reach that decision. When I think of all you endured during the Anschluss, to accuse you, of all people, of disloyalty!"

"Perhaps I should have shown him the Nazi arrest warrant with my name on it." Miss Wilson smiled. "Tell me Hilda, are you really going to contact his bishop?"

"Perhaps, I'm certain that his is not an approved view."

"It may be more prevalent than you'd think," warned her friend, "after all the Establishment view has, since the Reformation, been that Catholics had two masters and therefore could not be trusted."

"The Reformation was over four hundred years ago Nell, we have passed the stage of Catholics being required to take the Test Act before being allowed public office." This last was said with some acerbity.

"Just as well, if it made me feel half as angry as I did over that idiot priest, I'd have ended up in the Tower!" Nell Wilson smiled grimly, "It's probably for the best that you got to him first, if you hadn't I may have resorted to physical violence!"

Hilda glanced over at her friend, "Now that would be worth seeing!" she smiled. "If I call him back would you be able to perform?"

"Hilda Annersley I am not going to prison just to afford you with an afternoon's entertainment!" Nell's indignation was acute. "Anyway, what makes you think he'll come back, I should imagine he's still running! You've not lost your touch when it comes to reprimands!"

Both women dissolved into laughter!

Eventually Hilda had to stop, clutching her head she explained, "I don't think my brain approves of laughter just yet. Owww!" This last was forced from her.

Nell Wilson stopped laughing. "Sorry Hilda, I forgot your condition for the moment."

Hilda Annersley waved the apology aside and a short time later was able to report that the pain had gone.

"Enough of this Hilda," Nell stood up. "Hurry up and get ready, I have permission to take you out to lunch at the local hotel. It's not the Ritz but it does boast of better food than this establishment!"

As Hilda was still unable to walk far, Nell calmly appropriated a hospital wheelchair and expertly wheeled her friend down the long corridors and out of the hospital. Once outside the hotel however Hilda insisted on walking in, supported by her friend.

The two women ordered and began their meal, conversation ranged from discussions of the latest fiction, to the state of the War in both Europe and elsewhere, including the recent RAF raids on Hamburg, Nell mentioning her concerns about Con Stewart/Mackenzie and even the weather. Miss Wilson however flatly refused to discuss the Chalet School, to Miss Annersley's obvious annoyance.

"No Hilda, that surgeon fellow of yours was quite adamant, no discussions about work, nothing that's going to worry you or in any way slow your recovery. You had been over-working even before the accident and made yourself ill, now you have no choice but to rest."

"Well I do think, as my deputy Nell, that your first loyalty should be to me, and not some surgeon who has no idea about the concerns involved in running a school." Miss Annersley was the complete Headmistress here.

Miss Wilson shook her head smiling, "He knows what he's talking about." She held up her hand to forestall the inevitable remark about her English. "And if it comes to that," she continued. "I'm not your deputy." She glanced over at her friend with dancing eyes. "When she realised how long you were likely to be away, Madge Russell installed me as Headmistress, not deputy or 'Head Pro-Tem' but the Head herself." Her smile grew wider.

"I see, I've been deposed then?" The reply was half amused, half indignant.

Nell nodded, "I think the term is 'a bloodless coup'. However I *may* be persuaded to relinquish command in the future." She looked over at Hilda and added firmly, "But only once your surgeon says that you are fit, not before!"

Both women laughed and Hilda Annersley admitted defeat; their talk moved on to different things.

Once they had finished their meal they decided to go for a

walk, at least Nell Wilson walked; she insisted that Hilda get back in the wheelchair. For once the August weather had lived up to its promise and was warm and sunny. The two friends walked along the riverbank for quite a long way, having to turn back only on reaching the docks. They also visited the city gardens and joined many others listening to the bands in the park.

By four o'clock, Nell Wilson, noting that Hilda was tiring, suggested that they return to the hospital. Once back in her room Hilda Annersley admitted that her head had started to ache and the nurse on duty helped her back to bed.

A short time later, with an eye to the time, Miss Wilson leapt up. "Hilda my dear, I must dash! I know it's still holiday time but some of the staff have come back early and tomorrow we will be having a Staff Meeting. If I miss this train the next won't get me into Armiford until after one am—I can just hear Matey on the subject if I arrived back that late!"

Hilda smiled faintly. "I'm glad to hear that she inspires the same awe in the new Head as the old! You get off then Nell, and thank you for a lovely afternoon."

Nell Wilson moved to kiss her friend goodbye before leaving. "You'll be leaving yourself day after tomorrow to go to your cousin?"

"Yes, Nurse Wetherall will be coming with me—to help my recovery. My cousin has a huge house and rarely uses half the rooms, she has promised me an entire wing for the next few months."

Nell nodded, "Well get your nurse to write with the address won't you? And I'll see if I can get away for a few days at half term and come visiting." She smiled her farewell and left.

CHAPTER SIX

THE SEVERN BORE

The move to Helen Randolph's house took place on the second of September; the San provided an ambulance to ferry Miss Annersley and her nurse to Chepstow. The journey took some time as, even with good shock absorption, the continual shaking affected Miss Annersley quite severely. Jan Wetherall insisted that the ambulance stop every 20 minutes or so, as she said, it was obvious when the pain had become too much for her patient, Miss Annersley tended to turn so white that she blended in with the blanket wrapped around her!

Eventually the ambulance arrived outside a large Georgian house situated on the outskirts of the town. Helen Randolph was there to welcome them and immediately showed her cousin up to her room where Hilda slept for the next few hours.

Once they had recovered from the stress of the journey, Miss Annersley and Nurse Wetherall quickly developed a set routine, continuing to practice both her walking and reading skills, Hilda also arranged for her tutorials to recommence. One day a week Jan would visit her home and, on that day, Helen remained close in case Hilda required anything.

* * *

"Well how did the walk go?" Helen Randolph said brightly as her two guests appeared. Miss Annersley and the nurse looked at one another.

"My walking is improving Helen, we managed to go quite a lot further into the town. It was hardly an inspiring sight though!"

"Oh I know," returned her cousin. "To see good countryside you either have to have a car or take the local bus. There are some wonderful walks not far away but you have to be able to reach them! Before the War we had a car and chauffeur, but for the amount I'd use it, it wasn't worth keeping, once Andrew was away. He's the driver not me. Can you drive Hilda?"

"I can, but I doubt that's allowed just yet." She turned to Jan.

"Not for a long time, Miss Annersley," the nurse replied.

"Pity, I have a car, after all, and it will be just sitting at the School not being used. We wouldn't need much fuel either…" She stopped as a thought struck her, "Jan, can you drive?"

The nurse looked over from the fire. "Yes, ma'am, although its mainly been ambulances I've driven in the past!"

"Excellent," Hilda looked pleased. "I'll ask someone from the School to run my car down here and you can drive it."

* * *

Miss Wilson dispatched two mistresses, the following Sunday to deliver Miss Annersley's car. They arrived, driving both Miss Annersley's car and one of the School cars. They both greeted Miss Annersley warmly. Hilda was sat in Helen Randolph's drawing room and they both immediately rushed over to kneel at her feet.

"Hilary, Gillian, it's wonderful to see you both!" Hilda Annersley looked across to where Jan Wetherall was standing by the door. "Jan, come here, let me introduce you." She waited until the nurse was standing next to her then said, "These are Gillian Linton and Hilary Burn, both mistresses at the Chalet School, and both ex-pupils of the same school! Gillian, Hilary, this is Nurse Jan Wetherall, she has been the main nurse responsible for my care from the beginning."

The two eagerly shook hands with the nurse. "I hope Miss Annersley has been a good patient, Nurse Wetherall," Gillian said, her serious face smiling and welcoming.

"Please, Miss Linton, call me Jan," Jan smiled. "I find it easier to work with my patients if they can be a bit less formal.

Especially with head injuries."

"Then I'm Gill."

"And I'm Hilary," the slightly younger woman continued, "after all, we're both about the same age as you, anyway!"

The two women stayed for tea, whilst eating the small fancy cakes made especially by Helen Randolph's cook, they discussed the school very briefly.

"Miss Annersley," Gillian Linton began apologetically, "Miss Wilson made us promise we wouldn't speak of the school. She said you didn't need to know."

Hilda smiled. "That doesn't surprise me," she said softly. "Tell me then, are you looking forward to this term?"

"Definitely," Gillian smiled.

"Especially as Bill has taken over," Hilary said without thinking. "It just wasn't the same with that other woman in charge. She was a complete..." Her voice tailed off as Gillian kicked her, Jan noticed and turned to her patient.

"You are looking tired, Miss Annersley, I think you could do with a sleep."

Miss Annersley, frowning slightly at Hilary's words, was distracted. "Er, yes Jan, once my guests have left."

A short time later the two young women announced that they ought to leave soon, they both made their farewells to Miss Annersley, promising to write. As they left Miss Linton smiled at Jan. "Thanks, Nurse," she whispered.

The next day Jan tried driving the car for the first time and pronounced it easy to drive. "It's a lot easier than the ambulances I've driven," she smiled, "plus it's got far greater suspension—hopefully your head shouldn't be adversely affected!"

"Good, we'll arrange some different destinations then, I'm getting tired of seeing the same thing every day!"

"There are any number of different sights I'd recommend," said Helen Randolph, when questioned that evening, "but I would definitely get to see the Severn River, when the tide comes in the view is spectacular."

"Where would be best, Mrs Randolph?" Jan, frowning down at a number of different maps spread on the table, asked.

Helen Randolph joined Jan at the table and the two women spent some time going through different destinations. Hilda Annersley, forbidden to look at the maps, sat back in an easy chair listening to their conversation.

"This is probably the most direct route, the only trouble is that, at the moment, there are no road signs and if you miss your turn you could end up anywhere!"

"What do you recommend then?"

"This way," Helen Randolph traced a route, "it'll take longer but you're less likely to get lost! It's a pity I can't join you tomorrow but I'm chairing a committee, another time though."

The following morning, after breakfast, Miss Annersley and Jan Wetherall set out, the weather warm and sunny. Before disappearing Helen Randolph had wished them well, at the last minute pressing a small leaflet into Jan's hands.

"That gives you the time the tide starts to come in," she said. "You'll need to be sure you're not on the flood plain," With that she left.

The two women travelled along the roads, after some discussion they decided to go as far as the village of Lydney. They arrived about an hour before the projected turn of the tide and the low tide sands looked very inviting. After sharing a flask of coffee the two decided to go for a walk on the sands. There were steps cut into the side of the bank leading down to the sands, and a hand-rail fixed into the wall. Jan saw that the high water mark was about twelve feet above their heads and realised that watching the tide come in was likely to be interesting.

They walked for some minutes, Hilda with her arm through Jan's occasionally having to rely on the nurse's strength. After walking about 200 yards Jan stopped saying she thought they'd come far enough, Hilda agreed.

"I've been looking through this leaflet your cousin gave me," Jan said. "Apparently the difference in tide between low and high water is one of the biggest in the world! At one spot, further downstream, the difference has been measured as nearly fifty feet!"

"Impressive," Hilda Annersley replied a little wearily.

Jan looked over at her patient. "I think we'd best return now, we'll have plenty of time to see the turn of the tide—there will also be this thing called the Severn Bore, to look out for..."

Miss Annersley suddenly stopped and grabbed Jan's arm. "What did you call it?" Her voice was hoarse with shock.

Jan looked across at her with concern, Hilda had turned pale. "It's called the Severn Bore," she said, "weird name..."

Hilda Annersley interrupted her quickly. "Bore—it's a type of wave—comes up an estuary ahead of a tide—very fast." She looked around the low water sands. "And we're on the flood plain; what time did that leaflet say the tide turned?"

Jan quickly checked the times, she swallowed. "In nine minutes," she said quietly.

"Then that's how long we've got to reach the bank!"

The two women immediately started to retrace their steps, as best they could over the shifting sands, Jan Wetherall doing her best to help her patient.

"Jan..."

"If you're going to suggest I go on ahead, save your breath!" the nurse said fiercely.

They carried on, moving as quickly as possible, Jan glancing at her watch every so often, not sure just how accurate it was. Hilda Annersley was white now and her eyes half closed in the way that showed the pain in her head was increasing. She stumbled once, and only Jan's strength stopped her falling.

"We've got to keep going," she whispered urgently. "Only fifty yards to go!" She was seriously concerned about if Miss Annersley could make it that far. Help was at hand when a voice from the bank suddenly shouted down.

"The tide'll be here any minute, get out of there!"

Jan looked up to see a local fisherman starting down the stairs, he ran across to the two women. "Move it, girl, the Bore'll cover all of this in water, and the current will sweep you off your feet!"

While speaking he took in the condition of Miss Annersley and swept her over his shoulder in a fireman's lift. Then, grabbing Jan's arm he ran to the steps, pushing Jan ahead of him.

Reaching the top of the steps he gently placed Hilda Annersley on a nearby bench and then turned furiously to the nurse.

"Are you crazy? Did you want to get yourself killed?"

Jan, still panting from that last run, flared up. "Oh yeah, I did it deliberately! What the hell happened to some sort of warning signs..."

They were interrupted by Hilda's voice cutting across both of them.

"Look!"

All three turned to look at the river—downstream a large wave, filling the entire width of the Severn River and the flood plain. It was fully six feet in height where it travelled over the river itself and even on the sands to either side it reached more than three feet. The Severn Bore had arrived, preceding the return of the tide. It moved swiftly upstream, moving so fast that there was a wind in front of it—similar to the wind in front of tube trains—Jan thought inconsequentially. There was a low rumble accompanying the wave and, as it covered the sands at Lydney, a host of sea birds rose to escape it, adding their cries to the noise. Once it passed the sands were covered in water that was rapidly rising.

Miss Annersley turned to the fisherman. "Sir," she said softly, "I believe you just saved both of our lives, thank you."

The man flushed slightly. "You're welcome ma'am."

Jan looked across at him. "Yeah well, thanks mate," she said quietly. She then added, "And I know we should have found out more, but there were no warning signs about it either."

The man looked over to the steps. "There's normally a sign just here," he said, "wait a minute." He scrabbled in the bush beside the steps and brought out a huge sign written in red, "I'll bet this blew down in the strong winds day before yesterday, no wonder you didn't see any signs." He laughed. "Good job you were already on your way back then!"

Jan also laughed. "Good job I had with me someone who knows the meaning of words!"

Hilda Annersley still looked very white and shaken, however

there was a slight smile upon her face. "The first time my knowledge of English has had such an important effect." she said.

The fisherman, Jim Allen, disappeared into a nearby house and returned with two cups of tea. The two sat drinking the tea and watching the rising tide, Jan keeping a close eye on her patient's appearance. The drink seemed to revive Miss Annersley who slowly regained some of her pale colour.

"How's your head?" Jan asked softly.

"Aching," Hilda Annersley smiled slightly. "But it's nothing compared to just a few months ago."

"We'll wait a while longer, allow the aching to ease before getting back into the car."

As they finished their drinks Jim collected the cups.

"We should give him something, to thank him," Miss Annersley noted.

Jan looked over at the man. "I'll take care of it," she said, "he'll take it from me." She walked over to the man and stood talking to him for a while, Miss Annersley watched as he initially refused the money she handed him then, eventually, grinned and accepted.

On her return Miss Annersley asked her a question. "Why did you say 'he'll take it from me'?"

Jan smiled. "That's the class situation rearing its head again, ma'am. Taking the money from you would be," she paused, searching for the word, "fealty, obligation. His pride wouldn't allow it. From me, not a problem."

Hilda Annersley nodded. "Understood." She paused then added, "I expect that money to be claimed as expenses!"

Jan smiled. "I'll claim half of it ma'am, after all he saved my life too!"

Back in the car Hilda turned to Jan. "If possible, Jan," she began, "I'd rather this episode wasn't mentioned to anyone, I know that Helen delights in telling people of stupid episodes in my childhood, I'd rather others didn't know just how stupid we were as adults!" Her smile removed any sting to her words.

Jan nodded. "You've no idea how happy I'll be about that

ma'am." On receiving a questioning look from her patient she elaborated, "I didn't really want to have to confess to nearly losing my patient on our first trip out!"

"It will not mean trouble from your employer?"

Jan smiled. "I don't think so Miss Annersley, at the moment that's you!"

By the time they arrived back at the Randolph house Miss Annersley had regained her colour and the pain in her head had receded to manageable levels. They both looked none the worse for their ordeal. That evening Mrs. Randolph asked them about their day while they were all having dinner.

"Did you get to see the Severn Bore then? I understand it was a quite spectacular sight today."

"It definitely was that, Mrs Randolph," Jan's voice replied smoothly, "I'd certainly never seen anything like it before."

"It can be very dangerous for the unprepared," continued their host blithely, "walking on the sands at Lydney, there have been a number of accidents in the past."

"Can't understand how people could be so stupid, myself ma'am," returned the nurse calmly. "It's not as though they're not given enough warning!" Both she and Helen Randolph looked across at Hilda Annersley, who seemed to have been attacked by a fit of coughing!

"Something went down the wrong way," Hilda said quietly.

Helen nodded then continued. "There are even those who didn't know exactly what the Bore was and so were unprepared."

"Criminal!" Jan's voice sounded shocked, "As though they were just tourists! Well that type deserve all their ill-fortune, I suppose it's the locals who have to rescue them!"

Another fit of coughing came from the third member of their company, Jan moved over to stand beside Miss Annersley while Helen Randolph said she would fetch some water. As soon as Helen had disappeared Hilda turned to Jan, still giggling. "Stop it Jan!" she begged, "I can't keep pretending to cough!"

"Why, did you find something funny in what we were saying, ma'am?" Jan's expression was innocent.

"You know I did," Miss Annersley was laughing as she said this, "and you are an evil child!"

"Not sure I like that Miss Annersley—may have to continue talking with Mrs Randolph about our trip for the rest of the evening!"

There was a strangled yelp from her patient. "Oh no, please Jan! My head is already aching and I won't be able to eat!"

Jan considered. "Oh very well, can't have my patient fainting from hunger!" She grinned at the older woman and returned to her seat.

When Mrs Randolph returned the conversation moved on to other things!

* * *

Once a week, normally on a Saturday, Jan had the day off. On those days Hilda spent the day indoors with her cousin. Jan normally visited home for the day, travelling down by the early train from Chepstow. Therefore Miss Annersley was surprised to see the nurse sitting at the breakfast table when she appeared one Saturday morning.

"Good morning, Jan, aren't you going to miss your train?"

Jan Wetherall smiled up at her patient. "'Morning, Miss Annersley, can't go I'm afraid—the bombing last night damaged the line and no trains are running. I've already let mum know."

Hilda nodded and helped herself to some breakfast, thinking deeply, she suddenly looked up. "Jan, why don't you take my car? You may as well, neither Helen nor I can drive it. And there's plenty of petrol."

"Oh, thank you ma'am, if you're sure?"

Hilda nodded.

Helen Randolph, also at the breakfast table, spoke to Jan, "Go and ring your mother, Jan, I'm sure she will be pleased to see you."

The nurse disappeared, returning a few minutes later with a slightly worried expression, "Mum's pleased," she said, "and she asked me something, Miss Annersley, my mother has asked if you would like to go today for a visit as well. She says she would really appreciate having the chance to meet you."

Miss Annersley looked into the nurse's eyes for a moment, "If you're sure, Jan, I'd love to."

The nurse smiled, and the worried expression disappeared. "I'll let her know."

Helen Randolph clapped her hands. "Excellent, that solves a problem I had—I wanted to visit a friend of mine—she's been unwell—but couldn't see how I'd get the chance if I had to be with Hilda today!"

* * *

Almost as soon as Jan got out of the car she was enveloped in a hug from a tall young man, he picked her up and swung her around, laughing. "Jan, I thought you couldn't come! Where'd you nick the car from?"

Jan struggled, futilely, to free herself. "Let me loose, Adam, you big ape, and I didn't nick it!"

Adam grinned, a very similar grin to the nurse, and obediently released her. "Well it's certainly not yours is it? Not unless you've suddenly been paid a really huge bon..."

He stopped there as he saw Miss Annersley getting out of the passenger side of the car.

Jan grinned. "Adam I'd like to introduce you to my employer, this is Miss Annersley—mum's invited her for the day, and it's her car." She grinned again at the sudden flush to her brother's face. "Miss Annersley, this is my 'little' brother Adam."

Miss Annersley, herself a tall woman, looked up at the young man, Adam was touching six feet! "Hello, Adam," she said smiling, "Jan has told me a lot about you!"

Adam Wetherall swallowed slightly before replying, "Good to meet you, Miss Annersley, knowing Jan it was probably all lies though!"

Hilda smiled and there was a distinct twinkle in her eyes. "Well I wouldn't know about that, she says that she's proud of you, that you are doing well at school, and that you are still growing!"

Adam grinned shyly.

Jan smiled, "This way, ma'am," she said, indicating the family home. Inside the house Hilda Annersley met the rest of Jan's family, her brother Ben, three years younger than Adam's 16, was a slightly smaller copy of his brother, while 10 year old Christine was only small. Mrs. Wetherall, after greeting her guest warmly, bade her sit.

"I see you glancing at the size of my boys compared to me," she said, chuckling, Jan's mother was barely five feet tall! "My sons take after their father, Miss Annersley, while Jan, and, I think, Chrissie follow me!"

Miss Annersley smiled. "It was very good of you to invite me, Mrs. Wetherall," she said. "I must admit, after all that Jan has told me I almost feel I know you already!"

"Well Jan has told us a lot about you too! I'm grateful for you helping Jan with her studies. I'll fetch in some tea."

Jan's young sister sat on the sofa next to Miss Annersley, "Are you the lady who hurt her head?" she asked suddenly.

Hilda smiled, "Yes, that's right."

"Is that why your hair's so short? Most ladies have really long hair."

Jan made to hush her sister but Miss Annersley stopped her. "It is, when I first hurt my head the doctors had to operate. They cut all my hair off." She smiled at the young girl.

Chrissie giggled, "You mean you were bald!"

"I was." Hilda Annersley was laughing.

Chrissie thought for a minute, then, "Good job it's growing back then!"

"I think so!"

* * *

Hilda Annersley sat back from the dining table. "Mrs. Wetherall, I'm afraid I cannot eat another bite, that was magnificent. Jan told me that you were a good cook but until now I didn't realise just how good!"

The little woman smiled. "With a family like mine I've had to become a reasonable cook at the least," she said, "after all, how else were the boys to grow so well!"

She looked around at her children. "Clear the table now, and wash up, Miss Annersley and I will return to the front room."

"I'll bring some tea in, mum." This from Jan.

"Mummy, can I play outside?" Chrissie pleaded.

"After you've helped your brothers with the washing up, Chrissie," her mother smiled.

Miss Annersley and Mrs. Wetherall sat and spoke together for some time, Jan's mother was only a few years older than Hilda and, despite their different lives, they found they had a great deal in common. Jan joined them for a time but her younger sister came in asking if Jan would join in a game.

"Go with your sister, Jan" Hilda Annersley said gently. "You're not on duty today, remember?"

Jan grinned and left.

"You should be very proud of your eldest daughter, Mrs. Wetherall," Miss Annersley said softly. "She told me what happened when her father died. For her to achieve so much since then is remarkable."

Mrs. Wetherall turned saddened eyes to a family portrait on the mantle; the man in the photograph was an older version of Adam. "I am proud of her, and I think John would be very proud of her too." She turned back to her guest with a smile. "Neither of us had much schooling, but we could see the benefits of education for our children. I was very upset at Jan having to leave school when she did."

"Well she has made up for that since," Hilda returned gently. She was about to add something when all four Wetherall children erupted into the room at once, all trying to speak at the same time. Jan, seeing her charge wince at the noise, quieted her brothers and sister.

"Sorry ma'am, mum," she said quickly, "but there's trouble!"

"What tro..." began Mrs. Wetherall, but stopped as the Air Raid sirens started their wailing.

"That," Jan said grimly.

Mrs. Wetherall stood up quickly. "OK, Adam, Ben you know the drill, quickly round the house, boards up at the windows, Chrissie—into the shelter now."

"You have a shelter here, Mrs. Wetherall?" Hilda Annersley sounded surprised.

Mrs. Wetherall smiled. "Because of the Blitz, Miss Annersley, after living through that it was the first thing we built on moving here!" She turned to her eldest, "I'll take our guest to the shelter, Jan, check the boys are OK and then bring yourselves down."

Jan nodded, looking over at her patient worriedly, the noise of the siren was causing her to turn white with pain.

"I'll be all right with your mother Jan," Hilda said gently.

Less than five minutes later the Wetherall family and guest were in the shelter built at the end of the garden. Although small, the shelter was comfortable with camp beds along two walls and a small primus stove where Mrs. Wetherall immediately began brewing some tea.

Miss Annersley sat in one corner, leaning her head against the wall. Jan sat next to her. "I'm really sorry about this..." she began.

Hilda Annersley smiled. "Jan, I don't think even you have control over the German High Command! Besides it may be a false alarm." The Air Raid warning stopped and she looked up hopefully.

"It's not a false alarm," Jan said quietly, "that's why we came in before the siren—could see the planes. And when they start dropping their bombs you're going to be in far more pain."

"Because of the noise?"

"No, not exactly the noise—the vibration. Mr Roberts explained it to me, the brain floats inside the skull, any vibrations hitting the skull are immediately magnified and impact on the brain. Sound is vibration itself, but even worse are percussion noises—like bombs!" The nurse thought for a moment then turned to Adam who was standing by the entrance of the shelter looking out.

"How long Adam?"

"Few minutes yet."

"Time for you to get your motorbike helmet?" Jan asked.

"Easily." Adam looked toward his mother who merely said, "Be quick!"

As Adam returned carrying a leather motorbike helmet the first of the bombs could be heard some distance away. Jan took the helmet and returned to Miss Annersley, the noise of the bombs, even so far away, were already impacting on her head and she lay back with her eyes half-closed.

"I think this may help," Jan said above the noise. "Put it on, it has a layer of padding, it'll cut down on the vibration."

Hilda Annersley looked at the helmet and laughed. "Hardly dignified!" she protested.

The nurse leant forwards so that only Miss Annersley could hear. "Which would you prefer? Pain, or loss of dignity?"

Miss Annersley glanced up at the nurse then winced as the vibrations from another falling bomb impacted, she sighed. "Give me the helmet, Jan."

Once the helmet was on Miss Annersley had to admit that it did help cut down on the pain, it did not prevent it totally though.

"Lie on the bed, ma'am," Jan continued. "If you have these pillows all around it'll reduce the impact still further. While the bombs are falling overhead keep your hands over your ears and your mouth slightly open."

Hilda Annersley smiled slightly. "More information from Mr Roberts?" she asked.

"No, the Blitz!"

The air raid continued for over an hour before the All Clear was sounded, but it was some time before Miss Annersley felt well enough to leave the shelter. Eventually, when the pain in her head had receded a little she was able to walk back into the house. Out in the street at the front there was evidence that at least some of the destructive power of the bombs had got through, with a few broken windows and pieces of shrapnel embedded in doors. There did not appear to be any casualties however which pleased Jan as she did not want to leave her patient.

Ben came into the sitting room to report to Miss Annersley. "Afraid your car's been hit, Adam says one of the tyres and the windscreen."

Jan and Miss Annersley went outside to look, they found Adam already half-way through changing the tyre. "This is not a major problem," he reported. "The spare will do just as well, but you can't drive without a windscreen."

They looked over at the front of the car, the windscreen was completely smashed. Making their way back in Miss Annersley turned to Jan. "Is there a garage nearby? Perhaps we could call them..." She stopped as Jan shook her head.

"Lines are down," she said. "I tried just now to see if any help was needed at the hospital—after all they provided us with the phone in the first place! No, we'll have to think of something else."

* * *

Returning to the front room, Miss Annersley looked out of the window and stopped in alarm when she noted that the road outside was empty. "Jan, where's my car?"

The nurse looked up, startled, and then moved swiftly outside, she returned a minute later muttering under her breath. "I'll kill him, young idiot, if he damages that car..." she stopped, seeing Hilda looking at her. "Miss Annersley, I know he's too young, but he's a good driver, he won't harm your car..."

"You mean your brother, Adam?" Hilda asked quietly. "But where has he taken it?"

"He works part-time for a local garage, Miss Annersley," came the voice of Ben Wetherall, "He said he'd take it there to get the windscreen fixed."

* * *

"You are welcome to stay the night Miss Annersley," Jan's mother smiled at her guest. "You don't really look fit for a long car journey."

"That's very kind of you Mrs. Wetherall, but my cousin would worry and, as the phone lines are down, there is no way to tell her of our intentions."

Jan returned at that moment. "I think I've sorted out a way you can sleep for part of the journey," she said to Miss Annersley. Hilda followed her out to see that the back seat of the car had been transformed into a makeshift bed, using cushions, blankets and a quilt.

"I think there's enough padding to deaden the vibrations, especially as Adam tells me he tuned the engine while his friend was replacing the windscreen."

The young man flushed. "Least I could do," he said, his voice still occasionally see-sawing high and low. "Sorry again for the shock I gave you," he nodded toward Hilda.

Hilda Annersley smiled. "As you replaced the windscreen and tyre free of charge I think I gained on the deal," she said gently. "Jan, you seem to have stripped out half the bedding materials from your house! How will your mother manage?"

"These are spare," Jan replied, "I'll return them on my next visit."

* * *

Miss Annersley was awoken by the sound of voices, the car was stopped and Jan was outside. "So this isn't your car then, love," the deep male voice was faintly patronizing.

Jan's voice... "I told you that, it belongs to my passenger—but I'd rather you didn't wake her—she's not been well."

"Very noble of you, but this strikes me as very suspicious, it's late, getting dark and yours is the only vehicle on the road. We've had reports of people taking advantage of the blackout to steal cars; mostly they've come down from the big cities. They're even using the dodge of having the owner in the back..."

"You have got to be joking..." Jan's voice was angry.

Hilda decided to take a hand, moving quickly she got out of the back of the car and walked around to where Jan and the policeman were standing. The policeman had hold of Jan's arm.

"Is there a problem, Constable?" Her well-bred tones pierced the gloom.

The policeman spun around, seeing Miss Annersley for the first time. "Err, no ma'am, just checking out the story on this vehicle."

"Well I believe I heard my companion tell you that I owned this car, was there anything else?"

"No, no ma'am, I won't detain you, thank you ma'am." The policeman appeared suddenly to be in a hurry to move on.

Jan and Hilda both got into the front of the car, they drove in silence for a few minutes, then Jan started to laugh. "You nearly scared that copper out of five years growth!" she said. "He was all set on taking me down to the station when you appeared — what it is to have an upper class accent! He was definitely not expecting that!"

Miss Annersley smiled, and then softly pointed out, "Jan, I do not have an accent."

The nurse glanced across at her passenger, trying to gauge if she were serious, Hilda met her gaze with a deadpan expression.

"No ma'am, 'course not," replied the nurse. She paused then added, very quietly, "And Adolf Hitler is a nice man!"

Hilda Annersley laughed.

They finally made it back to the Randolph house an hour after dark, where Helen Randolph was waiting anxiously.

"I was starting to get worried," she said smiling. "I thought something must have happened to you."

Miss Annersley glanced over to Jan before replying, "Oh nothing much happened Helen, we were caught in an air raid, my car was stolen and we were stopped by the police, fairly normal day really." She and Jan both giggled!

CHAPTER SEVEN

SIX MONTHS ON

"Good afternoon Hilda, Jan, beautiful day today isn't it?" Thus Helen Randolph, newly returned from visiting friends for the last two days, as her guests appeared back from their walk. Miss Annersley stalked past her cousin and on into the sitting room. The other two stared after her...

"Was it something I said?" Helen queried of the nurse.

Jan shook her head. "Not unless you said it two days ago, ma'am, because that's how long this has been going on. I've been lucky to get three words out of her today and every instruction I've given has been queried. If it were anyone else I'd say she was very angry about something, but in the six months I've been looking after her I've never seen her angry."

"No she's always been known as a calm person, perhaps this is the exception."

"Well she definitely doesn't want to speak to me," Jan concluded ruefully. "Perhaps she'll tell you."

"I'll try," Helen Randolph promised.

The two women walked over to join Miss Annersley in the sitting room. Hilda was standing, staring into the fire, her face seemed drawn and tired. The nurse walked over to her, "I think you may be tired Miss Annersley, would you like to rest before Tea?"

"No, I do not want to rest," the reply was given flatly.

Jan sighed softly. "Well at least sit down, please? I'll bring you a drink."

"I do not wish to sit down, nurse, I'm speaking to my cousin. Helen, you mentioned that you were attending a concert tomorrow night, have you any spare tickets?"

Helen Randolph looked over at Hilda. "I didn't think you were well enough to attend any concerts just yet Hilda," she said with surprise.

"I would not recommend it ma'am," Jan's voice cut across. "I don't think your head could cope with the volume."

"I was not aware that I had to ask your permission, nurse!"

"No, ma'am, but the whole point of my being here is to ensure that your convalescence proceeds smoothly, you are not yet fit enough to be attending a concert," Jan Wetherall replied reasonably.

"Enough, Jan!" The words were shouted out, surprising both the nurse and Helen Randolph, Hilda Annersley stood there facing the nurse; her face flushed with anger and her eyes a steely grey.

"I think you forget yourself, nurse, remember you are in my employ, if I find myself dissatisfied I may remove you immediately!" The voice, normally rich and low, was icy." I did not ask your opinion about my intentions; I will be attending the concert tomorrow. If you have any difficulty accepting that I suggest you return to your previous post."

"I'm sorry Miss Annersley, but I would be failing in my duty if I did not point out times when you may be acting against medical advice." The nurse's tones were soft but determined.

"And you are well qualified to know that advice are you? Considering that you do not have any professional qualifica..." Hilda suddenly stopped, aghast, aware of what she had said and noting that Jan had gone white. There was silence as the two stared at each other for a long minute and then Hilda took a step towards the nurse, Jan swung round and walked out of the room. Miss Annersley looked with despair at her cousin.

"Go after her, Hilda," Helen said gently.

※ ※ ※

There was a gentle tap on the door, Jan ignored it; she continued to stare out of her bedroom window. She heard footsteps and a low voice began, "Jan..."

"I-I'll arrange transport back to Exeter for myself tomorrow, Miss Annersley," Jan interrupted, her voice expressionless. "I'll speak to the Matron, she will be able to send you a suitably qualified nurse for the rest of your convalescence."

Further footsteps, then a hand on her shoulder, Jan turned and looked up into the blue-grey eyes of Hilda Annersley, "Jan, I don't want another nurse, I want you," she said softly. The eyes looked down at the floor quickly before, once more, meeting her own, "I am truly sorry for my remarks, they were said in anger and they were not meant."

Jan's deep blue eyes reflected her hurt as she replied; "I've often heard that words spoken in anger are generally the truth."

Hilda shook her head slowly. "No, when someone is angry, especially if they don't normally get angry, they tend to strike out at those to whom they are closest; and they say things they know will cause the maximum pain."

There was silence for a few minutes, then, "So your words some months ago, about how you judged by results and thought I was a good nurse—they weren't just you being kind?"

Miss Annersley swallowed before replying, "I said I thought you were an excellent nurse, and I meant every word. My remarks of a few minutes ago were of me being very unkind." Hilda grasped the nurse's hands in her own then continued. "Jan, I'm really sorry, I had no right to say those things to you, please forgive me."

The nurse looked down at the floor, her mind replaying the phrases said and the aftermath. She then looked back up at Hilda Annersley, who had tears in her eyes. Jan nodded. "OK, apology accepted," she said softly, taking a deep breath. "I think though that I'm entitled to some sort of explanation." She noted that her patient was trembling and added, "Perhaps we had both better sit down first." She indicated the chair and Hilda sank gratefully into it, Jan sat on the bed.

"Why were you so angry?" she asked gently.

Hilda Annersley didn't answer immediately, staring at the floor, then, "Two days ago, the ninth, it was exactly six months since the accident. Six months since my entire life changed.

When I first recovered consciousness, I thought that, six months on, I'd be back to normal. That I could put all of this behind me. But I find I am continually being told, 'No, you can't do this, no, you can't do that', the number of restrictions I still have are almost overwhelming. And, deep down, I know that they are all justified." She paused for a moment. "But I have started wondering if they are likely to remain indefinitely. If I will ever return to the person I was before I stepped on that bus, ever return to the life I had." She stopped and took a deep, shuddering breath.

"The more I thought about it, the angrier I became, at the situation, the accident, the stupidity. Then, the angrier I became toward you—because your instructions and rules seemed to epitomize my situation. As if, without you being there, I would suddenly return to the old me. And that's all that was going through my mind at the end... It wasn't until I saw your face, and realised what I'd said, that the anger suddenly disappeared."

Jan thought for a moment, then..."Six months and two days ago, an ambulance crew was asking if you were Catholic, 'cos if you were they felt you were so badly injured you needed the Last Rites—yes, Miss Wilson told me—five months ago, you were in such pain that you could hardly move, four months ago you received the news that there was a very real possibility that you would never walk or read again. Do I need to go on?"

Hilda gave a half smile, "You mean I am improving?"

"Yes, and remember, the improvement is, quite literally, from the brink of death. You nearly died. Whenever you start to feel like this, remind yourself of how far you've already come."

The nurse got off of the bed and knelt beside the chair. "You will return to your old life," she said persuasively. "You will return to that school of yours! Your friend is only filling in for you, until you are fit."

Miss Annersley looked down at the nurse. "Thank you Jan," she said.

"Now," Jan said, standing as she spoke. "At a risk of repeating myself, I really do think you need a rest. Let me help you to bed."

She saw the older women into her own room and into bed, as she was leaving the room a soft voice stopped her. "Jan? You will be staying, won't you? Please."

"I'm staying," Jan replied. "Now get some sleep!"

Hilda nodded. "Yes ma'am," she said.

* * *

Down in the sitting room Helen looked up as Jan entered the room. "Are you alright, Jan?" she asked.

The nurse smiled. "I feel a little shell-shocked Mrs. Randolph, but I'll be OK."

Helen Randolph pressed some tea into Jan's hands and bade her sit down. "You know that Hilda didn't mean what she said, don't you?"

"I know, it didn't make it any easier to hear though," Jan replied softly.

* * *

The next two or three days passed slowly, Hilda Annersley was extremely subdued, tending to remain quiet and not join in the normal conversation. Until then she had been a willing participant and both her cousin and Jan Wetherall noticed the difference.

On the third day Jan decided to take action, she spoke to Mrs. Randolph and arranged that the sitting room would be free. When they returned from their walk Jan guided Miss Annersley into the sitting room and shut the door.

"I'd like to ask you something, ma'am," Jan said softly.

Miss Annersley looked up quickly but refused to meet the nurse's gaze. "Of course, Nurse."

Jan walked round to stand directly in front of the seated woman. "Who are you? And what have you done with my patient?"

The question startled Hilda so much that, for the first time in three days, she met Jan's gaze with her own. "I-I don't understand," she said.

Jan smiled. "For the past three days I have had a 'text-book' patient," she said gently, "she does exactly what I say, when I say it, she never complains, she rarely speaks, she will not look me in the eye and she agrees with my every opinion." Jan paused to take a breath, then, "Now there are some nurses who would love to have such a patient, but speaking personally, I'd rather get back the Hilda Annersley I've come to know over the past six months!"

Hilda looked away. "You don't understand, Jan, I hurt you, I allowed myself to become angry and..."

"And you are feeling guilty," finished Jan. She smiled. "There's no need, you know, I may be small but I've broad shoulders, and anyway a certain amount of verbal is expected when nursing. Now if you'd tried physical abuse..." she grinned.

For the first time in three days Miss Annersley returned a smile, "I wouldn't dare!"

"That's better! Now, why don't you put what happened three days ago into the past, I'd really like my patient back."

* * *

"Chalet School here, Rosalie Dene, School Secretary speaking."

"Hello Rosalie, may I speak to Miss Wilson please?"

"Oh Miss Annersley! How wonderful to hear from you! Are you well?"

Miss Annersley smiled. "I'm slowly recovering my dear! Far too slowly at times!"

"Well you mustn't rush things, Miss Annersley, and you sound far better than when I saw you in the holidays! Oh, here is the Head, I'll put you through."

"Hilda? Nell here! Everything OK?" Miss Wilson sounded worried.

"Everything's fine, I was just calling to find out what time you thought you'd be arriving, that's all."

"Oh, well it'll probably be sometime in the early evening,

maybe late evening on Thursday. I'm having to wait for a car as the doctors still won't let me drive!" Miss Wilson sounded somewhat annoyed.

A short laugh from her friend was followed by an amused comment. "Nell, you'll be driving long before I am! Be thankful." Hilda's tone was light as she teased her friend.

"We'll expect you when we see you then! You'll probably get here too late for dinner — I know how long it takes waiting for a car — but I'm sure Helen will be able to find something for you to eat! Scraps maybe, or any leftovers!"

She rang off leaving the current Headmistress of the Chalet School spluttering at the receiver in indignation. After replacing the receiver Miss Wilson suddenly laughed before returning to the pile of letters on her desk.

* * *

"Anyway, Edgar, Hilda and I had decided to do a little exploring — we'd been told only to ensure we were back for tea. We came across this small pond that had a little bridge across it, the bridge was only a few feet long, and Edgar was teasing the pair of us by stopping us from crossing. Hilda got annoyed and said she didn't need to cross the bridge, as the pond was only small, she'd jump across. She took a run up and sailed across the pond landing on the green grass on the other side."

Helen's eyes danced wickedly as she continued, "Except it wasn't grass, it was pond weed, and Hilda went straight into the pond up to her waist! Just to add to the problem, uncle Harold's guest had arrived early so there was Hilda's father, a Bishop, having to introduce to his guest — the Archbishop — this object covered in green slime, as 'my daughter Hilda!'"

As Helen Randolph finished her tale the rest of the company erupted into laughter! Hilda Annersley, somewhat pink with embarrassment, protested.

"Helen, this is most unfair! Telling these tales to Jan didn't matter," she flashed a smile to the nurse. "At least she would keep them under the 'medical in confidence' umbrella. But these people are my staff, my colleagues. How on Earth will I maintain discipline if, every time they look at me, they're picturing the state I was in after being pulled from that pond! I was only eight years old!"

"My dear, if I'm telling lies I'll stop! But all the things I've said are the absolute truth! Surely you would want your friends to know the real you?" Mrs. Randolph finished with a chuckle.

"You are a truly evil person Helen Randolph!" The statement would have sounded far more serious had Hilda been able to suppress her laughter!

In the distance there was the sound of the telephone ringing and, a few minutes later, a knock at the door.

"There is a telephone call, Mrs. Randolph," the young maid said. "It is the Chalet School, for Miss Wilson."

Nell stood up. "No rest for the wicked!" she smiled, as she reached the door she turned to her friend. "Remind me again Hilda, it is 'Cleanliness' that's next to 'Godliness' isn't it?"

Jan Wetherall also stood, walking over to stand behind Miss Annersley she spoke softly. "You need to have a break ma'am, I think a rest in bed for an hour or two would be best."

Matey smiled in approval. "Exactly what I was thinking, Nurse!"

Hilda Annersley opened her mouth to protest, glanced at both medical personnel watching her, and decided not to bother.

"Wise decision Hilda!" laughed Dollie Edwards, watching the proceedings with humour. Both Matey and Jan Wetherall looked across at the Junior Mistress with the same expression, Dollie tried to fend them off, holding her hands in front of her as a shield. "Now before you say anything, I've been classed as fully fit, my leg is fine now."

Jan looked across at the imposing School Matron. "I think Miss Edwards may benefit from a short break too, Matron." She said, very properly, but with eyes alight with mischief.

"As do I child!" Matron smiled over at her young colleague. "You deal with your charge, I'll speak to Miss Edwards!" She managed to wink the eye not seen by Dollie. Jan nodded and left, helping Hilda to her room.

When Nell Wilson returned it was to discover Matey and Dollie Edwards having a furious discussion about the need for rest, while Helen Randolph watched in amusement.

"Hilda not here? That's good," Miss Wilson said quickly.

Her two staff looked round. "A problem?" Matey enquired.

"An accident, the new girl Dorcas Brown, broken clavicle and nasty bump on the head. Not her fault apparently, she was saving young Betsy Lucy from falling downstairs and overbalanced herself."

"Shall we return now?"

"No." Bill was certain. "Mary Burnett says she's comfortable in hospital, there's nothing to be gained by racing back tonight—besides it would worry Hilda. We'll go first thing tomorrow as planned. There's no need to let Hilda know anything about it."

"I wouldn't recommend that, Miss Wilson," Jan's voice cut across.

Nell Wilson and the others turned to look at the nurse.

"Miss Annersley will know if you lie to her or try to hide something, I've found that out myself in the time I've known her." Jan continued, "She already knows that you've had a call from the School and is likely to ask about it once she re-joins the company."

Miss Wilson thought for a moment then smiled. "You're right Jan, I'd forgotten how quickly she can trace when someone is lying. One of the reasons she's so good at her job!"

Miss Wilson therefore explained what had happened at the School to her friend when Miss Annersley re-joined them. Miss Annersley accepted the explanation and checked that it was not necessary to return earlier. The following morning she waved goodbye to her three friends, promising that, her condition permitting, she would join them for the Christmas Play.

CHAPTER EIGHT

A TROUBLED CHILD

"Well the good weather has most definitely gone now!" Mrs Randolph was speaking from her vantage point in front of the large bay windows in the sitting room. "The rain is coming down in sheets and it's really foggy! A typical mid-November day!" Mrs Randolph turned to her companion.

"I agree, there's no way we'll be venturing out today." This from Jan Wetherall, "I'm sorry, Miss Annersley but I'm afraid there will be no walk today!"

The third occupant of the room looked up from where she was seated in front of the fire, "It's not so important anyway," she said softly, "my walking is practically normal now. I quite agree with both of you, today is not a day to leave the house. Helen you'll not be going visiting will you?"

Helen Randolph shook her head, "No, I'm staying put. I've already contacted my friends to warn them. I assume you'll be teaching for a while this morning Hilda? Well I have any number of things to do so I suggest we meet again at lunchtime." She smiled at both of them and hurried out of the room.

One o'clock saw them both joining their hostess for lunch, after which they retired to the drawing room for coffee.

Mrs Randolph asked how the tutoring was progressing and conversation continued in that vein for some minutes.

"I must say, when we were growing up, I would never have thought that Hilda would have entered the teaching profession," began Mrs Randolph. "It was never something that was even remotely associated with the family and, in any case, it's not as if Hilda ever needed to work."

"What made you choose to enter teaching then, Miss Annersley?"

Hilda looked thoughtful. "It was the influence of one of my own schoolmistresses, a lady who encouraged a love of both literature and learning. A lady who also decided to help and understand me, when everyone else in the school only wanted to see me punished." She smiled, "And I did deserve punishment, I had been extremely badly behaved at the time!"

"You? Badly behaved?" The expression burst from Jan. "I can't believe it!"

"Oh, I can," put in Mrs Randolph. "I can remember a huge fuss when Hilda would have been 13 or 14. I know that Uncle Harold was summoned to her school but never found out why?" Mrs Randolph looked inquisitively over at her cousin.

Miss Annersley flushed. "Surely you don't want to know that! It's ancient history now, well over twenty years ago, I'd rather not go into all that again!"

"But I'm intrigued Hilda, and I'm sure that Jan is too," said her cousin. "We knew you were in disgrace but not the reason! Come on my dear, I think we must insist!" She glanced across at Jan as she spoke and that worthy nodded vigorously in agreement.

Hilda looked around wildly. "Oh very well, but it's not something of which I'm proud," she began, "and you must both promise never to tell anyone else!" She glared at her listeners, especially her cousin, and they both nodded assent. "I..." her voice dropped down too low for either of them to hear.

"Sorry, didn't catch that."

"I took a bottle of my father's brandy and tipped it into the Staff teapot just before Break!" It was now impossible for Hilda Annersley to go any redder.

There was a stunned silence, and then both her listeners burst out laughing, "Hilda, I'm surprised you weren't expelled!" Helen Randolph gasped.

"I nearly was," Hilda replied ruefully. "Had it been left to the Head that's exactly what would have happened, luckily the Deputy Head, Miss Cullen, intervened."

* * *

"Hilda Annersley, stand up!" Hilda stood, she glanced around quickly, seeing the looks of sympathy on the faces of the twins Ruth and Naomi, then faced the irate mistress.

"Explain to me why your history prep has not been completed!" ordered Miss Burton.

"I, erm, forgot," Hilda replied lamely.

"You forgot?" the sarcastic tone made Hilda shiver. "Well we'll have to see if we can jog your memory. Take out your history textbook and turn to the chapter on Tudor England," Hilda did so and Miss Burton continued. "Now that chapter has ten pages, I want you to write out the entire chapter ten times. Until it is complete you will attend no other lessons and no Games!"

Hilda looked wildly indignant and opened her mouth to protest but the history mistress waved her silent. "I think that is all for now Hilda and I do not want you in my class until that work is complete. Leave the room!"

Biting her lip Hilda stalked out of the room; although knowing that she should take herself to the library to work, Hilda instead ran outside and climbed up the big apple tree growing beside the hockey pitch. She had been there only ten minutes when a horrified shout disturbed her.

"Hilda Annersley! What are you doing out of your classroom? Come down at once!"

It was the Head. Miss Hull was a tall, slim lady in her early fifties. She had light blue eyes and fair hair. She was generally considered to be a hard but fair teacher although she did not suffer fools gladly and rarely allowed sentiment to interfere with her work. She had been one of the founders of the school.

As soon as she had reached the ground Hilda was ordered, "Follow me!"

The Head led her back to Miss Burton's history class where she ascertained the reason why Hilda had been sent from class. She then instructed her charge to go to the Head's study.

Once in the study the Head motioned Hilda to stand in front

of the desk; the Head sat down. "I have had bad reports of you from a number of different mistresses over the past two terms," she began. "In fact the only good reports I've had are from Miss Cullen and Rev King." The Head glared over at Hilda who tried, unsuccessfully, to shrink into the floor.

"So can you explain to me why, with the exception of English and Religious Studies, your work has deteriorated so much?"

Hilda stared at the floor, not answering.

"Hilda!" The tone made her jump.

"Don't know," she mumbled.

"I seriously doubt that!" The Head was very angry. "You have systematically disrupted almost all your classes and your standard of work has dropped dramatically. Why?"

Hilda said nothing, instead staring defiantly at her Head.

"Hilda Annersley I am losing any patience with you!" The Head's voice was tight with anger. "If I cannot see an improvement in your behaviour and work I will have to seriously consider whether you should remain here. You are a disruptive influence on your fellow pupils." She glared at her charge.

Hilda wriggled violently and mumbled something.

"I beg your pardon?" The Head's voice was icy.

"I don't care!" Hilda's voice was loud and shrill. "I hate being here, and can't see the point of all this work. I want to be at home and wish I'd never met you! Why can't you leave me alone and stop interfering!"

The Head went white, controlling her own temper with difficulty she rose to stand directly in front of Hilda. "I don't know if you realise just how rude you have been Hilda! I will not speak to you again today, you will be sent home and I will explain things fully to your father tomorrow."

✽

The next day saw Hilda Annersley being taken directly to the Head's study first thing in the morning by her father. The Bishop was a tall, sad looking man with brown, wavy hair flecked with grey; his blue-grey eyes mirrored those of his daughter. He stood in the Head's study listening as Miss Hull listed his daughter's faults.

"Your Grace, I am sorry to have to bring this news to you."

The Bishop shook his head, "I'm glad that you did Miss Hull, I am extremely upset and disappointed that Hilda has chosen to behave in this way." His voice was deep and soft. "Hilda owes you an apology."

Hilda's eyes flashed and she looked angry, however she obviously held her father in great esteem for a forced "Sorry!" left her lips.

The Head was wise enough to see that that was the entire apology she was likely to get at present and nodded slightly in acknowledgement. She then discussed with the Bishop what punishment would be suitable and it was decided that removal to a Junior Form for the rest of term would have most impact.

"You understand Hilda that this is a form of disgrace," the Head spoke to the silent girl, "it is also a way you can show me you have reformed. It is hoped that the shock of this move will allow you to become a more sober and conscientious member of the community. Otherwise I will have to think seriously about whether I can keep you here."

Once released from the Head's study Hilda stalked out into the grounds at the back of the school. Ruth and Naomi caught up with her by the large apple tree.

"Hilda, what's going on? Are you in trouble again?" Naomi's face was grave.

"You'd better not be seen with me," Hilda replied. "The Head might decide to contact your father and then you'd be in trouble for 'sociating with me."

"Not likely Nan," the elder twin, Ruth, put in. "Dad's not going to say we can't associate with his boss's daughter! What happened?"

Hilda explained all that had occurred in the Head's study both on the previous afternoon and that morning. The twins were suitably horrified at the punishment handed out, although privately Naomi at least thought it was well deserved. Her twin, although the elder in age, still had a lot of growing up to do.

"You'd better knuckle down now Hilda," said Naomi gently. "I'm sure your father will have enough to say to you tonight."

Hilda Annersley's face darkened somewhat. "I don't care, I'm sick of school anyway." She laughed suddenly. "And I've just thought of a beautiful way to get back at the Head and all her staff!"

"What are you going to do?"

Hilda told them and the twins both reacted with guilty laughter.

"You wouldn't dare!" This from Naomi.

"Oh yes I would!" Hilda was adamant.

Hilda spent the day in her new class. Being forced to join with girls almost four years younger than her was humiliating, and she was not helped by the attitude of the ten year olds who seemed to think it was a big joke to have 'a big girl' in class with them – by the end of the day she was seething.

Most of the Staff had looked on the punishment with mainly relief and amusement. After all Hilda Annersley had spent the past six months doing her best to disrupt their lessons. It is true that Miss Cullen, the Deputy Head and Senior English Mistress, had attempted to speak to Hilda. However on receiving monosyllabic grunts in reply she had given up, resolving to speak to Hilda once her pupil had regained her temper.

Hilda herself, after spending the day in a foul temper, had by evening, given herself a bad headache. Normally a very placid person, her rage had caused her to feel quite unwell and she had been thinking of forgetting her latest idea. However Ruth had been prompted to whisper to her that she didn't think Hilda would dare attempt the deed and Hilda had an inordinate amount of pride.

For the next few weeks everything remained quiet. Miss Hull was congratulating herself for her original punishment—it appeared that, contrary to everyone's expectations, Hilda Annersley was settling down. She was working well and had requested additional work as she was finding the repeated lessons too simple.

One morning saw Hilda arriving at school early. In her satchel, along with various textbooks and exercise books, was a small, innocuous looking bottle full of fluid. Before morning classes began she had hidden the bottle away. Morning lessons were quiet; Hilda worked steadily—finding the Third's lessons ridiculously easy. A few minutes before the end of the last lesson before Break, she raised her hand and quietly informed the mistress that it was her turn to collect milk and biscuits for the form. The mistress checked the rota and waved her off.

Once outside the classroom Hilda raced around to the apple tree in the grounds; from within its trunk she retrieved the small bottle, she then ran to the window leading into the Staff Common Room. Agile for her age, Hilda wasted no time climbing through the window into the room. As planned it was empty but the maid had already brought in the jug of milk, hot water, crockery and, most importantly for her, the teapot—already full and brewing.

The bell rang for morning Break as Hilda quickly lifted the lid of the teapot and poured the contents of her bottle inside. In her haste a small amount also dripped into the nearest cup. Five minutes later Hilda Annersley was, very properly, carrying the milk and biscuits on a tray for her Form. The ten year olds making up the Third hadn't even noticed that she was a little late.

Retribution descended less than 15 minutes later! The end of Break bell rang but, instead of being led back to their classrooms, all girls were ordered to the main Hall. On the raised platform at the front of the Hall stood all the Staff and the Headmistress, Miss Hull. At sight of Miss Hull, Hilda swallowed nervously as the Head had never seemed so forbidding. Miss Hull's face was thunderous and her blue eyes flinty as she watched the school file in.

Once all the school had been assembled Miss Hull began, "I have brought you here because of a serious incident," Miss Hull's voice was tight with anger. "Less than 15 minutes ago an attempt was made to poison the entire staff body!"

There was a gasp from the entire school but Hilda could distinctly hear two horrified cries, it seemed that the Head also heard for she swung around to the Fourth. "Ruth and Naomi Tasker! Stand up immediately! Are you responsible for this?"

The twins looked around imploringly as Ruth tried to answer, however Hilda was already on her feet. "It wasn't them Miss Hull," she called out, "it was me!"

"You! Hilda Annersley come out here now!" Miss Hull was white with anger and her voice shook. Hilda slowly mounted the stairs to the raised platform and stood facing the Head. She could see the entire school staring at her, some with horror, some with satisfaction. She also saw all the staff regarding her with mixed feelings, some with almost as much anger as the Head, some with a little amusement. She saw only one sympathetic glance—from the Deputy Head.

"Perhaps I should have expected it from you Hilda," the Head's voice was tightly controlled, "after all you have done your best to disrupt this school for the last two terms. Have you anything to say that will make me reconsider expulsion?"

There was another gasp from the school at large; the last expulsion had been more than ten years before.

Hilda glanced around wildly, although part of her was exultant at the success of her plan, she found herself feeling a large measure of fear and concern. She also felt that, if she were to try to say anything, she would either laugh hysterically or burst into tears—and she wanted to do neither in front of the entire school! To try to prevent this she resorted to reciting lines from a play to keep her calm.

"I asked you a question Hilda!" The Head's voice thundered, breaking through Hilda's calm.

"Yes Miss Hull, I mean no Miss Hull," Hilda answered distractedly. She continued, talking to herself but, unfortunately, was loud enough to be heard by the entire staff body! "Romeo, Romeo, wherefore art thou Romeo?"

Miss Hull looked livid and stepped forwards intending to shake her errant pupil when a calm voice intervened. "I think, Miss Hull, that Hilda is a little upset at present. Suppose you allow me to deal with her? Once I've got to the bottom of this incident I'll report back."

The Deputy Head's voice recalled the Head to her senses and she agreed immediately, turning to order Hilda to go with Miss Cullen, she then dismissed the school back to normal classes.

"Come with me Hilda." Miss Cullen's voice was calm and gentle and she was able to guide the girl out of the Hall and along the corridor to the Staff rooms. Miss Cullen was a short woman with brown hair and soft brown eyes. She suffered from arthritis and walked with a stick, therefore the journey to her study was slow and allowed Hilda to regain a measure of control. Miss Cullen opened the door to her own small study and beckoned Hilda inside. There were two chairs near a small log fire, Miss Cullen limped over to one and indicated that Hilda should take the other.

"Hilda," Miss Cullen's voice was soft, "why did you do this?"

There was silence.

"You must realise how serious this is?" The mistress continued. "Did you buy the alcohol?"

Hilda looked up sharply. "No! It was from my father's study. He had left it out after his guests had gone home."

"I see, so you stole the bottle?" The voice was still soft but Hilda winced at the words, "Did you also drink some of the alcohol?"

A sharp, horrified, "No!" burst from the girl.

"Thank Heavens for small mercies!" Miss Cullen's voice was almost amused. "Now, tell me Hilda, why did you do this?"

Hilda looked around wildly for a few moments, then her eyes rested on those of her favourite mistress, she swallowed once before replying. "It was when Miss Hull told me I was being sent to the Third Form, and that almost all the staff wanted this," she began. "The Head said that it would hopefully make me a more sober and conscientious member of the community. I thought I'd show them what it meant not to be sober!"

There was silence for some time as Miss Cullen strove to

control herself; except for her lip twitching she was largely successful!

"And what is your excuse for your behaviour over the last two terms? There has to be a reason why a clever and talented girl should suddenly decide to change her behaviour so dramatically. Did you want to be expelled?" This last said with sudden insight and Miss Cullen was pleased to see a slight flush appear on the girl's face.

"You did want to be expelled? But why?" The Deputy Head's voice was perplexed.

"Doesn't matter why, so long as it happens," the muffled reply was quiet.

"It does matter Hilda." Miss Cullen's voice was firm. "I wish to know why my star pupil, the person I considered to be the best at English in the school, should be trying to get herself expelled."

Hilda's face had flushed with pride at Miss Cullen's praise but she shook her head and refused to answer.

"Hilda, I want an answer from you! What happened six months ago to effect this change in attitude? What changed in March?" Miss Cullen's voice remained soft but with a steel ring to it.

Hilda looked up and reddened. "I can't say," she whispered, "I promised Miss Hull."

Miss Cullen nodded. "Very well, I am going to ask her. Remain here Hilda, you may choose a book to read from those shelves. I'll send a maid with some milk." The Deputy Head left the room.

Miss Hull was attempting to wade through a mound of paperwork when a knock on the door heralded the entrance of her Deputy.

"Oh Elizabeth, have you managed to get to the bottom of Hilda Annersley's behaviour?" The Head had regained her temper.

Miss Cullen shook her head. "Not yet, Grace, though I have discovered that Hilda wants to be expelled!"

"In that case I think we can oblige." Miss Hull's reply was swift.

"No," cautioned the Deputy Head. "I'd like to know exactly what has caused her to suddenly act in this way. Had you asked me at the beginning of the year I would have said that Hilda Annersley was an exemplary student. Something happened to her early this year, she refuses to tell me, says she promised you something."

Miss Cullen glanced across at her Head and saw a slight flush spread across Miss Hull's face. "You do know, Grace!"

Miss Hull shook her head. "I am aware of nothing in her school life that could have caused Hilda Annersley to behave badly."

"And in her home life?"

"You know I will not allow problems at home to influence the school..."

"You may not Grace, but most people do not have your discipline." Miss Cullen was firm. "Did something happen in her home life?"

"Her mother died of Influenza early in March." The statement was bald.

Miss Cullen stared at her Head. "You mean to tell me you have known of this and not thought it could be related to her behaviour? We're talking about a thirteen year old child, Grace! This is inexcusable! That girl has had to deal with this on her own? And you wouldn't allow her to tell anyone would you? That's the reason she said she couldn't tell me!" Miss Cullen turned to go then swept back suddenly. "I'm going to find out all the background to this, Grace, and you are not going to expel her. If you try I'll ensure your actions here are made public knowledge!"

The Deputy Head swept angrily out of the study leaving the Head speechless behind her!

Back in her own study Miss Cullen appeared as Hilda was finishing her milk. The girl looked up apprehensively as the English mistress entered the room. Miss Cullen sat next to Hilda and smiled sympathetically over to her pupil.

"Miss Hull has told me about what happened in March to your mother, Hilda." Miss Cullen's tone was gentle. "Why don't you tell me in your own words."

Hilda Annersley's face had brightened slightly and she seemed somewhat more relaxed. "We were all ill with the 'flu. Daddy and I were not too bad although my eldest brother John was off work for two weeks. Simon, my other brother was away in France and didn't get 'flu—he got injured at the Front though. Mummy was quite ill too. She took a long time to get well and spent half the day in bed 'cos she was ill."

Hilda stopped there to scrub her eyes quickly before continuing. "One day I was late for school—I'd overslept and was in a rush. So I ran out of the house without breakfast, I also forget to kiss mummy goodbye." Hilda looked down at the floor for a long time before going on. "I-I-I didn't mean to forget, honest! It's just I was in a rush an' I didn't think it mattered and mummy wouldn't mind." She swallowed convulsively. "That day John came to the school to take me home at lunchtime. He s-s-said mummy had gone to visit Jesus."

Hilda looked up at the Deputy Head. "I never got to say goodbye!" she sobbed.

Miss Cullen gathered the crying girl into her arms; Hilda continued to talk between sobs. "I didn't even know she was that ill! No one told me anything. An' now she thinks I didn't care about her 'cos I couldn't be bothered to say goodbye!"

Miss Cullen tightened her grip on the child and softly murmured, "Of course she doesn't think that, silly! She's in Heaven now and she knows all your innermost thoughts. She knows that you love her!"

"Are you sure?" The voice was muffled.

"I'm sure." The certainty in the Deputy Head's voice calmed Hilda somewhat. "Your mother knows that you love her and she loves you. She also knows that it wasn't your fault that you couldn't say goodbye."

Hilda cried for a few more minutes, but this time Miss Cullen sensed that they were tears of relief. When she had finally recovered and was seated again in her chair, Miss Cullen continued.

"Is that what all of this has been about?"

Hilda nodded.

"But why did you want to get expelled?" The English

mistress sounded perplexed.

Hilda gulped then said, "I didn't want to be away from Daddy. If I were at school it could happen again. Daddy wouldn't let me give up school."

"I see, and how do you feel about that now?"

"Well perhaps I don't need to be home again." Hilda looked worried. "But how can I stay here now? The Head said she was going to expel me!"

"You let me worry about that." Miss Cullen was very positive. "Now I think you had better go home for now — I'll take you. Will your father be in?"

"Yes."

"Good, I'll have a word with him; explain what's been going on, I'll also speak to Miss Hull. I'll see you back here first thing tomorrow morning."

The following day Hilda reported back to the Deputy Head, she was feeling a great deal better, Miss Cullen had spoken with her father for some time the previous day and, after the mistress had left, her father had spoken to her and hugged her. He had even apologised for not telling Hilda that her mother was so unwell, and he'd confirmed that her mother would continue to love her and not blame her for not saying goodbye.

When Miss Cullen showed her pupil into the Deputy Head's study she was pleased to note that Hilda appeared to be far happier and that the air of defiance had disappeared.

"Well Hilda, yesterday's events have still to be rectified," Miss Cullen began softly. "What are you going to do, to make things better?"

"Don't know." The reply was muffled.

"Yes you do Hilda, what is the first thing you must do to start to put right this poor joke?"

"Suppose I should 'pologise."

"Apologise, Hilda, you have an excellent speaking voice, you should ensure that you always use English correctly. You enjoy English lessons don't you?"

Hilda looked up, "My favourite," she said.

Miss Cullen smiled, "And mine! Now, you will have to

apologise to the Headmistress, the staff and the girls. Yes I mean it!" This last as Hilda had looked up in indignation. "You owe the Headmistress an apology for the trick and your rudeness. You also must apologise to the girls for disrupting their lessons yesterday—although I expect some enjoyed the disruption—and, of course, you must apologise to the staff. You do realise that any of the staff could have become quite ill if they had drunk your mixture—even myself?"

"Oh no, Miss Cullen! I knew you would not be ill—you don't drink tea!" Hilda's reply was quite innocent and caused Miss Cullen to bite her lip again and turn away.

When composed once more she continued. "Now, your punishment will be severe, but you will not be expelled. If you can accept your punishment and grow from it, I expect Miss Hull will eventually stop being angry with you—however you should be aware that she wanted to expel you straight away. I have managed to persuade her to give you one more chance. I hope you will not disappoint me?"

Hilda looked up with tear-stained eyes violently shaking her head.

"Your earlier punishment has been rescinded and you are to rejoin the Fourth; however you are to be in isolation for the rest of the term. That means you sit apart from all the other girls and are not allowed to speak unless a mistress or master addresses you. This punishment only applies while you are at school of course. You will continue to take Games lessons but are not allowed to take part in any matches—I understand you are a good hockey player?"

"Yes ma'am, I play Right Wing."

"Well I'm afraid the school will have to do without your skills."

The Deputy Head paused to view her charge thoughtfully for a moment. "Hilda, for the past six months your work has been appalling—well below your normal levels—in almost all subjects. This was reflected in your poor exam results last summer and in your being placed in the B stream rather than the A this term. I believe you can do far better than that. If you would like, I am prepared to help you by some additional tutoring after school so you can make up the work you missed when you were trying to get yourself expelled!" Miss Cullen's tone was warm as she said the last!

Hilda looked up eagerly and with determination. "Thank you Miss Cullen, I'd like that!"

* * *

Miss Annersley finished speaking and her audience stretched and blinked in the gathering dusk.

"Good Heavens!" exclaimed Mrs Randolph. "Where has the time gone?" She quickly rang the bell and requested that tea be served.

"How long did your punishment continue, Miss Annersley?" Nurse Wetherall was curious.

"The isolation continued throughout the term," Hilda Annersley replied. "Not a pleasant punishment! Although luckily only during school hours. I believe Miss Hull would have continued the punishment for longer, but my ranking at Christmas persuaded her that I was working hard once more."

"What was your ranking?"

Hilda coloured slightly. "I was top of the class," she said shyly.

"I continued seeing Miss Cullen long after I had caught up on my work. She was possibly the best mistress I have ever come across. Not only did she cause people to love her subject, but also she tried to understand the reasoning behind her pupils' behaviour. She became Headmistress herself only a year later and was excellent," she smiled. "She even made me Head Girl in my final year! She died a few months after seeing me achieve a First at Oxford, unfortunately she didn't live to see me teach." Hilda concluded sadly.

"She inspired you to be the same type of mistress?" Jan said with understanding.

Miss Annersley nodded. "Yes, it's the best epitaph I could envisage for her."

CHAPTER NINE

SYBIL

The first of December saw Jan Wetherall packing up to return to Exeter; her three month leave of absence from the hospital was finished and she had to return to the neurosurgical unit. Mr Roberts had been on the phone the night before telling her that he was expecting two new patients and wanted her there to receive them. Miss Annersley joined Jan in her bedroom as the nurse was completing her packing.

"I really wish I had asked Mr Roberts for a longer leave of absence for you," Hilda Annersley confessed.

Jan smiled slightly. "You don't need my help any longer Miss Annersley, your walking is fine—it's just a case of building up times and muscle. The same with your reading, just a question of time, no more."

Hilda Annersley nodded. "I know all that Jan, but I don't want to keep you here to help with my convalescence, only because I'll miss you."

"I'll miss you too, I'll also miss our tutorial sessions. If I pass those exams next March it'll be due to you."

Miss Annersley shook her head, "Not true—you've done the work, all I did was guide you in the right direction."

"I think that's what teaching is all about!" Jan said softly. She finished packing her case and turned to the older woman. Miss Annersley was standing there with a rather worried expression on her face. Jan noticed she was holding an envelope.

"Is something wrong?" the nurse asked.

Hilda Annersley smiled. "No," she took a deep breath, then, "Jan, this is for you," she handed over the envelope. "Now I know you're going to try to refuse but I don't want to hear any ideas of class differences—we've passed all that. The money in that envelope is my personal thank you to you. Regardless of the skills of the surgeons, if it hadn't been for you I would still be in that hospital bed. Don't ever allow anyone to tell you that you are anything less than an exceptional nurse." She flushed slightly, remembering, "Even if they happen to be your current employer!"

Jan opened the envelope and her eyes widened at the sum of money inside. "This is not necessary, ma'am, you've already paid my salary for the last three months..." she began.

"Yes it is necessary," the quiet voice replied. "It will in no way repay the debt I owe to you, but it can at least be used to bring pleasure. Use the money as you wish, perhaps use some of it on that family of yours!"

Jan looked down for some time before meeting Hilda's gaze. "Thank you," she said softly.

A little later Jan's luggage was being loaded into a car and she stood at the door with both Helen Randolph and Hilda Annersley. Helen stepped forward first, holding out her hand. "Jan, I've really enjoyed having you as a guest, I will definitely know who to call should I ever require a nurse. Please don't be a stranger—if you are ever in Chepstow I expect you to visit!" With a glance at Hilda, Helen Randolph waved goodbye and vanished back indoors.

Jan and Hilda stood looking at each other for some time, then.

"The car's waiting." This from Miss Annersley.

"Yes," Jan stepped forwards, holding out her hand, "I'll *really* miss you," she said quietly.

Hilda Annersley looked down at the hand and shook her head, stepping forward she took the younger woman in her arms, Jan returned the hug and the two woman stayed thus for some time. Eventually they broke apart.

"You look after yourself, Miss Anner..." Jan stopped as Hilda Annersley placed a finger on her lips.

"My name is Hilda," she said firmly. "I expect you to remember that when you write!"

Jan nodded. "I will, and don't worry, you'll get back to that School of yours, I just hope they realise how lucky they are!" She turned away then, brushing her eyes and walked over to the car. She got in and the car pulled away.

Hilda Annersley watched her go, a lone tear running down her cheek.

* * *

For the next two weeks or so, Hilda continued with her convalescence; her cousin joining her for her walks on a number of occasions. She even managed to attend church for the first time since before the accident—it had proven impossible previously owing to the organ music which affected her head. Hilda Annersley, an intensely spiritual person, had greatly missed her church and was extremely grateful that she could now go, especially in the weeks leading up to Christmas.

A letter from Nell Wilson reminded her of her promise to attend the school's Christmas play and, after checking with Mr Roberts whether it would be advisable, she wrote back expressing her intention to attend. Madge Russell immediately contacted her offering a place to stay overnight at the Round House.

She arrived at the Round House to be met with glee from both Madge and Joey Maynard who had brought her young son, Stephen with her. Hilda had not seen Stephen since March and so noticed a dramatic transformation between the month old baby then, and the ten month old trying hard to walk now! She spent an enjoyable few hours with her friends and both Stephen and Madge's baby Ailie. Later that afternoon Jem Russell joined them; Hilda took the opportunity to have a quiet word with him.

"Jem, I've just spent the last few hours with Madge, Joey and their babies without any ill effects, my head feels fine. I know I'm not yet strong enough to return to work full time, but surely I could at least return on a part-time basis?"

Jem looked across at Hilda. "You know what Mr Roberts

said, Hilda," he said uncertainly, "not before Easter."

Miss Annersley sighed, "Jem, I didn't know just how much I would miss work, and I haven't even the solace of tutoring any longer, Jan has returned to the hospital. My cousin is a dear, but I'm not designed for a country life!"

Jem Russell thought for a moment. "See how you get on at the Play today Hilda, and we'll discuss it further tonight."

* * *

"Are you ready, Hilda?" Miss Wilson said somewhat impatiently. "We do not want to get there late. Seeing you arrive would stop the play in its tracks!"

Hilda laughed. "I'm sure you're exaggerating, Nell! Why should my appearance do that?"

"You underestimate the influence you have, my dear! Oh the girls like me well enough, but I think they almost worship you! I only hope none of the actors catches sight of you during the performance—they'll forget their lines."

As she spoke Hilda appeared and the two friends hurried into the waiting car.

* * *

Jem Russell and Jack Maynard were both waiting for her when Miss Annersley returned to the Round House that evening. Neither of them said anything as she settled herself in the chair pulled close to the fire by Madge. Eventually Hilda sighed and turned to address both doctors.

"I was back with the school for three hours at most, some of it watching a play, then answering questions and addressing the school in the hall!" Her hand lifted to her head. "And yes my head has started to hurt once more. You are correct, I'm not ready, yet!"

Jack smiled sympathetically. "You will be Hilda, just give it a few more months."

Jem nodded. "Jack's right Hilda, you'll be ready soon, and

considering how ill you were, your progress has been remarkable." His keen eyes reminded Hilda that he was the only one of her friends who knew just how much progress she had made.

"Hilda would you like to rest before dinner?" Madge noted that her guest was very heavy-eyed.

Hilda nodded and allowed her hostess to lead her to her room.

* * *

Hilda slept for just under two hours and, on awaking, realised that her headache had gone. She noted that it was about an hour before dinner and decided that she was hungry. A quick visit to the bathroom and a change of clothes and she felt fit to descend to join the Russells. On her way she had to pass the nursery and noted that the door was ajar. Thinking to check on baby Ailie she entered quietly and immediately noted a slight figure standing beside Josette's bed.

"Sybil? What are you doing here child? You should be in bed." Her voice had regained much of its richness and the low tones did not wake either of the younger children. Sybil, however spun round quickly.

"Oh, I'm sorry Auntie Hilda, I didn't disturb them I promise." Sybil's voice sounded tearful. Miss Annersley walked over to the eldest Russell girl and put her arm around those thin shoulders.

"I can see that," she smiled. "Now, why don't we go back to my room and you can tell me all about it."

She guided the young girl back to the small guest room and sat her down on the bed. Hilda Annersley had been told all about the difficulties caused by Sybil earlier in the year. She had been responsible for seriously injuring her younger sister, solely because she had disobeyed a strict order. However Hilda was puzzled, she had heard from Joey that Sybil had redeemed herself during the summer, and had appeared to turn over a new leaf. Yet here she was, out of bed past her bedtime and sneaking into the nursery. What was going on? Hilda was determined to find out!

"Now Sybil, tell me why you were in the nursery." Hilda Annersley's low voice was sympathetic and comforting and the young girl scrubbed her eyes before replying.

"I woke up thinking that Josette was ill again, Auntie Hilda, I had to check, cos it was my fault she was hurt."

"But Josette is well now, Sybil, why should you think she was hurt again?" Hilda's voice was gentle.

"I dreamt it" Sybil whispered. "I keep dreaming it, I see Josette all burnt and screaming, and I wake up sure it's happened again. As I was home tonight I thought I had to check." Sybil turned a tear stained face towards Hilda, "I'll never forgive myself for what I did!" She burst into tears and buried her face in Hilda's lap.

Hilda drew the sobbing child to her and wrapped her arms around her.

"Sybil" she said softly, "stop crying now, I want to talk to you."

The girl swallowed her sobs, recognising in the tones her Headmistress rather than Auntie Hilda.

"Now Sybil," Miss Annersley began. "I thought this had all been dealt with months ago, yes you caused the accident that led to Josette being burnt—but your parents have forgiven you and Josette has almost recovered. Your Auntie Joey told me how good and helpful you were when she took you on holiday in August and September, and Miss Wilson has said how well you're doing in class. Why have you suddenly started feeling like this again?"

Sybil looked up into Miss Annersley's face. "'Cos of what's written in the Bible," she whispered.

Hilda Annersley was surprised but did not allow her surprise to register on her face.

"What do you mean, Sybil?" she asked gently.

The young girl gulped and then continued. "The new father at church, he said it," she whispered. "He said that man could not forgive sins, only God could forgive sins. When I asked him later if hurting Josette was a sin, he said it was. So mummy and daddy forgiving me doesn't count does it Auntie Hilda? 'Cos it's in the Bible so it must be true!"

Miss Annersley was mentally thinking some extremely uncomplimentary and irreverent thoughts, about vicars who failed to consider the impact that their words could have on impressionable young minds! However she allowed none of this to show in her demeanour. She smiled at Sybil. "My dear, as you get older, you will realise that there are some things written in the Bible that have different meanings, depending on just who happens to be reading them!"

She reached into her small case and removed her personal copy of the Bible, turning to the Gospel according to St Luke, she flicked through until she reached the point she wanted. "Now Sybil, the vicar was correct, up to a point, we cannot be truly forgiven for our sins until we ask God." She pointed to Chapter 11 in the Gospel, verses 2–4. "Read those three verses Sybil," she said gently.

She waited while the girl did so, Sybil turned to her aunt. "That's The Lord's Prayer," she said quietly.

Hilda Annersley smiled. "Yes Sybil, now, in the middle of the Lord's Prayer there are some lines that are vitally important: 'Forgive us our trespasses, as we forgive those who trespass against us.' Do you know what they mean?"

Sybil nodded. "It means we are asking God to forgive our sins... oh!" Her face brightened. "But I've said The Lord's Prayer lots of times since Josette's accident, so I must be alright then!"

Miss Annersley looked at her in amusement. "Well that depends, Sybil," she began, "did you mean to ask God to forgive you? And were you truly sorry? I don't think you have thought about it until now."

She smiled at the downcast face in front of her. "Sybil," she said gently, "it's never too late, you know! If you ask God now, and you are truly sorry, He will forgive you! All you have to do is repeat His prayer and mean every word."

"Really?"

Miss Annersley nodded. She watched as the girl scrambled to her feet and then knelt by the bed, she began to speak but stopped at Miss Annersley's signal. "Sybil, there's no need to speak out loud, He can hear you just as easily if you say it to yourself!"

She watched as the girl closed her eyes. A few minutes later she opened them again and smiled at her Auntie Hilda.

"All finished?" Miss Annersley's voice was gentle. The girl nodded. "Then you are forgiven Sybil," she watched as a tremulous smile appeared on the girl's face.

"I feel all clean inside," Sybil whispered, "as if everything is new!"

"That's because God has forgiven you." Miss Annersley stood up. "Now, I don't think you'll have any more nightmares about Josette any more, will you. So let's get you back to bed!" She walked with the girl back to her own bedroom and tucked her in, kissing her goodnight before leaving the room and closing the door, Sybil already almost asleep. As she turned she saw Madge Russell standing there watching anxiously.

"I was just coming to wake you," Madge said quietly. "Is Sybil alright?" Her voice betrayed how worried she was about her eldest daughter.

Hilda smiled. "She'll be fine, now, Madge. She just needed a little help, that's all." She quickly explained the scene in her room and how Sybil was unlikely to now have any more nightmares. As she finished she glanced across at her hostess and was surprised to see Madge Russell quietly crying.

"Why Madge, whatever is the matter?" Miss Annersley's beautiful voice brushed over Madge Russell who looked imploringly at her. Hilda glanced around and then quietly pulled her friend back into the small guest room.

Once she had sat Madge on the bed and fetched a glass of water for her, she settled herself in the chair opposite and waited. After a few minutes Madge looked up.

"Hilda, Jem and I have known there was something wrong with Sybil for some weeks now. Both Matey and Nell had tried to find out what it was, without success. She kept having nightmares, but wouldn't tell any of us why. That's why she's here tonight even though term hasn't finished yet. Nell Wilson was hoping that if she were in more familiar surroundings, she might let us know!"

"Well it worked, Madge, I just happened to be the one closest, that's all!" Hilda's voice was soft, she looked more closely at Madge, then continued gently. "There's something else though isn't there?"

Madge Russell sat staring at the floor for a time before replying. "Hilda, I feel that both Jem and I have failed badly as parents, at least as far as Sybil is concerned." She gave a short laugh, "I can remember any number of occasions when her faults were pointed out to me, before the accident, yet I ignored them, wanting to see only the good in her, not seeing the bad."

"There is a lot of good in Sybil, Madge," Hilda Annersley agreed. "How could there not be? But, yes, she also has bad within her, after all she is only human, we all have both good and bad."

"But until Josette's accident I refused to see it, refused to act. If I had acted, then the accident would not have happened..."

Hilda shook her head. "You cannot be sure of that, Madge, however much you give children a foundation, you cannot be sure of exactly how each individual child will react. Consider the alarms and excitements your own sister put you through! Yet she is now extremely responsible." She paused, smiling, then continued, "When she wants to be!"

Madge Russell shook her head. "Even Joey saw it, she warned me that Sybil's attitude was becoming ugly, I still did nothing. If my baby sister, more than twelve years younger than I, could see it, yet I missed it—I must be a poor mother!"

"Madge, if you were a poor mother, you wouldn't be sitting up here punishing yourself for something that is not your fault. Instead we'd both be downstairs eating!" Hilda Annersley smiled and received a slight smile in return. "Being a mother, or a father, doesn't come with an instruction manual, there isn't a helpful book that you can refer to whenever things go wrong, or a list to check up if you've forgotten something. On the evidence of this evening, I would say that Sybil has most definitely changed for the better, I think she will become a child and a woman that you will be proud to call your daughter."

She moved over to the bed and sat next to her friend, placing her arm around Madge's shoulders. "You are a very good mother, Madge, and you will, like every mother, learn to become even better with experience."

Madge Russell smiled and kissed her friend on the cheek. "Thank you, Hilda, how do you always know the right thing to say?"

Hilda laughed. "I don't Madge, I just say what I believe to be true, it was never a habit that endeared me to my brothers when I was a child! But perhaps I've learnt to be rather more tactful as I've grown up!"

Madge looked over at her friend wonderingly and Hilda caught the look. "What is it, Madge?"

"Forgive me, Hilda, I was just trying to work out why you had never married and had a family." She paused then continued hurriedly, "Oh, please don't think I'm prying..."

Hilda Annersley shook her head, smiling. "I've no objection to answering, Madge, the short answer is because I never found someone that I wanted to marry. If I'm honest though, I could never envisage being married, I value my independence too much. I suppose, were I to meet someone that I could love, as you love Jem, or Joey loves Jack, that my opinion would change. I rather doubt it though!"

"Don't you have regrets though, Hilda?" Madge continued, "About never having the chance to be a mother yourself?"

Hilda Annersley smiled gently. "Oh but I am, Madge," she said quietly. "After all, as far as the school is concerned I am the Abbess—a Mother Superior. And, to paraphrase the book, 'I have, and God willing will continue to have, hundreds of children, most of them girls!' I have always felt a very special affinity with Mr Chips."

She waited while Madge Russell tidied her face and then the pair of them descended for dinner.

CHAPTER TEN

CHRISTMAS

On returning to the Randolph household, Hilda Annersley settled back into her normal regime; her plans for the Christmas period had been to remain with her cousin. Helen was expecting her daughter Nell home from school on the Wednesday (the 22nd) and had already made a number of plans for the holidays. She had assured Hilda that Nell was a quiet child, Hilda, Headmistress at a girls' school for more than six years, had smiled and forbore to correct her cousin. She felt that her condition was improved such that she would be able to manage with one child, although she knew that returning to the school was not possible at present.

The weekend before Christmas, however, Helen received a telephone call early one morning, while the cousins were still having breakfast. She returned to the table looking decidedly vexed.

"What's the matter, Helen?" Hilda asked gently.

Helen Randolph looked across, a worried expression on her face. "That was Nell's school," she began. "It seems they have an epidemic of mumps, nine girls have just developed it, they are not going to allow any of the girls home for Christmas!"

"How is Nell?" Hilda asked quickly. "Has she developed the illness?"

Helen sat down at the breakfast table distractedly. "No," she sighed, "and she's unlikely to catch it, but they can't risk sending the girls home. As the quarantine for mumps is so long it seems simplest to just keep them there for the entire holiday. They have extended a welcome to any mothers who wish to join them for Christmas but..."

"Helen," Hilda Annersley spoke firmly, "if your only reason

for not joining your daughter is me, then that is not a good enough reason. I can find alternative arrangements for Christmas!"

Helen Randolph looked across hopefully. "Are you sure, Hilda? I don't want to seem as though I'm pushing you out, but if I were to go to Nell, the house would be deserted, I always give the servants the Christmas and New Year period off."

"Don't worry about it, Helen, I'll just make a phone call—I'm sure something can be arranged!"

Miss Annersley was away for less than ten minutes, when she returned she was chucking softly.

"What is it?" Helen Randolph was intrigued.

"I've just spoken to Nell Wilson, my friend from the school, you remember? She was about to call me, she has a small cottage in Devon, and a cousin of hers is using it at the moment with her three children. The family has moved back to Portsmouth for the holiday as her cousin's husband is on leave—he's a sailor—the cottage is empty and Nell was going to call me to see if I fancied spending Christmas there with her."

* * *

Arrangements were swiftly made; as neither Miss Annersley nor Miss Wilson was able to drive owing to the accident they arranged for one of the school cars to take them. Hilary Burn, spending Christmas with Gillian Linton and her sister, volunteered to drive them down and to return and pick them up again in the New Year. The Chalet School term finished on the Wednesday before Christmas therefore the Thursday saw a car, loaded with provisions donated by Karen, Madge and Joey, and carrying Nell Wilson and Hilary Burn, arrive at the Randolph house. Hilda Annersley bade goodbye to her cousin, who was waiting for a taxi to take her to the railway station, and got into the back of the car, joining her friend Nell.

"Good to see you again, Hilda," Nell Wilson smiled. "We have enough provisions to last the entire winter, so we shan't starve!"

The journey to Dartmoor progressed in easy stages; although much improved, Miss Annersley was still affected by the vibration from a car if travelling for long periods, therefore Hilary stopped for a break every hour or so. After a short, quiet discussion between Hilary and Nell, one rest stop occurred in the middle of Exeter and Nell Wilson suggested to Hilda that she stretch her legs.

"There's something I want to show you," she said mysteriously.

Hilda got out of the car and looked around her in some puzzlement. She was in an ordinary street at the bottom of a hill. There was a wall at the base of the hill opposite the road. The road turned sharply to the right. She looked across at her friend with a questioning glance.

"You don't recognise it, do you?" Miss Wilson said softly.

Miss Annersley shook her head slowly.

Nell smiled and pointed to the hill. "This is where we had the accident back in April, that's the hill we were coming down in the bus," she said, "and that's the wall the bus slammed into before overturning!"

Hilda looked more closely at the wall; it showed signs of having recently been rebuilt.

"Where did I finish up?" she asked, interested.

"You were thrown out of the bus," Nell explained. "I think because you were still standing when the accident happened, the rest of us were seated. You ended up over there, near that tree. Dollie, Jeanne and I were still in the bus, Dollie had to be cut out, though I was able to crawl out by myself before the ambulances got there."

"Nasty." This from Hilary Burn who had joined them. She spoke to Hilda. "You have no memory of any of this, Hilda?"

Hilda Annersley shook her head. "I cannot remember anything after the last day of the Spring Term until I awoke in hospital," she said softly. She looked again at the hill, the wall and the distance she had been thrown from the bus. "For the first time, I believe that to be a blessing!"

The three women got back into the car to resume their

journey. They arrived at Nell's cottage early afternoon, Hilary helped Nell unload all their provisions and luggage; both of them flatly refusing to allow Hilda to carry anything. Hilda instead went to explore the cottage; she had not been there before. Described as a cottage there were two bedrooms and a bathroom upstairs and a kitchen and fairly large lounge downstairs. It had an outside lavatory. The cottage was situated in a large garden and had views from the lounge and one of the bedrooms onto the moors. It was less than half a mile from a nearby, fairly large, village, yet appeared to be completely alone, with no other human habitation visible.

Hilda quickly found the kettle and lit the gas stove; a cup of tea would be welcome for all. The kitchen soon warmed up because of the gas hob, but a chill in the December air drove Hilda into the lounge, intending to light the fire. She found Hilary already there, placing small amounts of coal onto an already burning fire. She smiled around at her old Headmistress.

"Thought you'd need this lit before long, Hilda," she said shyly. "The forecast for all of Christmas is very cold, there's even some snow expected on Christmas Day! It'll be good to have a White Christmas, I miss the winters in the Tyrol."

Hilda smiled, the Games Mistress, an Old Girl of the school, had been a pupil when the school had been in the Austrian Tyrol.

"I doubt that the snow will be anything like that experienced in the Alps, Hilary," Hilda said softly. "However, it would be pleasant to see the ground covered in snow, if only for a short time!"

She disappeared out to the kitchen to retrieve the boiling kettle from the hob. As she was searching for the tea, Nell appeared with a large box of provisions.

"My cousin took a great deal with her to Portsmouth," she explained, "so I've brought a lot just in case." She searched through the box and retrieved a packet of tea.

Some minutes later the three women were seated in the lounge with tea and a box of biscuits, the fire started by Hilary already giving out heat and taking the chill from the room.

Hilary didn't stay long; finishing her drink she sprang up, stating that she should go soon to take advantage of at least the small amount of light left. She left after hugging Hilda and Nell and wishing them both a Merry Christmas.

The next hour or so saw the two friends unpacking and ensuring all provisions safely stored. Nell Wilson went out to check on the level of coal in the bunker and also noted that a large pile of logs was stored near the garden shed, halfway down the garden.

"We shouldn't have any trouble with fuel then, Hilda." She commented once back inside and warming herself in front of the fire. "It's probably just as well as I think it's going to be cold over the next few days, and we'll need to light the fires in our bedrooms as well!" She glanced across at her friend. "Sorry if it seems a little basic though, I've only ever used it as a holiday home!"

Hilda smiled. "I think your cottage is perfect, Nell," she said softly.

Later, after their evening meal, the two friends sat in companionable silence, Hilda reading, while Nell sat attempting the Times crossword. After managing to complete most of the clues she sat back, relaxing into her chair. Hilda Annersley looked across.

"You look as though you needed to relax Nell," she observed quietly, "have you had such a terrible time this term?"

Nell Wilson smiled, "Hilda, I refuse to discuss the school with you!" she said mock sternly, she then relented slightly. "No, the term was fine, but I must admit to enjoying being away from the responsibility for a short time, here I'm just me."

Hilda nodded. "Understood, Nell!" She smiled, and returned to her book.

Nell disappeared out to the kitchen and returned a short time later with tea for both of them. Hilda finished the chapter of her book and placed it to one side.

"I am sorry, Nell" she began, "I'm hardly being good company for you, I'll leave finishing the book until later."

Nell laughed softly. "Hilda, seeing you reading again gives

me so much pleasure I'll gladly forgo any conversation from you!"

Hilda looked across sharply. "Why, what do you mean?" she asked quickly.

Nell shook her head. "Hilda, did you think I didn't know? I've known about your problems with reading for months now!"

Hilda looked somewhat annoyed. "Jem Russell told you!"

"No one told me," Nell replied, she moved across to kneel beside her friend's chair. "Ever since I've known you, Hilda, you have always been reading. In the Staff Room and then later in your study, you always had at least one book on the go! Now I came to visit you in hospital over the summer holidays three or four times, you did not have any book in evidence. Not even the Bible! Added to which, when you answered my letters it wasn't even your handwriting!" She looked across interrogatively at her friend.

"That was Jan, she answered all my mail, I dictated my replies."

"I guessed as much." Nell's voice was soft. "So are you going to explain?"

Hilda Annersley sighed slightly before explaining the problems there had been earlier in the year, in particular with her reading ability. She tried to gloss over just how serious they had been but Nell Wilson was able to see the truth.

"Hilda, that must have been devastating news for you," Nell sounded quite horrified. "Why didn't you tell me? And why tell Jem Russell?"

"I didn't tell Jem, he discovered from Mr Roberts," Hilda was quick to reply, "and I didn't tell you because you had enough to worry about. You'd just got back to the school, and I know more went on there than I've been allowed to find out! You didn't need additional worries about me!"

"Hilda, that's ridiculous!" Nell sounded almost angry, she paused to take a breath and calm down before continuing. "Remember what we said to each other, back in April, when you had just recovered consciousness? We said we would be family to each other. Well families share things, Hilda! At the very least you would have had another person to talk to about it. You should not have had to deal with this on your own!"

She took one of Hilda's hands in her own and looked deeply into the blue-grey eyes. "Now you promise me, Hilda, that you'll never try to hide something like that from me again."

Hilda looked across at her friend for a short time before gently inclining her head...

The following morning, Christmas Eve, saw the two friends up early, the night before had been a clear and very cold one and there was a heavy frost with ice along all the pathways. After breakfast they decided to walk into the village. Being used to alpine winters they were both prepared for the cold and had dressed appropriately. In addition they had both packed their nailed boots and the icy surfaces held few worries. The village itself was a typical rural village, with a church in the centre and a large green. There were a number of shops displaying a few festive decorations, but the shelves appeared very bare owing to the impact of rationing.

"Probably as well that we brought most of our supplies with us," Nell remarked softly. "I doubt there's much to spare here."

Hilda nodded gravely. "Yes, we tend to forget, occasionally, that we live in a privileged environment. Even so, I wouldn't have thought that the rationing has affected everyone here as badly as in the larger towns and cities. At least they should have dairy products here—we'll have to stop off at that farm we passed on the way back."

Walking past the village green Nell looked down a side street and stopped in disappointment.

"What's wrong?" Hilda asked.

"The Catholic Church there has been boarded up," Nell replied. "It doesn't look as though it's in use any more."

They went into the local corner shop/post office to send off a few letters. While there Hilda also bought some stamps, while Nell chatted with the local vicar who was sheltering from the cold. On the way back she turned to her companion. "There's a Catholic Church in the next village down," she said. "It's only a mile away. I'll walk over there tonight for Midnight Mass."

"Nell!" Hilda was laughing. "Please don't tell me that's what you were speaking to the vicar about!"

Nell Wilson winked at her friend. "Trust me, Hilda, they always know where the opposition are located!" She grinned.

On the way back to the cottage they were able to purchase some milk, butter and eggs. The farmers wife also asked if they needed anything else.

"Oi 'eard on the wireless that not many families would be having a turkey dinner this year," she said, her Devonshire accent quite pronounced. "We've no turkeys but might be able to spare a small chicken for the two of you?"

Nell, sipping the cup of tea that both of them had been provided with, shook her head. "That's very kind of you, Mrs Cooper, but we brought a great deal with us. The cook at the school has provided us with a chicken for tomorrow!"

Later, that afternoon, Hilda and Nell were both in the kitchen preparing food for the following day.

"Do you know, until coming here for Christmas," Hilda remarked, "I cannot remember the last time I actually cooked for myself."

Nell looked across at her friend and surreptitiously attempted to take over preparing the chicken. Hilda saw what she was doing and laughed.

"I'm not a health hazard, Nell!" she protested. "I do know what I'm supposed to be doing! I was just saying that it's a long time since I cooked. After all we get no opportunity when at the school and I don't have anywhere else I can call home. Whenever I go away it's generally to hotels or friends who have servants."

"Well I'm afraid this guest house is very basic, Hilda," Nell responded with a grin, "and I'll expect you to help with the washing up and the cleaning too!"

That evening the two friends were sitting next to the fire, the weather remained clear but very cold. They had listened to a few items on the wireless and had also heard the BBC News, now they were both sitting in silence, thinking. Nell Wilson retrieved her cigarette case from the side of the chair and extracted one; she looked across at her friend. "Cigarette, Hilda?"

Hilda Annersley roused from her day dreaming and looked over at Nell who repeated her question. "Oh, no thanks Nell," she murmured. A few minutes later she looked at the clock, it was almost ten-thirty.

"Nell, what time were you planning to leave for Midnight Mass?"

Nell shrugged. "The vicar said it was about a mile away so if I want to be there for half eleven I should leave by ten past eleven at the latest. A brisk walk should get me there in time."

"Oh," Hilda paused for a moment, then. "I'm unable to make a brisk walk just yet, but if we left a little earlier I could easily manage the distance. Would you mind if I accompanied you?"

"Of course not, Hilda." Nell looked across at her friend, slightly surprised. "If you're sure? I mean, the daughter of an Anglican Bishop!"

Hilda smiled. "Different path, Nell, but the same God," she said gently...

The following morning there was a soft knock on Hilda's door and then Nell Wilson appeared. "Merry Christmas Hilda, I brought you some tea."

Hilda Annersley glanced over at her clock before replying, "Merry Christmas Nell, but why so early?" The clock said only six-fifteen am.

"You came to Midnight Mass with me," Nell replied. "If you stir yourself we'll make First Eucharist at your church—I checked, it's at seven-thirty today."

Hilda smiled. "In that case you're forgiven for disturbing me so early!"

"Early! This is normal rising time at school!"

"I'm convalescing! And it's Christmas!" She drank the tea. "I'll be right down, thanks Nell."

They arrived back at the cottage, following the service, a little before nine o'clock for a late breakfast. The Christmas Day morning was cold and dark, with a great deal of cloud banked up on the horizon that Nell Wilson, with her expert weather eye, said promised snow before the day's end. As the temperature was plummeting, Nell decided that the fires in the two bedrooms should be kept alight and disappeared upstairs. Hilda, after clearing away the breakfast things, thought that more fuel would be required and quickly slipped on her outside shoes and coat to bring in some of the logs stacked by the garden shed.

She had made two trips up the icy path and back with some logs when she heard Nell's voice. "Hilda Annersley get back here this instant!" She looked around, Nell was stood just outside the kitchen door staring angrily in her direction.

"What is it, Nell?" Hilda asked softly, as she brought back another load of logs. Nell didn't reply immediately, instead taking her by the arm and pulling her back into the warm kitchen. Once there she spoke.

"Hilda, have you completely lost all your common sense?" Nell's tone was extremely exasperated. "You are still convalescing from a severe head injury, you're still not totally steady on your feet and you're prancing around outside in icy conditions with no more than ordinary shoes on! Suppose you'd slipped over?"

"But I didn't slip over, Nell," Hilda pointed out, reasonably she thought.

"That's beside the point," Nell returned. "You could have, and if you'd hit your head it could have had serious consequences! For goodness sake Hilda!" She went to say more but then obviously gave up, instead pulling on her own shoes and coat to retrieve the rest of the logs.

Hilda watched through the kitchen window as her friend stalked angrily up the path toward the logs, halfway there she had to step over a small rock, as her foot came down on the other side of the rock she slipped slightly, overbalanced and slipped backwards! She fell back, sitting abruptly on the grass, standing up again immediately she shot a glance toward the kitchen but was unable to discern if her fall had been seen. She collected some logs and retraced her steps, being particularly careful when coming to the small rock.

On entering the kitchen she saw that Hilda was standing by the window and realised that her friend must have seen everything. However Hilda was stood with a totally expressionless face, watching as Nell entered the kitchen.

"Everything alright, Nell?" Hilda's voice was very quiet, Nell looked across suspiciously but her friend's face remained impassive.

"Everything's fine, Hilda. Why do you ask?"

"Oh, no reason." Hilda's voice seemed a little cracked and Nell swung round to look at her friend again. Hilda's face remained impassive but, suddenly, Nell noticed that those blue-grey eyes were almost swimming in tears of laughter, while Hilda was biting her lip in an effort not to smile! Hilda turned to look out of the window again. Nell walked up behind her.

"You wouldn't be thinking of laughing at another's misfortune now would you, Hilda?" Nell spoke softly into her friend's ear.

"Wouldn't dream of it, Nell," the quiet voice almost whispered.

Nell remained suspicious but could see that Hilda had her features under control, she stormed out of the kitchen muttering something about taking the logs upstairs, once in the lounge however, she swiftly removed her shoes and crept back into the kitchen. Hilda Annersley stood, facing the window, her head down and her shoulders shaking, she was crying with silent laughter!

"You rat, Hilda!" Nell burst out. "Laughing because I slipped over, that's hardly charitable behaviour now is it?"

"I'm not laughing because you slipped over," the surprising response; "well, not totally. I'm laughing because I didn't!" Hilda turned to face her friend with a huge grin on her face, "And after all, Nell, even if I had slipped, it would hardly have been a head injury would it?" She began giggling again and, after a few more seconds of injured pride, Nell joined her...

Christmas dinner that afternoon was a quiet affair, the two friends had prepared a traditional English fare with chicken rather than turkey, small sausages, roast potatoes, carrots, peas, cauliflower and Brussel Sprouts. There was a small Christmas pudding afterwards, donated by Joey's Anna, and a little pot of Devonshire cream that Mrs Cooper, the farmer's wife, had pressed upon them the day before. After eating, Hilda and Nell sat back in the armchairs almost unable to move! They listened to the King's Christmas broadcast on the wireless and then washed up.

On their return to the lounge with coffee, they exchanged gifts. Hilda gave Nell a small package, on opening it Nell found a new set of Rosary beads and a silver St Christopher medallion on a chain. She passed over to Hilda a larger parcel, inside was a leather bound volume of the Complete Works of William Shakespeare. The first flakes of snow started to fall just as it was getting dark, and both women went out into the garden at the back. Dressed for the cold and, this time, both wearing their nailed boots, they watched in silence as the snow covered the landscape, turning everything white.

The snow stayed on the ground for only a few days, although it remained cold. Hilda and Nell took the opportunity of the holiday to relax further. They walked up on the moors for hours on end, Nell ensuring that the pace was slow enough so that her friend could keep up. Hilda found her walking improving even more and her strength returning. During these walks Hilda even persuaded Nell to talk, a little, about the School and any concerns that she had; offering advice borne from experience.

"After all Nell, I am hoping to return after Easter," Hilda said on one occasion, halfway through the week between Christmas and New Year. "I feel I can at least start to take an interest in the School affairs!"

"So long as it's from a distance then, Hilda, I will keep you informed. I may even write asking for your advice on occasion!" Nell replied, "But I do not expect to see you on the School Grounds before Easter, you know! The Chalet School is 'out of bounds' as far as you're concerned!"

"I wouldn't dream of returning to the school before my surgeon gives his permission, Nell," Hilda responded quickly, with an amused look. "I've heard just what an ogre their new

Headmistress can be!" She smiled sweetly at her friend.

New Year's Eve saw both women sitting, listening to the wireless to see in the New Year. As the sound of the chimes from Big Ben sounded over the airwaves, Hilda and Nell clicked together the small glasses of sherry they were both drinking in a toast.

"Happy New Year, Hilda," Nell said, kissing her friend on the cheek. "Let's hope it's a good one, perhaps by the end of it, we'll be that much closer to the end of the War. And I hope it will be a far better year for you than 1943."

Hilda reached out to grasp her friend's hand. "Happy New Year, Nell, regardless of everything else that happened, I don't consider that 1943 was a bad year. I feel that the accident had one very good result, I discovered I had a sister!" She smiled across at Nell.

Hilary Burn appeared on January 2nd, she dropped Hilda back at the Randolph House before going on to the school.

CHAPTER ELEVEN

THE TYROL

Midway through January some official-looking visitors appeared at the Randolph Household asking to speak to Miss Annersley. Hilda met them in the sitting room. Her cousin Helen accompanied her.

"Forgive us for disturbing you, Miss Annersley," the taller of the two men began, his arm outstretched to shake Hilda's hand. "I am Colonel Jackson, this is Mr Howard, my colleague and I are from the War Office, this is our card." He passed over a small card. "We have been assigned to the 'War Crimes Commission', as you may have read, it is the government's intention that all those of the enemy responsible for crimes against the conduct of war will be asked to account for their behaviour."

"I have read a small amount about those intentions, Colonel," Miss Annersley's voice was, as ever, calm. "How may I assist you?"

"We understand that you were present in Austria during the time of the Anschluss?" Mr Howard asked.

Hilda nodded. "Yes I was the Headmistress of a school situated in the Tyrol area, near Innsbruck."

"We understand that the school had to vacate the area very quickly owing to some trouble involving some of the mistresses and girls of that school and a local mob of Nazis?"

"It did." Miss Annersley paused, looking at both of the men gravely. "Gentlemen, I am not the person to speak to about those events, my friend and colleague, Helena Wilson, was the mistress involved. You may find her at the Chalet School; I will give you the address. She is currently the Headmistress there."

"Our thanks, Miss Annersley, but it was not, precisely, the events involving the mob that we were interested in." The Colonel smiled slightly before continuing, "One of the officers involved in the rapid and forced evacuation of your school is under investigation. He may be charged with war crimes and we want some background on his earlier deeds. Do you remember a Rudi Bhaer? He would have held the rank of Lieutenant at the time?"

Hilda Annersley nodded. "I remember Lt Bhaer, Colonel, what information do you require?"

"Just all you can remember of that time, Ma'am." This from Mr Howard. "I'll be taking notes as this will be useful as background."

* * *

Hilda Annersley, Headmistress of the Chalet School for well over a year, was attempting to pack up all the items in her study. The amount of correspondence alone was exceptional and she was not sure exactly what the Nazis were going to allow them to take. She sighed; leaving the Tyrol was going to be a huge wrench for all the staff concerned, and for her in particular. A resident in the quiet Austrian Alps for almost five years, she had grown to love the land and its people. She was; however, well aware that recent events showed just how unsafe the land had become.

A knock at the door heralded the History Mistress, Con Stewart. "Hilda, you wanted to know when Otto had a good fire going?"

"Oh yes, thank you Con." The Head glanced around at the files. "Perhaps you could give me a hand?" she asked.

"Of course, what are you doing?"

"Trying to decide what files should be burnt," replied Miss Annersley dryly. At her colleague's expression she chose to elaborate. "I do not believe the Nazis will allow us to take these files with us, Con. And we have records here of every German and Austrian pupil who has ever attended the Chalet School."

Miss Stewart's eyes widened as she realised the implications. She swallowed quickly then replied, "It never occurred to me but you're right. These cannot be left. What about staff records?"

"The same, all records of any Austrian mistresses or masters will be burnt. Although a number of them are hoping to join us, not all of them will. These types of records could be very informative in the wrong hands."

Between them the two women managed, after making a number of trips, to take all the files to the fire. Hilda sighed with relief as she watched the last of them burn and then the pair of them returned to the Head's Study.

"How many of the girls are packed?"

"Matey said over half, she thinks the rest will be completed easily tomorrow," Miss Stewart replied. "Have you managed to book the train? "

"I believe so; it leaves Innsbruck 8am day after tomorrow. Rosalie Dene, Dr Jem's secretary, was on the phone earlier, she'll be bringing the tickets across sometime this evening."

Con Stewart clicked her fingers, suddenly remembering something. "Matey asked me to speak to you, said could we have bedtime for all the girls brought forward an hour—the next few days are likely to be tiring and tomorrow will be busy."

Hilda nodded. "I'll announce the time during the notices. By the way, either you or Jeanne will have to take prayers for the Catholics tonight; it doesn't look as though Nell will be back in time."

"No problem." 'Charlie' made to leave and then stopped. "Hilda, there's something else isn't there? I mean apart from all this dreadful situation."

The Head looked over at the younger woman, debating with herself whether or not to mention a concern. "It may be nothing," she began, "but, it's almost 6pm, I expected Nell Wilson back from Spartz long ago. I have a terrible feeling that..." she stopped and gave herself a little shake, saying with a laugh, "Oh it's nothing Con."

Con Stewart looked across at her Head thoughtfully.

"I know you Hilda Annersley, you are not one to worry unnecessarily. The last time I can remember you having a feeling like this there was a reason—Stacie Benson remember?"

Hilda paled; she could easily remember the sense of urgency that had caused her to rush her group of girls back from the dentist three years ago. She had been certain that something dreadful had occurred back at the School, but unable to say what it was. Of course, on reaching the School they had discovered that Eustacia Benson had run away, the girl had nearly died.

"Yes I remember, Con," she said softly. "And I pray that I'm wrong this time!"

The normal business of the Chalet School continued for the rest of that evening. When Nell Wilson and the others had not returned by 8pm Hilda rang up Die Rosen. She spoke to a Madge Russell almost out of her mind with worry.

"I've heard nothing Hilda." Madge's voice plainly told of the strain she was under. "The last thing Joey said to me was that she'd get Daisy and Robin back by 6pm as we will be up early tomorrow to catch our train. Margot's frantic too, in fact Jem has sent her to bed, she was worrying so much she was making herself ill!"

"Has Jem contacted the Police and the hospitals?"

"Yes, but they've been extremely unhelpful. The only thing we've heard is from one of the English doctors attached to the San, he said he was in Spartz earlier and there was some sort of riot."

"Well I wouldn't expect Nell Wilson to allow any of the girls to get involved in that!" The Head was positive. "Look Madge, perhaps they've just got caught up and missed their transport. They'll probably be contacting us soon."

She rang off and her sense of unease grew dramatically. She sat thinking for a short while and then pressed the bell on her desk. When the maid appeared she asked her to go inform the Staff that she was calling an emergency Staff meeting in ten minutes...

At the meeting all the staff were subdued, they listened while

Miss Annersley related her concerns about the non-return of Nell Wilson and party.

"Do you feel something has happened to them, Hilda?" This from Mademoiselle de Lachenais.

The Head nodded. "Yes, Jeanne, I'm convinced of the fact, especially after what Madge said about hearing there had been a riot in Spartz."

"But there's no way Nell would allow any of the group to get mixed up in that!" Miss Norman protested.

"I know that, Ivy," Miss Annersley replied, "but I think they may have inadvertently become a part of it. Jem Russell has contacted the authorities but received little information." The Head paused to glance around at her Staff before continuing. "Now you all know why we moved here at half term, and you are as aware as I, of the current unrest in this part of the world. I believe they are in serious trouble."

"Do you think they have been arrested, Hilda?" The quiet voice belonged to Miss Edwards; she was voicing the question all the Staff wanted answered.

Hilda Annersley shook her head. "I don't know Dollie," she said quietly. "I pray that they have not, that instead they are running. Regardless, it will not take the authorities long to turn their attention to us, and we have more than 120 girls here, for whom we have responsibility."

"What do you want us to do, Hilda?" The calm, matter-of-fact voice of Matron Lloyd, 'Matey' to most people, cut across the rest of the Staff's thoughts.

Miss Annersley smiled at the Matron. "I am going to attempt to bring our departure forward as much as possible, we will need to ensure everyone is packed ready. Include the belongings of the girls who are missing, but ask one of their friends to remove any items the girls hold dear. If the authorities arrive they may want to search their belongings—I doubt they will be gentle!"

After a little more discussion the staff all left to help with the packing, Hilda signalled to Con Stewart to remain.

"Con, I know this is hard for you, Nell's your closest friend.

But if you could check through her belongings please? Try to retrieve anything she holds dear, any mementoes or photographs, anything you can think of that she would want saved."

Miss Stewart nodded gravely. "She's your friend too, Hilda, is there anything you can think of?"

The Head considered. "Any photographs of her family, and her Rosary," she smiled. "I'm sure you can think of other items," she watched as the younger woman left.

Returning to her Study, Miss Annersley placed a call through to the main Railway Station at Innsbruck. After a number of different functionaries she was finally placed through to the Stationmaster. She asked him if it were possible the reservations made for the day after tomorrow for the Chalet School, could be changed to tomorrow. The Stationmaster was suspicious of her motives and unable to give a definitive answer. He did, however, promise to return her call as soon as he had made enquiries.

For the next two hours there was frantic activity within the school; although the Juniors had already gone to bed, the rest of the school were awake and pressed into helping to complete all the necessary packing. The girls were told only that there was a possibility that the School would be travelling tomorrow rather than the next day. For the most part the girls accepted this, although one or two of the elder girls looked grave and concerned.

Miss Annersley did, however, speak to Polly Heriot, Joyce Linton and Ilonka Barcokz, the three remaining Prefects. Mindful of the advice Matey had uttered when Mademoiselle had fallen ill, the Head told the three girls something of the truth. She explained that Miss Wilson's party, including a number of their own select group, had not returned from a shopping trip and that she had serious concerns about their safety.

"Did something happen in Spartz, Miss Annersley?" This from Ilonka.

"I don't know, but I suspect that they have become caught up in something."

"Then they could be in serious trouble, couldn't they?" This from Polly, she flushed slightly as Miss Annersley's calm gaze swept over her. "My guardian allows me to read *The Times*, Miss Annersley, I have read about incidents in both Germany and Austria."

The Head nodded. "Yes Polly, they could be in serious trouble." She replied softly.

"What can we do to help, Miss Annersley?" Joyce asked, and Miss Annersley marvelled anew at the change in character from someone who, when a Middle, had come very close to expulsion.

"For now girls, support the others, look after the Juniors and pray." The Head's request was uttered with simplicity.

By ten o'clock news arrived; Rosalie Dene, Dr Russell's Secretary and an Old Girl of the School arrived clutching the tickets for the School's train journey. She asked to see the Head.

Once in the Head's Study, Rosalie waited until the maid had left before turning a worried face toward Miss Annersley.

"Dr Jem sent me, Miss Annersley," she began rather breathlessly, "there are soldiers and police everywhere and he believes they are listening to the telephone calls. I had a genuine reason to visit because of these." She indicated the tickets she had placed on the Head's desk.

"You have news for me, Rosalie?" Miss Annersley's voice was calm and betrayed none of her mounting concern.

The young secretary nodded swiftly. "About an hour ago one of the herdsmen from the upper shelves brought Daisy Venables to Die Rosen."

"She was on the shopping trip?" Miss Annersley asked.

"She was," Rosalie confirmed. "She has told us exactly what happened in Spartz and where the rest of the party are now!" She informed the Head of all that had happened during the afternoon and evening, including where Miss Wilson and party were currently hiding.

On hearing the news Miss Annersley, still showing her young guest her normal, calm demeanour, rose and walked over to stand beside the window. Hidden from the secretary's view, the Head's expression cracked as her horror and concern for her friend and pupils threatened to overwhelm her. She looked out at the mountains and then took a deep breath; her eyes closed as she silently uttered a prayer for help and courage. A few moments later she returned to her seat, her countenance as calm as ever, she asked Rosalie what the Russells had decided.

"Dr Jem and Madame agree that they must all flee, they are trying to decide where would be best, and both Dr Maynard and Dr Mensch are planning to join them."

"Are the party unhurt?"

Rosalie nodded. "We think so, at least from what we can tell," she smiled. "Poor little Daisy is only twelve and very tired! She said they were all well but she also said that Miss Wilson's hair had turned white, so I'm not sure just how accurate her description is!"

"That does seem most unlikely." Miss Annersley's face showed her scepticism at her colleague's change in hair colour. "You didn't mention Robin, I know she was on the trip, is she with Miss Wilson?"

"No," Rosalie replied, "from what Daisy has been able to tell us, Miss Wilson left her with the innkeeper, Herr Borkel, she hasn't appeared yet, but we hope that she, at least, is safe."

Miss Annersley nodded, then seeing that the young women was also somewhat upset by the news she had delivered, rang her bell and asked the maid for some coffee.

While drinking and persuading the younger woman to eat some of the fancy twists included, Miss Annersley voiced something that had surprised her. "How on Earth did you manage to convince Dr Jem that you should make the trip across to here? I would have thought he consider it far too dangerous!"

"I think he would, normally, Miss Annersley," Rosalie replied, "but I was planning on coming across with the tickets anyway, and it was felt that he should be at Die Rosen in case of any visits from the police."

"Well I think, Rosalie, that you should remain here tonight, and not attempt to go back to Die Rosen." The Head's voice showed her concern. "If necessary we can introduce you as a member of staff here—perhaps even my secretary, I most definitely need one!" she smiled and Rosalie smiled back.

Miss Annersley passed on to the Staff that the party were safe, but didn't mention any of the details that Rosalie had told her. She was also able to say that the Stationmaster at Innsbruck had rung back and was able to change their reservations to 10am the following morning. The Head sent everyone off to bed quickly, although she, personally, did not believe they would be allowed to sleep for long...

Less than two hours later there was a frantic hammering at the front door; Miss Annersley, who was only dozing, awoke immediately and got up, she reached the door at the same time as Matey and nodded to the Matron to open the door. Outside stood a tall man, very Germanic in appearance with blond hair and blue eyes. He was dressed in the uniform of the SS, the secret police. Miss Annersley, her mouth suddenly very dry, stepped forward.

"May I ask your business, Sir?" Her tones remained calm but, to Matey at least, the Head's voice was slightly shaky.

The officer looked toward her and clicked his heels. "Fraulein Annersley?" His voice was soft and friendly. "I am Leutnant Rudi Bhaer, my apologies for the lateness of the hour but I have some very important questions that need answering." He smiled, suddenly looking only sixteen years old and, despite themselves, both women found themselves relaxing somewhat.

"My men will remain outside, Fraulein, the questions should take only a few minutes."

Hilda Annersley nodded slightly. "Of course Lieutenant, would you please follow me?" She led him along the corridors into her Study and bade him sit. "What are your questions, Lieutenant?" she asked softly.

The SS Leutnant sat back in his chair. "There was an incident in Spartz today, some of your girls and staff were involved. I should like to speak to them." His tones were reasonable, friendly.

"I know of no incident in Spartz, Lieutenant," the Head's voice remained calm.

"Nevertheless, an incident occurred, and I wish to speak to the following people." He read from a list: "Helena Wilson, Hilary Burn, Maria Marani, Jeanne Le Cadoulec, Evadne Lannis, Cornelia Flower, Lorenz Maico and Cecilia Humphries. I understand the first is a mistress at this school, while the rest are pupils?"

"That is correct, Lieutenant, they went on a shopping trip to Spartz earlier today, they have not returned."

A flicker of something, Hilda Annersley did not know what, crossed the officer's face, it disappeared in an instant and the officer smiled. "Where are they?"

"I do not know, I spoke to the owner of the school earlier this evening; her husband had tried the authorities and hospitals without success..." She stopped as a sudden increase in noise was heard by both of them. Miss Annersley could hear doors being flung open, shouted commands in German and the sound of many girls crying, sobbing. She looked across at the SS officer. "What is happening, what are your men doing?" she asked, her voice loud, commanding.

The man smiled, it was not a pleasant smile. "My men are looking for these fugitives, Fraulein, it will go badly with you should they discover them. The rest of your staff and girls will be held in the hall until they, too, can be questioned."

The Head's face darkened in anger. "They are only children, Lieutenant, and you lied to me! I must go to them." She made to stand up...

Suddenly the man was beside her, one hand holding her down in the chair, preventing her from moving. "No Fraulein, you will not move until I tell you. You will do exactly as I order, now where are the fugitives?" Suddenly the man had become infinitely more menacing.

Miss Annersley saw he now held a pistol in his right hand, while still holding her with his left, her mouth dry and her breath coming in short gasps, she repeated her words.

"I can only tell you what I know Lieutenant, my Senior Mistress and some pupils went on a shopping trip to Spartz, they have not returned. I do not know where they are."

"You lie, Fraulein." The words were cold, emotionless. "Do you know what I can do to you?"

"I am a British citizen, Lieutenant..." Miss Annersley's words were cut off.

"Verdammt!! Your government has stood aside and done nothing so far! Why should that change? Do you really think they will care about a few women and children?"

Miss Annersley remained silent, her eyes on the muzzle of the pistol.

"Have you heard of the term 'protective custody', Fraulein Annersley? Or perhaps 'political prisoner'?" Lt Bhaer's voice was soft and conversational once more.

"Yes, I've heard of them," the reply was a whisper.

"You would not last a week there, that is if I allow you to go." The SS officer's voice became even more smooth and soft as he traced the muzzle of his pistol down the Head's cheek. "After all, you are still a fairly young woman..."

The man swung away and stood on the opposite side of the desk once more, he looked across at the woman in the chair. Despite herself, she was trembling and the man, on seeing this, smiled.

"Get up, Fraulein, we go to speak to your school." His voice darkened. "If I do not like the answers they give me, I may just decide to allow my men some target practice. Remember that, Headmistress," he said the word mockingly, "remember what will happen if your school gives me the wrong answers!"

Miss Annersley rose and walked around to stand next to the SS officer, she looked across at him and spoke, her voice, normally deep and low, now cracked, a parody of it's normal rich tones.

"Lieutenant, not the children, I'm begging you..." she began.

"I am looking for these fugitives," Lt Bhaer interrupted, "if they have not yet been found they may be hiding among the rest of your girls or staff. I intend to question all of them and check their details against their files. You do have files?"

Miss Annersley nodded, pointing to the cabinets across the other side of the room.

"Excellent."

There was a knock at the door and two soldiers walked in.

"Now remember, you will follow my commands exactly, Fraulein, you will not deviate," the Leutnant's blue eyes bore into the blue-grey eyes before him. "If you say or do anything that I have not approved, you will lose one of your pupils. Do you understand?"

"Yes, I understand," came the faint reply.

Bhaer turned to the soldiers. "I want all the personal files, staff and children. Bring them to the hall!" The two men picked out the cabinets and prepared to transport them.

*

In the hall there was bedlam; all the Chalet girls had been roused from their beds and herded into the large room, many of the younger girls were crying while some of the older girls attempted to soothe them. The staff had also been roused and were all standing along one wall, two guards preventing them from helping the girls. Those domestic staff still attached to the School had also been awoken. Around the walls at set intervals stood the soldiers, dressed in black and carrying sub-machine guns, these men watched the despair with hard eyes and expressionless faces.

Lt Bhaer appeared at the main door, beside him walked Miss Annersley; the Head was white in the face and trembling slightly, although this was seen only by the sharp eyes of Matey. The officer walked onto the dais and toward the lectern set up for the Head's use. As the noise continued he suddenly drew his pistol from its holster and slammed the butt into the top of the lectern three times. The wooden lectern cracked and split beneath the onslaught and the noise was sufficient to quiet the room.

Everyone's eyes turned to the lectern, Lt Bhaer smiled in satisfaction and ordered the Head to join him in the centre, she swallowed slightly before addressing the crowded Hall.

"Lieutenant Bhaer is looking for some people," she said

softly. "Miss Wilson and her party. He intends to check each person's identity against our records and will require that each of you come up onto the dais individually. I have told the lieutenant that we have not seen any of the missing party since this morning. If anyone here has seen them, they should inform the lieutenant, it is exceptionally important that you are absolutely accurate and honest." While saying this, Miss Annersley's gaze swept across the staff, lingering for a split second on the white face of Rosalie Dene...

* * *

Miss Annersley paused in her recital of events from almost six years before to drink from her tea cup, the two men suddenly awoke to the lateness of the hour.

"I do apologise ladies," this from Colonel Jackson. "I had no idea how late it was, Miss Annersley, what you are telling us is fascinating and exactly the type of information we require as back up."

The other man, Mr Howard, nodded his agreement. "Most definitely," he said. "This type of eye witness account gives us a feel for the man, he certainly appears to enjoy the power his rank and position gave him."

"We should go now," the Colonel said, standing. "May we return tomorrow for you to complete your story?"

Hilda Annersley nodded. "Of course, gentlemen," she said softly, "I have yet to tell you of his behaviour in front of the entire school."

CHAPTER TWELVE

ESCAPE FROM TYROL

The following day, before the men from the War Office arrived, Helen had the chance to speak to her cousin.

"Doesn't it bother you, Hilda? What that beast said, the things he threatened you with? You seemed to be able to relate everything so calmly and it doesn't seem to have affected you in the slightest. I know you've always been composed, but I would have expected some sort of reaction!"

Hilda Annersley smiled, "What makes you think that I didn't react, Helen?" she asked softly. "As to dwelling on what happened in the past—that's a waste of energy. God allowed me to survive, he allowed Nell and the others to escape, those are the only important results of those dreadful days." Miss Annersley's face remained composed although Helen could see a slight hint of the feeling that she had endured.

A knock at the door heralded the return of the two men from the War Office.

* * *

The two soldiers appeared with the files and placed them on a large table that they carried onto the dais. They also brought a chair for the SS Leutnant; he sat down and beckoned the Head to his side.

"As each person is brought up here, Fraulein, you will tell me their name so my man can retrieve the file," he ordered.

Miss Annersley nodded and the SS Leutnant signalled his men. One at a time the girls were told to mount the steps to the dais, as each one did so, the Head told the Leutnant the girl's name and form. Standing in front of the Nazi the girls appeared young, scared and vulnerable. Miss Annersley ached to be able to do something for them but the threat from the Leutnant held her in place. Each girl answered the questions, saying they had seen nothing of the party, sometimes the man accepted this, but on other occasions he shouted at the girls, accusing them of lying.

On one occasion, when the shouting Leutnant had reduced a girl to tears there was a commotion from the staff ranks; Miss Stewart, her red hair an indication of her hot temper, broke ranks to go to the girl. She was roughly seized by one of the guards and pushed back, some of the other staff attempted to hold her back but she shrugged them off, rushing toward the girl. Before she had taken more than a few steps a guard had stepped across and raised his rifle; the rifle butt caught Con Stewart across the cheek, splitting the skin there and raising a welt of blood. She fell back and was immediately caught by some of her colleagues. The sudden violence stopped the girl from crying and she was able to answer the Leutnant's questions and be dismissed.

Con Stewart stood still, shaken, her temper still roused but now fully aware of her own danger, she whispered angrily to her nearest neighbours.

"Why doesn't Hilda do something? She's just stood there, hasn't said a word, hasn't objected or anything!" Her lowering expression caught the Head's eyes accusingly and Miss Annersley flinched, well able to read the accusation.

One of the guards heard this whisper and replied, "If your Headmistress says or does anything not sanctioned by the Leutnant, he will order one of your girls shot!"

The staff stared at him in horror and he nodded quickly before turning away, not wishing his own people to see him passing on information to the enemy.

Con Stewart, a handkerchief pressed against her cheek to stem the bleeding, looked over toward the Head once more. This time, when Miss Annersley's fleeting glance caught her own she mouthed the word 'sorry' and was rewarded by seeing the Head blink twice in acknowledgement.

Biddy O'Ryan, when accused of lying became richly Irish in her replies, forgetting to speak German and instead rudely insulting the man in her native tongue. Luckily for her, the Nazi did not understand what was said and simply signed for a soldier to drag her away. At the first touch from the soldier the young Irish girl fell into a fearful silence, as though just realising what she had risked.

Most of the hall was in silence, apart from the Head's voice murmuring names as each girl approached. Occasionally there was a delay when a file could not easily be accessed. Finally all the girls had been questioned, the last, Polly Heriot, giving the same reply as the rest—she had not seen the party, she had no idea where they were.

The Leutnant stood up and began to pace angrily, he turned to his sergeant,

"Are there any other girls in the building?" he snapped.

The sergeant shook his head. "None, Sir! We have checked the surrounding buildings and out houses as well."

The officer nodded. "Very well, bring the women here, one at a time!" he ordered.

The staff were ordered to the dais individually, they also had nothing further to say, then halfway through their number, Rosalie Dene walked to the dais, as she mounted the steps Miss Annersley spoke, her tones carrying to the young woman.

"Miss Rosalie Dene, School Secretary."

There was a pause as the man with the files searched through the few left, he then reported back that there was no file of that name. The Leutnant smiled slightly.

"At last," he said with satisfaction, "Fraulein Wilson I assume?" He picked up Miss Wilson's file and retrieved a small photograph from it. Glancing first at it then at Rosalie Dene he frowned. "No, and you are not still a school girl."

He sat there, thinking, while Rosalie waited, then "Explain!" he ordered sharply.

Rosalie Dene gulped slightly. "M-m-my file is probably in the archives, Lieutenant. I was a pupil here and have only recently been appointed School Secretary. I have not yet had the opportunity to retrieve it."

"And these archives are where?" The question was asked of Miss Annersley.

"In England," the soft reply.

"Very well, Fraulein Dene, answer the question, have you seen the fugitives since they left for Spartz?"

"I have not," Rosalie's reply was swift and firm.

"Do you know where they are now?" The second of the two routine questions was snapped out, Rosalie swallowed slightly, her gaze not moving from that of the SS officer.

"I do not!" Her reply was just as firm and the Leutnant grunted and dismissed her. On her way off of the dais she caught the Head's glance, Miss Annersley's face remained expressionless but her eyes were smiling.

The remainder of the staff were seen without incident, when the last of the staff had been dismissed the soldiers brought the few remaining files, they were those of the missing party. The Leutnant looked across at the Headmistress.

"It seems then, Fraulein, that you spoke the truth, the fugitives are not here. No matter, we will find them, there are search parties out all over the surrounding countryside. It is only a matter of time. You are leaving here today?"

The question caught Miss Annersley off-guard and she quickly glanced at her watch, it showed the time as just after 4am.

"Yes, Lieutenant, our train leaves at 10am," she began, then stopped as the SS officer shook his head.

"No Fraulein, you will be leaving by an earlier train." He stopped and smiled as he saw a ripple of fear cross the woman's countenance. "The train leaves Innsbruck at 8am for Paris. You will be on it, the entire school, as well as a number of other 'undesirable foreigners'. Transport will arrive at 5.30am, be ready."

He turned away and then returned suddenly, "I notice that you are already packed, Fraulein?"

The Head nodded.

"You may take only your own, personal belongings. Those of the fugitives are to be left here—they will have no need of them once we find them!"

He turned and snapped a command to the waiting soldiers, they all came to attention and lined up in ranks before marching out of the Hall. A short time later they heard the front door slam shut...

* * *

Hilda finished relating her story and the four people in the room all relaxed back in their chairs.

"An extremely interesting account, Miss Annersley", the civilian, Mr Howard, said. "It gives us some insight into the type of person Lt Bhaer was, six years ago."

"From the information you have given us, ma'am" the Colonel put in, "there is really nothing in his actions to warrant a title of 'War Criminal', and yet..."

"And yet, gentlemen," Miss Annersley continued, "the potential was there." She smiled at the other three inhabitants in the room. "I have the reputation, at my school, of always being able to see the good in someone, of always wanting to give them another chance to reform. But I am able to recognise evil. Lt Bhaer did not threaten me purely to retrieve information, but because his position of power and authority allowed him so to do. I believe that he would, without a qualm, have ordered the execution of any of the girls. Purely to make a point."

The two men nodded in agreement. "Miss Annersley, should this case ever get to trial, would you be willing to give evidence as to his conduct six years ago? You would not be expected to tell the entire story, just the actual threats made, and perhaps your opinion as to whether you felt he was capable of carrying out said threats?"

Hilda Annersley considered for a short time then nodded. "I would have no objection to being called as a witness," she said softly.

The two men stood, after shaking hands with both women

they took their leave; after the men from the War Office had left Helen Randolph sat next to her cousin.

"You didn't complete the story, Hilda," Helen said quietly. "I'd like to know the rest, especially as you've already told me there was a reaction, and I'd really like to know the rest of the story of the escape."

Hilda looked across at her cousin and smiled. "I'll finish the story, Helen, but…"

She was interrupted. "My word, Hilda, I'll tell no one." Helen was sincere and her cousin nodded before continuing her story.

* * *

After the soldiers marched out there was a deathly silence within the hall; Miss Edwards, closest to the door, went outside after a few minutes and returned with the news that they had left the grounds. All eyes turned to the pale figure of the Headmistress. Miss Annersley straightened and walked to the centre of the dais. She looked out on everyone, Staff and pupils, her eyes glistening and her face calm.

"I want all of you in this room," the Head began, her voice reaching everyone without apparent effort, "to consider the people who have attended this school as pupils or staff, and count how many different nationalities you have known. In this room today, I see representatives from England, Scotland, Wales, Ireland, France, Hungary, Norway and America. In the past there have been many others including Italy, Austria and Germany. Remember all of the people you have known from those countries in particular, and also remember that the actions of one man or group of men cannot be held as representative of an entire nation."

Miss Annersley took a breath before continuing. "If a person is afraid, it may cause them to do something they know is wrong, or even stop them from doing something they know is right. Now the events of the last few hours have been frightening for everyone, but in a short time we will be boarding coaches to take us to the railway station and to France. When I board that train I want every single person in this room to be waiting for me. I do not want to lose any of you during the journey because you react to a comment or action. The people, who may make those comments or perform those actions, are almost certainly far more frightened than you are but, unlike you, have no method of escape.

"I cannot, yet, ask that you pray for the men who have just left, instead I ask that you join me in silent prayer for our missing group. That they manage to escape their pursuers and that you pray for the ordinary people who, in the conflict that is sure to come, will suffer because of a comparatively few evil men and women."

She bowed her head and the remainder of the staff and all the girls did the same. From the youngest junior, everyone was sending their prayers to the group who had innocently 'gone shopping'; the older girls and staff also considered the ordinary people they had known from Italy, Germany and, especially, from Austria.

Afterwards the Head looked around the hall once more, "The events that we have just witnessed, that have occurred this night, in this hall. They will have frightened you, I know, because they have frightened me, too. But do not allow your fear to colour your perception of this country and her people. You have all placed your signatures on our Peace League, in it you have vowed to promote peace between our different countries, if you speak of your experiences this night, to others, that will reduce the likelihood of peace."

Miss Annersley dismissed everyone to quickly get washed and dressed. Their transport to the station would be arriving within the hour. She quickly spoke to the staff, praising Rosalie for keeping her head, and asking Matron Rider to attend to Con Stewart's wound. Afterwards she swept back to her study. She entered the room and had just gone into the small bathroom attached at the rear of the study when her mask slipped, leaning against the hand basin she was violently sick, retching again and again until long after there was nothing left in her stomach.

An arm around her shoulders guided her back into the study proper and sat her in the Head's chair. Her eyes full of tears, Hilda Annersley could not, straight away, see the identity of her helper. She was handed a damp flannel and a glass of water. After wiping her face and sipping the water she looked up into the calm face of Matron Lloyd.

"I'm sorry, Matey," she began. "I didn't want anyone to see..."

"That you're human, Hilda?" Matey's brisk no-nonsense tones were gone, replaced with a far more gentle voice. "I must admit, on occasion I have wondered. You are always so calm, you see. My dear, I would be far more concerned if you had not had a reaction."

Miss Annersley shook her head. "I cannot afford any type of reaction, Gwynneth, I must be strong, everyone else is relying on me."

"By not allowing yourself to react, Hilda, by always placing others' needs above your own, you could cause yourself serious illness. You should at least let someone else take on part of the job." The Matron's voice was sombre.

"Who else is there, Gwynneth?" The Head's quiet voice returned. "Madge Russell is 'busy' and she'll have all of Die Rosen to deal with as Jem will be needed at the San. Could you do it? Or Con Stewart? Jeanne de Lachenais?"

Matey shook her head to all the suggestions and Miss Annersley nodded in acknowledgement.

"Let's face it, Gwynneth, there's only one other person who could do the job of Headmistress, who could help me and ease my burden, and she's currently running for her life."

There was silence in the study for a short time as both women sent their thoughts and prayers to Nell Wilson, then Matey turned to the Head.

"Granted then Hilda, there is no one else. But you have got to look after yourself, once we are on the train I'll bring you a small dose to help you sleep..." She stopped as Miss Annersley was shaking her head.

"No, Gwynneth, not until we are safe in France. At any time

the Staff or girls may need me, I cannot be unavailable."

The Matron sighed, recognising the truth in the Head's words, "Very well, Hilda, but I'll be watching you."

"I expected nothing less, Matey!" A small smile crossed Miss Annersley's face.

* * *

The station at Innsbruck had never before appeared to be such a cold and forbidding place; despite the warm, early morning sunshine, a number of the more sensitive girls and Staff found it difficult to repress a shiver as they entered the station. Unlike all the other times they had been there, the Chalet School found they were greeted with hard stares and barely muffled curses. Many people that, previously, had always met the School with friendly smiles and the traditional 'Gruss Gott', turned their backs or stared with flat, forbidding expressions. Even those few that wore friendly expressions quickly turned away or hid their faces, afraid to be seen 'consorting with the foreigners'. The Staff of the Chalet School hurried their charges onto the train that sat, waiting, at the platform, a few of them being responsible for ensuring that the luggage was also loaded. While watching the activity and ensuring all her charges boarded the train, Miss Annersley was pleased to catch sight of Madge Russell. The two women moved to stand away from any possibility of being overheard.

"Madge, are you leaving now too?"

The owner of the school shook her head. "Not yet, Hilda, Jem is hoping to get compensation for the San and so needs to stay. He has said that I must leave but I will keep him company a little longer. We will be sending Margot and the children out soon."

"You still plan to reopen the School in Guernsey?"

"We do, we'll, of course, keep you informed about our plans. Thank you for sending across the message that you had been ordered to leave, I had to be here to see you off, and to pass on any news."

"What news have you?" The Head's low voice asked while her eyes took in the dark circles under Madge's eyes and her air of exhaustion.

Madge Russell smiled slightly. "They came looking for Robin, so Jack Maynard took her with him. Daisy is safe though, she seems to have been missed, luckily."

"And the others?" Miss Annersley's voice was insistent.

Mrs Russell took a deep breath, "Sorry, Hilda, I forgot that you wouldn't know." She lowered her voice. "Jem met them last night, they are all fine, although worried and exhausted. He took a lot of supplies with him and the group are travelling to Umfert to meet up with Gottfried, Jack and Robin. The idea is to try and make it into Belsornia."

"When do you plan to leave, Madge? It will not be pleasant for you to remain once the Authorities realise that Nell and the others have escaped."

"I know that, Hilda, but I must have word about Joey and the others. If anything happens I'll be able to do something if here. I'll not be able to if in Paris or London."

Miss Annersley said nothing, privately she felt that Madge would be unable to do anything regardless, but realised that Madge needed to hold onto that hope. "Where is Jem? Has he come down too?" Miss Annersley could not see the doctor on the platform.

"No, he felt he had to go to the San first thing. He's arranging for all the patients to be evacuated, Therese Lepattre will have to be moved very slowly and carefully of course, and a number of others are almost as bad. I was brought down by one of the other doctors at the San as I had to be here. I brought Daisy with me, she's still very upset and I thought perhaps, seeing her friends, that would make her feel better."

"Why don't you send Daisy to join her friends? Allow her to come with us now," the Head suggested. "It would be safer for her, and probably ease Margot's mind. If you extract a promise from her not to speak of her experiences she will probably benefit from being with girls her own age."

"Oh yes, Hilda, that's an excellent idea," Madge seemed very relieved, "Especially as Margot is very unwell at the moment, I think this situation is sapping the little strength she has!"

"Do ensure that Daisy is aware of just how unwell her mother is, though, Madge." Miss Annersley's eyes darkened, a bitter memory from her own past surfacing. "I would not want her to have to discover, too late, that she should have made her farewells to her mother!"

Madge Russell turned a horrified face to her Headmistress. "I hadn't thought of that, although Jem did warn me that Margot had very little strength. Thank you, Hilda, I'll ensure Daisy knows, a little, about how serious her mother's condition may be."

The two women stood in companionable silence for a short while, watching as the last of the passengers and baggage were loaded onto the train, they slowly moved to the train themselves as the first warning whistle blew.

"What happened at the School, Hilda? I've spoken to Rosalie, she said that you'd been visited but didn't say much more."

Miss Annersley turned to the owner of the Chalet School, pleased that she had warned Rosalie to say little about the previous evening's events. Madge Russell looked very tired, unsurprising considering her condition and her concerns about her sister, her husband and her ward, Hilda had no wish to add to her worries.

"We were visited by the authorities, yes Madge," she replied. "They found nothing and did not discover where the others were hiding." The Head was grateful that she had long perfected the art of holding a totally expressionless face, Madge Russell was unable to detect any problems.

When the train blew its final whistle Hilda Annersley bade farewell to Madge Russell, the two women exchanging hugs, she then boarded the train just before it set off. Once on board the Head walked the length of the train, speaking to all the girls, attempting to soothe their fears. After only a short time the rocking motion of the train, and the interrupted night, meant that most of the girls settled down to sleep. Miss Annersley then took the opportunity to speak to her staff. On reaching one particular compartment, Miss Stewart made a point of singling her out, to speak in private.

"Hilda, how are you? Did that SS coward hurt you?" The History Mistress looked very shame-faced as she asked her questions.

Hilda Annersley smiled slightly. "I'm fine, Con," she replied, "he didn't hurt me."

Con Stewart looked down at the floor for some seconds, Hilda saw that the wound on her face was covered with some gauze and a dressing, however she could see additional bruising around her eye and jaw.

Miss Stewart spoke again, very softly. "Hilda, I'm so sorry, that I even considered that..."

She stopped as the Head held up a hand. "You could not know of Lt Bhaer's order to me, Con. From your point of view it must have seemed that I should do far more. I certainly felt that I should, but I believe his threat was genuine."

Con nodded. "I think so too," she smiled slightly. "The only good thing is that at least, by being on this train, we have left him far behind."

"True, Con." Miss Annersley's soft voice had a slight bite to it. "Unfortunately some of his colleagues have joined us." She indicated with her head along the corridor, two soldiers were walking toward them.

As the soldiers drew level with the two women they stopped, the older of the two soldiers held out a hand.

"Your papers!" he barked.

Both Miss Annersley and Miss Stewart retrieved their papers and passports from their coat pockets and passed them across. The soldiers took a great deal of time examining the paperwork before, reluctantly, passing them back to the two women.

"Fraulein Annersley?" It was the older soldier again.

"Yes," the Head replied. "I am Fraulëin Annersley."

The soldier smiled slightly, it was not a smile intended to inspire. "Leutnant Bhaer asked to be remembered to you, Fraulein."

The soldier bowed his head mockingly before continuing along the corridor. Both women watched them go, Miss Annersley keeping a restraining hand on her younger colleague's shoulder. As soon as the soldiers were out of sight Con Stewart turned to the Head.

"How can you just accept it Hilda? That scum wanted you to react, if it had been me I'd..."

"You would have been hit by a rifle butt again, Con!" Hilda Annersley's voice was soft and held some amusement, even though she had turned pale at the soldier's words.

The History Mistress stopped and laughed slightly. "Yes, I probably would have! It's lucky for me that you were here!" she admitted quietly. She paused to take a breath then continued, "Nell is right about you, Hilda."

"Oh? What does Nell say?" The Head's voice held a great deal of curiosity.

"She says that, of all her friends, you are the one that most complements her." Con Stewart's voice was grave. "I know that I do not, Nell and I are too alike..."

"You do yourself a disservice, Con," Hilda Annersley interrupted quickly. "Nell values your friendship more than any other." She stopped suddenly and Con saw a faint flush replace the pallor. "So much so, that I will admit to some feelings of envy." The last said very quietly.

"Jealous? You? I can't believe it!"

Miss Annersley smiled. "Well," she began, "I am only human, Con. Despite the pedestal that some people keep insisting I should stay upon!"

There was silence for a short time before the Headmistress gave herself a small shake. "I must continue," she said, smilingly, "everyone else will need to see that I'm still around!" She looked across at her History Mistress. "I received news from Madge, Con," she began. "Nell, Jo and the girls are safe at the moment, they are trying to reach Belsornia. Gottfried Mensch and Jack Maynard are both with them."

Miss Stewart nodded. "I'm pleased for Joey that Jack has joined them," she said, "that's another pair who complement one another! Thanks for letting me know, Hilda, I'm sure they will escape. God willing!"

* * *

Miss Annersley stopped there and smiled over at her cousin, "There's not a great deal more to add, Helen," she said. "The train did indeed take us straight through to Paris. It was not a particularly pleasant trip, but it was reasonably safe. Once we reached Paris the vast majority of the girls and Staff went on to London, and once the girls were all handed over to their parents or guardians and we had received information that our missing party were safe in Switzerland, I was able to sleep." Hilda laughed slightly. "I slept for 24 hours non-stop and I didn't need any 'dose' from Matey! The Chalet School was out of business for the next year or so. It restarted in the August of 1939 in Guernsey, and I was Headmistress once more."

"Some of the events you described sounded terrifying, Hilda. I imagine that, even now, almost six years later, they are discussed at your school."

Hilda Annersley considered. "Surprisingly, Helen, they are not discussed, I think partly because, certainly for the junior girls, they were unaware of the magnitude of the danger, and also that, apart from threats and Con Stewart's injury, nothing actually happened. Nell's party were in far greater danger, had they been captured I doubt if any of them would have survived."

"But you, personally, were threatened with the same fate or worse." Helen sounded indignant that her cousin should be so calm about the seeming lack of interest from the school.

Hilda nodded. "Yes, but the school would not be aware of those threats because, until yesterday, I had never told anyone of the events in my study that night. Apart from Matron Lloyd, that is, and she would never say anything."

"Does your friend know what you and that girl Rosalie did for her and her party?"

"Does Nell know that we lied for them?" Miss Annersley

smiled. "No, I don't believe I've ever told her. Should she ever find out I expect I'll get another lecture! But I did no more than she would have done, had our positions been reversed. I believe Rosalie's actions were far more laudable; after all she was only in her early twenties at the time. She really is the School Secretary now, so her story on that night was only a little premature!"

CHAPTER THIRTEEN

FAMILY

It was only a week or two later that news came for Miss Annersley; Helen Randolph joined her in the drawing room one morning where she was finishing a letter to Nell Wilson.

"Would you like that letter to go out with the afternoon post Hilda?"

"Oh yes, thank you Helen, I've nearly finished it." Hilda's voice held some amusement and her cousin looked at her questioningly. "Nell's letter included a lot of news, but also a small snippet from the school itself. She's got a new pupil there who sounds intriguing. Name of Tom Gay!"

"Tom? But I thought you only accepted girls!"

"We do, this child's real name is Lucinda Muriel would you believe! The girl has always been known as Tom when at home, and from what Nell said in an earlier letter, even looks like a Tom!"

"Well I can understand her not wanting to be known by either of those names." Helen was trying desperately not to laugh, "Poor child! What did your friend have to say about the girl?"

"Oh, just asking my advice about her, it sounds as though she's being affected by the change from a home to a school environment." While speaking Miss Annersley finished writing and carefully blotted her paper before sealing the pages in an envelope.

The two women then made their way into the sitting room and helped themselves to the tea set out there. Once settled Helen turned to her cousin.

"I wouldn't have thought your friend needed to be continually contacting you about decisions, Hilda." Helen began. "From the little I saw of her, back in October and again, just before Christmas, she seemed to be the type that could cope."

"Oh Nell is perfectly able to manage, Helen," Hilda was quick to assure her companion, "but anyone that has a great deal of responsibility, finds it useful to use another for advice and as a confidant." She smiled across at Helen. "Nell is just using me in the same way that I have used her ever since being appointed Headmistress."

"I understand, that's how I first met Andrew," Helen's gaze swept over to a family photograph on the mantel. "He was Edgar's '2-I-C' and his friend. One of the things Edgar said to me, when Andrew and I got married, was that Andrew was the most loyal person he knew."

"Exactly!" Hilda nodded. "I've been friendly with Nell from my first term at the Chalet School, and I've actually received Nell's loyalty from long before I was appointed Headmistress. At the same time though, she has never failed to give me her complete and honest opinion about any subject, even if that meant a completely different opinion to mine! Anyone that holds a position of authority would value that combination. I am just returning the compliment at present!"

"Will there be any difficulty once you return, Hilda?" Helen's voice was questioning. "After all, by the time you go back, hopefully after Easter, it will be more than a year since you were last there. Your friend will have been Headmistress for most of that time!"

"As far as Nell's concerned, there will be no difficulty," Hilda Annersley smiled. "As I said, she is loyal, and besides is my closest friend. I must admit though, I have considered that point myself. It does seem rather unfair to ask her to revert to Senior Mistress once more! I'll have to think on it!"

Later that day the second post brought a number of letters, one of them was addressed to Hilda Annersley, and had been redirected from the School. She opened it with some interest, after reading through the contents she turned to her cousin.

"Helen, I've just received a letter from my brother," she said soberly.

Helen Randolph, knowing that her cousin had very little contact with either of her brothers, looked interested. "John or Simon?" she asked.

"John," Miss Annersley's voice was rather subdued. "He writes to inform me that his wife, my sister-in-law, died just before Christmas!"

"And he's only just told you? Suppose you had wanted to go to the funeral?" Helen sounded annoyed.

Hilda shook her head. "I'm sure it never even crossed his mind, Helen. After all, Emma and I had absolutely nothing in common, other than that she happened to have married my brother. I've neither seen nor spoken to John for more than fifteen years. The only contact we had was through Christmas cards and the occasional letter."

"You've not spoken since your father's funeral?" Helen Randolph's voice was shocked. "I had no idea. But then you are so much younger than your brothers aren't you?"

Miss Annersley smiled slightly. "An entire generation younger, Helen. John is almost fifteen years older than I, Simon twelve years older. I believe I was very unexpected, an accident!"

"But your parents..." Helen began.

"My parents loved me wholeheartedly." Hilda's tones were warm as she remembered her parents. "My father did the best he could for me, once mother died. I couldn't have asked for a better father. He even supported me when I wanted to go to university and then into the teaching profession. When he died he left me enough money so that I was not reliant on either of my brothers. Otherwise..."

"Otherwise John would have insisted that you give up teaching and find yourself a husband!" Helen finished positively.

Hilda Annersley smiled. "Yes," she affirmed, "John never understood my need to learn and then teach, he has always firmly believed that women are there to be looked after and protected, that they are unable to cope on their own. I'm afraid I was a great disappointment." Her eyes twinkled with amusement.

"What about Simon?"

"I was never very close to Simon," Hilda replied, "but he never had a problem with my choice of profession. His wife was also a teacher, she and I were fairly friendly in the short time they were married. After her death though, Simon just retreated into himself. I do correspond with him occasionally."

"He never considered marrying again?"

Miss Annersley shook her head. "No, his wife died in childbirth, their first, the child also died. I believe a large part of Simon died at the same time."

Helen nodded understandingly. "Poor Simon," she murmured, she looked across at her cousin once more. "So is John's letter just to inform you of Emma's death then?"

"No," Hilda replied, "it's an invitation to the reading of the Will!"

At her cousin's puzzled look she elaborated. "Emma left a Will and the solicitor gave John a list of all those who were beneficiaries and needed to be at the reading—my name was upon the list!"

A few days later Miss Annersley arrived at her brother's house in Buckinghamshire. As the taxi driver retrieved her bags and rang the doorbell she pondered on her welcome. The February air was chilly and Miss Annersley shivered slightly, she was not really dressed for the cold. The door opened and a butler looked out, Miss Annersley gave her name and was welcomed into the house, her belongings taken in by another servant. After taking her coat, the butler led her along the passage to a room on the right, as he opened the door he announced to those inside the arrival of Miss Hilda Annersley.

Miss Annersley walked into the room, a tall man, grey haired but with the same blue-grey eyes as Hilda herself, detached himself from a group over in the far corner and welcomed her with a quick kiss on her cheek.

"Hilda, good of you to come," he said shortly. "I understand you are still on sick leave following that accident last year, are you well?"

"I'm recovering, John," Miss Annersley replied smoothly. "I hope to return to the school after Easter."

"The school, yes, still a big part of your life then?"

"Of course."

There was silence for a while, then Hilda turned to her brother. "I'm sorry to hear of your wife's death, John, my deepest sympathy." Her voice was full of empathy and, for a short time, the formal man in front of her relaxed enough to allow her to see his pain.

"Thank you for that, Hilda, I-I-I would have informed you before but I ..."

Miss Annersley touched her brother's arm. "No need to say anything else, John," she smiled. "I'm sure you had far too many things to arrange."

John Annersley smiled slightly in return, he turned. "Let me introduce the children to you, Hilda, it's been some years since you saw them, I doubt you'll recognise them!" He placed an arm around his sister's back, guiding her to one corner of the room.

"This is Edward," a younger copy of his father. Edward was in his late twenties, he wore the uniform of an officer in the Guards Regiment. "Celia, her husband is overseas, in the Royal Navy." Celia, in her mid-twenties, was tall for a woman, standing only a little below her aunt in height.

John Annersley moved to the other man in uniform. "This is Joseph, I believe that the last time you met he spent his entire time asking you questions—you'll be pleased to know he put that to good use and is hoping to become a university lecturer!"

"Once the War is finished, father," Joseph Annersley's voice was deep and low, he smiled over at his aunt. "In a way, Aunt Hilda, you were my inspiration and, once the War's finished and I'm back in civvies I'll be returning to Oxford to complete my studies."

"What subject are you studying, Joseph?" Hilda Annersley remembered the boy of seven who had bombarded her with questions throughout the long day of her father's funeral. It had made the day that much more bearable, knowing that she could stimulate a young mind.

"What else? English of course! I said you were my inspiration!" Joseph smiled then reached behind him to pull another member of the family forward. "And this is our youngest, Elizabeth, she was only a babe-in-arms when you last saw her!"

Hilda smiled at her youngest niece, marvelling at the contrast; with her two nephews and other niece it had been obvious that the children were all Annersleys, the same height, slenderness and blue-grey eyes, but Elizabeth was totally different. Darker hair, brown eyes and standing barely over five feet tall. The girl, Hilda remembered she must be no more than 17 years old, had the characteristic slenderness, but otherwise did not resemble her father at all, instead seeming to be an almost perfect replica of her mother, Emma.

"Hello Elizabeth, it's good to meet you." Miss Annersley smiled down at the girl, her voice warm.

Elizabeth Annersley flushed. "How do you do, Aunt Hilda?" she mumbled, refusing to meet her aunt's gaze. Almost before she had finished speaking she turned away and moved swiftly out of the room.

John Annersley made an angry sound. "Elizabeth, come back here, immediately!" he ordered. The girl did not appear to hear him, instead slamming out of the room. "I'm sorry Hilda," he said, somewhat embarrassed, "she's taken losing her mother very hard."

Hilda Annersley nodded. "Of course, John, I can sympathise, no matter." She stared thoughtfully after the girl—there appeared to be more to her reaction than grief. Almost as though, in some way, she was blaming her aunt for something.

After being shown her room, Miss Annersley readied herself for dinner, the dining room was a fairly small room but warm, with a number of touches intimating that Emma Annersley had been a good home-maker. Hilda sat next to her eldest nephew, discussing with him her time living in the Tyrol. She noticed that Elizabeth, sat on the opposite side of the table, avoided her aunt's gaze.

The following morning the entire family gathered together to hear a lawyer read out the contents of Emma Annersley's Will. She had left a certain amount of both money and jewellery as well as some stocks and shares. Most of this went to her husband and children, the jewellery being divided between her two daughters. She had also left certain bequests to various of the servants; however it was the final bequest that involved her sister-in-law. The lawyer read it out in full....

"And, finally, I know I leave my daughter Elizabeth with her future undecided. Elizabeth and her father have always found it difficult to agree and I had hoped that I would be there to mediate. As I am not, I therefore ask my sister-in-law, Hilda, to take on that role. Hilda, please advise Elizabeth on the course her future should take. We have never been close, but I have always admired you and your achievements. Please make Elizabeth see that she too can achieve great things."

Hilda Annersley sat there, in astonishment – unless she were mistaken, Emma Annersley had just asked her to take on the role of mother to Elizabeth! She turned to her younger niece, but Elizabeth, after showing her a look of some despair, turned and ran from the room.

John Annersley came up to Hilda. "Emma told me of this, Hilda," he began. "You may wish to have some background."

Miss Annersley nodded and followed her brother into his Study. Sometime later that morning found her knocking on her niece's bedroom door.

"Elizabeth, may I come in?" Miss Annersley's voice had fully recovered now.

"Go away, I don't want to talk to you!"

The words caused Miss Annersley to raise an eyebrow, deciding that now was as good a time as any, she replied, "Elizabeth Annersley open this door at once!" The Headmistress' tones flowed effortlessly and there was a shocked silence from within. Moments later the sound of the door being unlocked; Elizabeth stood there, her face blotchy from crying, her hair rumpled. She gazed in a mixture of defiance and trepidation up at her aunt.

"Thank you, Elizabeth." Miss Annersley said smoothly, she walked into the room and sat herself in the easy chair by the window. Elizabeth stared at her for a while before closing the door and walking over to sit in the chair opposite.

"The last time I saw you, Elizabeth, was more than fifteen years ago. You were barely two years old. Tell me, exactly how have I managed to upset you so quickly?"

There was silence for some time, Hilda looked across at her niece who flushed before mumbling, "Because they expect me to be like you!"

"They?"

"Father, Mother and Edward. Maybe Joseph too although he's not so intense about it."

Miss Annersley remained silent and her niece continued speaking to fill the gap. "Oh, don't you see? All my life, all I've ever heard is how clever you are! All of us children did. For Edward it didn't matter—he always wanted to follow father into the Partnership, Celia just wanted to marry, and did before she was twenty! Joseph wanted to do exactly the same as you, and father encouraged it."

"I see," Miss Annersley said softly. "I had no idea, Elizabeth, I've only received the occasional letter from your father. I did not know of this."

Elizabeth nodded. "Well when the school told mother and father that I was clever, that's all I heard. That I could follow my aunt's footsteps, go to university and get a degree, or even a PhD! I told them I wasn't keen on English but it didn't stop them. The next thing was that I go in for Science—maybe even become a doctor. No one listened to what I wanted!"

"And what did you want, Elizabeth?" Hilda's tones were soft.

The girl shook her head. "It doesn't matter, because now Mother has passed on the role to you, and you will agree with father that I should not waste my brains. That I should ready myself for further study—after all—you are a teacher yourself, you'll want to ensure that your own niece continues the tradition." The words were said with some vehemence.

"It does matter Elizabeth, I care a great deal about what you personally want. Your mother asked that I be there to advise you on your future. I cannot do that if I don't know your own hopes."

"But what about Father, won't he expect you to...."

Hilda Annersley smiled. "I stopped doing what your father expected me to do when I was younger than you are now," she said softly. "If I'm to fulfil your mother's wishes I need to know your story."

Elizabeth looked down at the floor for some time, then, "I like school, I really do, I've got some good friends and I enjoy the life. I've been to boarding school since I was ten years old, I really enjoy it."

"Yes, I believe, if it's a good school, that almost all girls thrive," Hilda Annersley said softly.

Her niece looked up, smiling slightly. "I'd forgotten, of course, you're Headmistress at a boarding school aren't you?"

Hilda inclined her head, smiling.

"I always wondered why my father and mother didn't send me to your school," she shrugged, "perhaps they felt I would get preferential treatment or something!"

Miss Annersley shook her head. "No, Elizabeth, that would not have happened."

The girl looked across at her aunt. "No, perhaps not," she said softly, "anyway, I had no problems with school, enjoying it all, but my favourite lessons were Games lessons."

"Games?"

Elizabeth flushed. "I know, it doesn't sound much, but rather than studying all the time, I found I really enjoyed Games, hockey, netball, cricket, swimming, all of it. I was in the First Eleven for hockey and cricket when I was only fourteen years old. I also swam for the county. I may not look it, but I'd found my forte, I'd found what I wanted to do. From that age I wanted to specialise in Games, in Physical Fitness." She stopped for a moment, remembering, before continuing.

"And then, my reports from school suddenly seemed to be getting scrutinised by mother and especially father, my every mark looked at—and I am good at my lessons, I'll admit. But to father that was all that seemed to matter, my views were brushed aside, as a silly whim. Instead he was checking through all my marks to find out exactly how I could specialise, eventually, as my Science marks were highest, he decided I should train as a doctor. He was prepared to fund me through medical school, but he would't hear of me training in Physical Education and becoming qualified to coach."

"You did ask him then?" Hilda asked gently.

The girl nodded. "Oh yes, and my Games Mistress at school did too, she said I was a natural, that my talents would be wasted if I was forced to do something else." Elizabeth looked down at the floor again before continuing. "Father didn't listen though, he said that I had only one choice—to study medicine—if I chose anything else he would refuse to give his permission and would cut off all funding."

"What about your mother?" Miss Annersley spoke softly.

"She said she wanted the best for me, but she could see how unhappy I was." A few tears fell as Elizabeth remembered. "And of course, she was so ill. At the end, she said she'd done the only thing she could think of that might help!" The girl laughed harshly. "I really thought she meant it, too, I thought perhaps she had left me enough funds of my own, so I could train as I wanted. Instead what do I find? She has passed on my case to the one person most likely to advise an academic career. My aunt!"

Miss Annersley sat there in silence for quite some time, remembering, before turning to her niece. "Your mother and I were never close, Elizabeth, but I believe she had your interests at heart when she asked me to help you. Perhaps it would help, if I told you, a little, of what happened when I was about your age."

CHAPTER FOURTEEN

DECISION

"Hilda, I say Hilda wait a minute!" The plaintive voice stopped the girl in her tracks, Hilda Annersley turned to see her friend Ruth Tasker running to catch up.

"Ruth, running in the corridor is not allowed," she said primly, a small smile playing on her face.

"It is when I'm trying to catch up with you," her friend retorted. "Honestly Hilda, when are you planning to stop growing? You must be the tallest girl in the school now!"

Hilda shook her head. "Mavis Carter is taller," she replied, her voice soft and low. "I believe she's almost six feet tall, I'm only 5'9"!"

"Well Mavis is a lot bigger, too, her height doesn't show so much, you're tall and thin, it's more obvious." Ruth Tasker, at only 5'4" noted with dissatisfaction.

Hilda laughed, her otherwise serious face taking on a sunny expression, her blue-grey eyes sparkling. "Well did you chase after me just to complain about my height?" she asked.

"No, of course not," retorted her friend. "Two things, first, when are we to have our first Prefects meeting of the term, as you're Head Girl I thought you'd be the one to ask!"

Hilda thought for a moment. "Check with everyone if directly after school this evening is suitable, we could stay on for up to an hour without any problem."

"OK!" Ruth made to move away.

"Wait a minute!" her friend stopped her. "You said two things?"

"Oh yes, I nearly forgot! The Head wants to see you!"

Hilda looked across at her friend in exasperation. "Well

really, Ruth, that's the more important message! You should have given me that one first!"

"No I shouldn't," Ruth replied. "If I had then I'd never have got an answer to the second question." She grinned at Hilda who shook her head in despair before turning to retrace her steps along the corridor to the Headmistress's Office.

When Hilda entered the Head's Study, the woman sat at the desk looked up and smiled. Miss Cullen still had the same warm and gentle smile, and her brown eyes softened considerably as she saw her Head Girl. The last few years had seen escalation in her arthritis and the Head was growing more and more disabled, however she still ruled the school with a firm hand.

"Hello Hilda, did you have a good Christmas, my dear?"

Hilda walked round to greet the Head, she then settled in the chair Miss Cullen pointed out to her. "Yes, over all it was a good time," she said thoughtfully, "busy, of course, but father's profession ensures that Christmas time is always his busiest period."

The Head smiled. "A necessary evil, my dear, for anyone in the Church, although perhaps 'evil' is not the correct description! Did you have a chance to discuss matters with your father?"

Hilda reddened slightly. "Not really, Miss Cullen, poor father always looked so tired when he returned home."

"Yet you have only another two terms here, Hilda, and if you wish to be considered for entry to Oxford the deadline is fast approaching. What of your brothers?"

Hilda shook her head. "They still consider me to be a child, Miss Cullen," she said ruefully. "Oh Simon is good enough, but he is busy in his profession, and besides I believe he is seeing someone." She blushed slightly.

Miss Cullen smiled. "It does happen, Hilda," she said gently. "And your elder brother?"

Hilda's blush vanished, to be replaced by an expression of some frustration. "Oh, Miss Cullen, he doesn't listen. His thoughts are that women need a husband, his wife Emma has already started including me in their dinner parties, and there are always young men there."

Miss Cullen shook her head. "Hilda my dear, they probably think they are being kind to you, even though we are now in the 1920s a woman alone frightens many men. You will have to tell your brother and sister-in-law that your plans, at least for the immediate future, do not include marriage. Later, perhaps, they will, but if you wish to go to Oxford to study, your father and brother need to be told now."

Hilda sat silent for a time, her eyes staring at the floor, when she looked up again it was with an imploring expression, "Miss Cullen, I don't think they'll listen to me. My brother has no respect for my opinions, and, to my father, I am his baby daughter. But I'm sure they would listen to you! Couldn't you speak to them, please?"

The Head sat, thinking for some time, when she replied she was very serious. "Hilda, my dear, I could speak to your father, yes, I could convince him that you are intelligent enough to go and study at the most prestigious university in the world. I'm sure that I could even manage to convince your brother of the same! But Hilda," Miss Cullen's voice deepened in tone and her eyes softened further, "if I do that, I will just be reinforcing their belief that you are not old enough to choose for yourself. That you cannot act as an adult, and confront your family as one. Is that truly what you want, dear?"

Miss Cullen sat back and watched as her protégé absorbed the impact of her words. She had high hopes that Hilda would make the correct choice, but could do no more to influence her.

Hilda Annersley sat thinking for some time, when she looked up there was a firm resolve in her face. "No, Miss Cullen, it is not. I'll speak to my father and brother myself."

The evening meal at the Annersley household was a quiet time; Simon Annersley, although still, officially, living at home, was out for the evening, Hilda suspected it was with his new lady friend. She wondered how long it would be until he brought her home to meet father, she thought it would be soon. Hilda looked across at her father, it was only over the last holiday that it had finally dawned on Hilda that her father was growing old. She had always been aware that he was somewhat older than the fathers of friends of hers—as the youngest in the family, and by quite a significant margin, that was obvious. Only she had not noticed before now. With a shock, when thinking about it, she realised that her father was nearly sixty-eight years old! No wonder he was always looking tired. Unlike most professions, the clergy was one that did not have any set retirement age; Hilda wondered how long her father would continue to work.

His Grace, the Bishop Harold Annersley, glanced across at his young daughter and realised, with surprise, that she was no longer a child. He sat back in amazement, looking at the graceful and almost regal presence of his youngest child. She seemed to have changed almost overnight from the troubled child of, and here the Bishop stopped, almost frowning, why it was almost four years since his beloved Mary had died, no wonder Hilda had changed!

Remembering a conversation he had had with his elder son, John, only last weekend, he decided to speak to her. "Hilda, my dear."

Hilda looked across. "Yes father?"

The Bishop moved across to kneel beside his daughter, taking her hands in his he spoke. "Forgive me, my dear, but I have only just realised that you are growing up, that you have only a few short months left as a schoolgirl. Where has the time gone?"

Hilda smiled slightly, and the smile lit up her face. "I will be eighteen in May, father, I am almost an adult."

"Of course, my dear," the bishop smiled. "And I realise that I have been very remiss in not securing your future until now."

"My future, father?" Hilda's voice was somewhat troubled.

"Yes dear, your brother pointed it out, last weekend. You do not want to remain as my housekeeper for the rest of your life, we must give you the opportunity to meet people, to widen your social circle..."

"To meet a husband?" Hilda's voice was quite emotionless and, to begin with her father did not register that there was anything wrong.

"Why yes, John did mention that he felt an early marr..." the Bishop stopped, suddenly noticing something. Looking into his daughter's eyes he saw that their normal blue-grey colour had changed, all the blue seemed to have drained out, leaving only a dull grey. He had never seen Hilda's eyes change colour before, but he knew exactly what the change meant—his own eyes had the same trick—whenever he was angry or upset about something.

"Hilda," he said softly, "what is wrong? Why are you upset?"

Hilda looked down at the floor for some time before replying. "Father, Miss Cullen believes that I will obtain high enough grades in my exams to qualify for a place at Oxford University, to read English Literature."

There was a silence for a while, then, "I see, tell me Hilda, is this something that you would like to do?"

Hilda swallowed slightly before raising her head and staring straight into her father's eyes. "Yes, father, with all my heart. I've wanted to go on to university for the last two years, obtain a degree, perhaps even more."

"And then?"

Hilda shook her head. "I don't know, father, but I think I'd like to teach. You know, last year, I was tutoring some of the Fourth? It was the most wonderful achievement, to realise that, because of something I had done that they finally understood Shakespeare! I cannot imagine any other role being more fulfilling." Hilda's eyes were sparkling.

Her father sat back on his heels, deep in thought, he said nothing for so long that Hilda grew rather worried. "Father, are you unwell?"

The Bishop shook his head. "There has never been an Annersley woman from this family, that attended university," he began, somewhat gruffly. He looked across at his daughter, sitting there with a determined expression on her face. He smiled. "Until now."

Hilda looked across, scarcely able to believe her ears,

"Really, father?"

"Yes my dear, as far as I'm concerned you may go to Oxford, with my blessing. And I will be so proud to see you obtain a degree from there."

Hilda smiled so widely that she felt her face must split! "Oh, but, what about John?" she said quickly.

"He'll just have to accept that his baby sister has her own life," her father replied, also smiling. "I'll tell him so."

"No, father," Hilda shook her head. "I'll tell him myself!"

* * *

Hilda didn't get a chance to speak to her brother until the following weekend; before that, however, back at school, she was able to let the Head know the good news, just prior to an English Literature class. The Senior Literature class was still taken for some lessons by the Head herself. On this occasion she was revising some of Chaucer's Canterbury Tales, preparing the girls for the exams they would be taking in the next term. She finished the lesson a few minutes early and, rather than start anything new, engaged the girls in a discussion about a recent debate they had watched. The debate had been entitled, 'Women and Science—are they compatible?'

Naomi Tasker, the Games Prefect, smiled as she replied, "Miss Cullen, the debate was very interesting, and the two teams very skilled. But I don't think there was any doubt about the result."

Her sister continued. "Agreed, oh the team agreeing with the subject were extremely clever, but even they conceded that as far as Science was concerned, women are just not suited for it!"

Miss Cullen smiled slightly. "Then you do not believe that women could, if they wanted, be good scientists?" The question was thrown open to the entire class, Hilda, thinking deeply, replied.

"I don't believe so, Miss Cullen, I think that women are far more suited to the Arts, we have the capability of being able to understand, analyse and write about emotion, in literature, for example. Also things like History and Art, all need some emotional expertise. Scientists, in general, seem to have to be too cold, too calculating, and far too emotionless."

Ruth nodded. "Agreed. I think that, as woman are able to move more into producing independent work, that more will appear as great novelists, artists and historians. There will also be more women in exploration, archaeology and similar. But pure science? I cannot see it. It's not something that will ever appeal to many women."

Miss Cullen listened, not venturing an opinion of her own, it being her remit that the girls should form their own opinions, rather than mimic her own, she smiled slightly. "What of the new ideas about teaching Science?" she asked softly. "It has only recently been started in this school and I am aware that not all girls schools teach it."

"I suppose it should be taught," Hilda replied once more, "there may be the exception that could be interested. But I cannot see that it will ever be very important for girls to learn about, and I cannot think of any woman that has ever done anything noteworthy in Science!"

The rest of the girls agreed with the statement and Miss Cullen nodded, thinking deeply. At that moment the bell rang and the girls were dismissed, Hilda was last to file out.

"Hilda, you have a free period now, don't you?" Miss Cullen stopped her just as she was leaving the room.

"Yes, Miss Cullen."

"I wonder, my dear, could you retrieve some information for me, from the library?"

Hilda smiled. "Yes, of course," she was well aware that the Head's illness made walking painful.

Miss Cullen smiled. "You have heard of the Nobel Prizes? Could you please find out for me the winners of the Nobel Prizes in 1903, and 1911."

Hilda nodded and swiftly walked over to the Library, once there she spoke to the Librarian and was pointed toward the reference books. She swiftly checked through to the pertinent dates and noted the names. On seeing some of the names she stopped, a little troubled. She sought the Head, finally finding her in the School Secretary's office.

"Miss Cullen? I have the information you wanted."

Miss Cullen dismissed the School Secretary and limped across to her Head Girl. "What did you discover, Hilda?" she asked, while pointing the girl into her study.

Hilda waited until both of them were seated before replying, "I discovered exactly what you intended that I discover, Miss Cullen," she said with a slight smile. She took a piece of paper from her pocket and read, "Physics prize awarded to Marie Curie 1903—a joint award with her husband—and Chemistry prize awarded to Marie Curie alone in 1911."

"I see," Miss Cullen also smiled. "And has that knowledge in any way changed your opinion?"

Hilda thought for a while, she then lifted her head. "Obviously my opinion was incorrect," she said quietly, "perhaps women can do well in science."

Miss Cullen nodded. "Perhaps they can," she agreed. "Hilda, I have had to live through a time when, the fact that I was a woman meant that my opinions and ideas were not accepted or acted upon. I suspect that you will have to do the same. But do not ever allow yourself to believe that women cannot do something, simply because they are women." She smiled at Hilda, after a short time in thought Hilda returned the smile.

* * *

At this point in her recital, Miss Annersley stopped, smiling, her niece looked across, puzzled.

"What is so funny, Aunt Hilda?"

Miss Annersley looked across at the girl. "Only remembering how painfully naïve I was at the age of seventeen, Elizabeth," she said softly. "Had I been told then, that I would end up counting as my greatest friend a woman who was an excellent Science teacher, and yet also someone with a hot temper, I would never have believed it!"

Elizabeth smiled. "Did you speak to father about going to

university?" she asked.

"I did, that weekend. He was not very happy about it!"

* * *

"Father, this is ridiculous! Why on Earth are you even considering this, this preposterous suggestion? The child does not need any more schooling, she already knows enough to get by. What more is necessary when she will soon marry and have a family to look after? A household to run?" John Annersley was quite red in the face and almost shouting at his father. Hilda, sat on the opposite side of the table, watched him. A tug at her arm caused her to look round, Emma, her sister-in-law, spoke to her quietly.

"Come, Hilda, we will withdraw to the sitting room, your father and brother have important matters to discuss."

Hilda's eyebrow rose and she gazed across at her brother's wife. "The important matters directly concern me, Emma, I am not going to leave the room and have my future decided for me. I will have an input to this discussion."

Emma jumped as though shot, her husband's little sister had been neither rude nor insolent, in fact her speech had been as calm and reasoning as that of any adult. She had also made it abundantly clear that she intended to defy the conventions of the day, and remain in the room. John Annersley, hearing his wife and sister speak, glared round at Hilda before turning back to the Bishop.

"You see that? No respect for tradition, no respect for her elders. She has already been at that school far too long, father, I insist that you discipline your child."

The Bishop's eyes grew flinty grey. "You forget yourself, John," he said sharply. "I will not be dictated to in my own house. This is none of your concern, I informed you of Hilda's plans only out of courtesy. This is none of your affair."

There was silence for a short time, John realising that his father was angry, into the silence Hilda spoke. "Father? May I say something?"

Harold Annersley looked round and smiled at his daughter. "Of course, my dear."

"Thank you, sir." Hilda walked over to stand, facing her brother, John Annersley was a tall man, over six feet, and glared down at his sister.

"John, I am no longer a child," she began. "However I have no wish, at present, to settle down with a husband and family. Now father has agreed that I may go to Oxford, to obtain a degree and any other qualifications. He has also said he is happy with my choice of profession. Why is this such a problem for you to accept? After all, you attended Cambridge, studied Law."

"That's different," John returned angrily. "I was studying for my family's future."

"And I will be studying for mine," Hilda replied.

John glared across at his sister. "That would not be necessary if you decided to be a proper woman and settle for a husband. Someone who can look after you, ensure that you do not have to concern yourself with anything outside the home. Women need a man to guide them, Hilda, you do not have the mental capacity to cope on your own."

Hilda's eyebrow rose at this remark and she looked across at her brother as though seeing him for the first time. "Is that truly your belief, John?" She asked quietly, "That no woman is able to live without a man to guide them? Can you really have so little respect for half the human race?"

"Respect? Of course I have respect for women, but it is tempered with the knowledge that as men we have a responsibility to take care of, and protect those too feeble minded to help themselves!"

Hilda looked somewhat shocked. "And that is your opinion of all women, John? I don't think that is a very respectful view of our mother," she turned to look across at Emma. "Or your wife!"

Her brother also looked, aware that he may have inadvertently insulted his wife. Emma sat across the table, a frown on her face.

"I was not being disrespectful," John stormed, "and how dare you suggest that? If this is the type of behaviour learnt from that school of yours it is high time you left there. Who on earth does that Cullen woman think she is? Installing such conduct in her pupils! Forcing all of them to feel that settling down with a family is not good enough for them. I suppose, because she never had a husband herself, she feels that it is beneath any of her pupils. I will be contacting the board of Governors about her, she's not fit to teach girls, she..." John stopped, suddenly aware that his little sister was staring at him, her eyes piercing.

For herself Hilda felt pure anger, but, apart from her eyes, she allowed none of it to show, her voice remaining calm she spoke. "How dare you! You have absolutely no right to condemn my Headmistress. She has been there for me ever since mother died and you shall not belittle her, or attempt to cause trouble for her."

John made to speak but was shocked into silence by the look he received from his baby sister. Hilda continued in the same calm, even, and, above all, cold tones.

"For your information, Miss Cullen does not consider that further education is something to which all girls should aspire. She recognises that, for some, their greatest wish is to have a home, husband and family. And she does not denigrate that decision. She does however, believe that a girl or woman should be able to choose for themselves." There was a pause as Hilda took a deep breath. "I choose to go to university, brother, my choice has been accepted by father and you have no right to try to influence that choice. If I ever chose in the future to marry, the one, the only criteria I will search for, is that he is someone that can respect me, and my right to choose. Or, to put it simply, that he is the complete opposite of you!"

* * *

There was silence in the bedroom after Miss Annersley had finished relating details of the meeting between herself and her brother. Elizabeth looked across at her aunt.

"Did you really say that to father?" she asked, her tones somewhat awed.

Miss Annersley smiled, "I did, although, had he not insulted Miss Cullen, I rather doubt that I would have summoned up the courage."

"What happened next?" Elizabeth was interested.

"Your father never mentioned the conversation again, and he didn't try to interfere with either my plans, or with Miss Cullen's Headship. Indeed he said very little to me, I think he was rather shocked at the reaction he received. I don't think he ever appreciated just how much I loved Miss Cullen, or how much she did for me. Even when she died, less than four years later, she still thought of me, I was the main beneficiary of her estate."

"You had kept in touch?"

"Oh, yes, we remained close, I was with her when she died." Hilda Annersley's eyes darkened as she remembered her mentor. Shaking herself she turned to her niece and smiled, "Now Elizabeth, what of your own situation?"

The girl looked across at her aunt, thinking deeply. "I think I owe you an apology," she said quietly. "You don't intend to push me toward one particular career, do you?"

"And be false to my own teacher? No, Elizabeth, I couldn't do that. At my School there are any number of girls that could go on to university, do well in a career. Some of them do exactly that, some take the first steps, then find that their greatest happiness is being a wife and mother. I do not deride their choice, as long as it is their choice, and not one forced upon them by family or society pressures."

"And my choice?"

Miss Annersley thought for a moment. "Your mother was there, when I spoke to your father about choice, Elizabeth. I believe her intention in asking that I help you, was to ensure that you had the opportunity to make the choice for yourself."

"But how can I do that? Father will not change his mind, and I have no money of my own, and in any case I'll not be considered an adult until I'm 21, until then I must obey father!"

Miss Annersley smiled. "Perhaps we can cause him to change his mind, Elizabeth. You will need to confront him yourself, he will not respect your determination if I plead your case. However, if I just let you know exactly what I intend to give you for your twenty first birthday..."

* * *

Two days later saw Miss Annersley back with her cousin; during afternoon tea she related her story.

"Elizabeth went and saw her father, I went along for support but said nothing. She agreed with her father that she would go to university and study Medicine."

"She did? But how did you get her to change her mind?" Helen was very confused!

Hilda smiled. "I didn't, Helen," she replied. "Elizabeth said that she would study medicine until her 21st birthday, she would then enrol at Bedford to start her course to become a Games/Fitness mistress."

"I don't understand."

"On her 21st birthday, Elizabeth, in the eyes of the law, would become an adult, and, my 21st birthday present to her will be enough money that she will not have to rely on her father, but can choose her own destiny!"

"Ah," Helen smiled, seeing her cousin's plan. "I suppose you hoped that John would realise that he'd just waste three years worth of tuition fees, sending her to medical school, when she had no intention in completing the course?"

"Exactly!" Hilda returned the smile. "And it worked, John relented, said that Elizabeth could go to Bedford when she left school."

"An excellent solution, Hilda," Helen said. "I wouldn't have thought John was too happy at your part though?"

Hilda Annersley smiled, a little sadly. "No, Helen, I think he was expecting me to insist on an academic career, even though it was not Elizabeth's choice. I do not believe my actions have brought us any closer as a family—although I hope to have regular letters from both Joseph and Elizabeth."

"My one surprise, considering his attitude when you wanted to go to university," Helen began, "is that he wanted Elizabeth to go anyway, it seems to be a complete change."

"Yes, I wondered about that too," Hilda confessed. "I believe he wanted to prove that anything his baby sister could do, his family could improve upon."

"You mean he was jealous?"

"Yes, it is a failing all Annersley's have, to a certain extent. We are competitive. John had just translated that to his entire family. I think Emma recognised that, and saw that perhaps I was the only one that could see and respond to Elizabeth's need."

CHAPTER FIFTEEN

THE TELEGRAM

March had been ushered in with heavy rain and storms, therefore it was with some pleasure that, in the second week of March, the weather had turned fine once more. Miss Annersley was able to go out on her walks without having to watch for bad weather. On a number of occasions her cousin joined her; one day, after walking into the village and back, the cousins arrived back at the house in time for lunch. As they were finishing their meal the second post arrived and they opened their letters in the sitting room with a large pot of tea to accompany them.

Miss Annersley was smiling at one of her letters and Helen looked across, a question on her face.

"It's from Jan," Hilda said quickly, "she tells me that she has just finished her exams and that she is very sorry, but she is convinced that she has failed all of them! I'll read it to you...

Dear Hilda
Many thanks for your last letter, it's good to hear that you're still doing well. When I think that it's almost a year since the accident—you were brought in to the unit on the afternoon of April 9th last year, and I don't think anyone expected you to survive. Just think of all that's happened since then. Oh by the way, you're not to worry about still feeling tired—I've seen it before with serious head injuries—they will feel tired for ages afterwards— sometimes more than a year later. The feeling will go in the end.

Mum and the family send their best wishes—Adam asked me to thank you for the Science textbooks your friend Miss Wilson sent him—they helped him in his exams. He spoke to Miss Wilson on the telephone, to thank her personally, she was very interested in his plans to study Engineering at University. She was able to tell him the best places to apply that could have scholarships, he got some information from one or two only last week. It'll mean him staying on at school until he's 18 but he's taking on more work at the local garage evenings and weekends so should be able to help pay his way. Hopefully by then (September next year) the War will be over and he'll not have to fight—I know he's as big as a man but, to me, he's still my little brother.

Mum said to tell you that if you have to come to Exeter for any reason to be sure and call in. I said you'd probably be seeing Mr Roberts in the next month or two, so perhaps you could call then? She'll be pleased to see you—so will Chrissie, she asked me the other day when you'd be visiting—she wants to see if your hair has grown!

Talking of exams, I finished the last of mine only last week, I'm sorry ~~Miss Annersley~~ Hilda, but I don't think I did very well. The Scripture one was all right, I managed to answer all the questions and remembered a lot of the details you'd said. But I didn't do so well in the English one. I was so nervous and managed to forget everything you had taught me, making stupid mistakes, I even found myself describing Romeo's character when asked about Macbeth! . I don't think I answered enough questions and I'm sure I didn't write enough detail. Perhaps I can retake them in the summer.

Anyway, must finish as my shift's about to start.
Yours Jan.

"I gather you do not believe that to be the case?" Helen asked.

Hilda Annersley shook her head. "Not in the slightest," she said emphatically, "Knowing her progress, while I was tutoring her, and her potential, I would say she has done well. But she will only remember the things she did badly, rather than the things she did well! I'll reply now, she'll need a little encouragement, something to remind her that she has the potential to do well!"

She moved out of the sitting room and up to her room to collect her writing paper. On her way back down the stairs she saw that the maid, Annie, was in urgent conference with the Housekeeper, Mrs Sutton. As she drew closer she heard Mrs Sutton speak to the girl. "I'll deal with it, Annie, you get back to your work!" The Housekeeper then turned to address Miss Annersley. "I wonder, ma'am, if I could speak to you, privately? It's very important."

"Of course, Mrs Sutton," Miss Annersley responded quickly, wondering what on earth was so important. The two women moved into the dining room and faced each other.

The Housekeeper took a deep breath before starting, her honest face very worried. "Miss Annersley, I know Annie should have given it with the rest of the post, but I'm sure you can understand exactly why she didn't? I mean Mrs Randolph is a lovely lady and Annie wouldn't want to upset her or nothing."

Hilda Annersley looked concerned. "What do you mean, Mrs Sutton? Why would Annie have upset Helen?"

"It's this." Mrs Sutton pulled an orange envelope from her pocket. "Annie can read well enough, and her neighbour had one of these that announced her husband had been shot down and killed when on some bombing raid." She offered the envelope to Hilda.

Hilda took the envelope, noting that the telegram was from the Air Ministry, she swallowed slightly. "Would you like me to take this to Mrs Randolph?" she asked softly.

Mrs Sutton nodded. "I'd be very grateful, Miss Annersley."

Hilda nodded. "Very well, Mrs Sutton, I'll deal with it. Please tell Annie that she was correct to bring the telegram to you. Mrs Randolph will need some support when she receives this, and otherwise, I may not have been aware of it."

The Housekeeper smiled gratefully before exiting the room. Hilda looked at the envelope in her hand for at least a minute without moving. Then, with a deep breath and squaring of her shoulders, she walked out of the dining room and across to where her cousin waited.

"Oh, Hilda, there you are, I wondered what on Earth kept you?" Helen greeted her cousin cheerfully. "My dear, when you write to Jan you will give her my best wishes, won't you?"

Miss Annersley mumbled something and Helen nodded and returned to her letter, after only a short time, though, she looked back up at Hilda.

"Is there something wrong, Hilda?" she asked solicitously, "Are you feeling well?"

Hilda walked over to stand next to Helen. "I'm well, Helen, but I have some news for you." She proffered the orange envelope.

Helen looked at the envelope, then back at her cousin's face, she paled considerably and took some deep breaths. "I-I-is that from..."

"The Air Ministry," Hilda said softly.

Helen swallowed again, then stretched out her hand toward the envelope, before her fingers touched it, though, she snatched them away. "I can't," she whispered. "Oh Hilda, please open it, read it." Her normal complexion was white, her face drawn, the brown eyes wide and pleading.

Hilda nodded slightly, reaching across to the desk, she picked up a paper knife and slit the envelope, inside was an official telegram, Hilda swallowed slightly and licked suddenly dry lips,

TO MRS HELEN RANDOLPH **STOP** REGRET TO INFORM YOU THAT YOUR HUSBAND SQUADRON LEADER ANDREW JAMES RANDOLPH, SERIOUSLY INJURED IN ENEMY ACTION **STOP** NOT EXPECTED TO SURVIVE **STOP**.

She looked over at her cousin, her face distraught. "Oh Helen," she said, her voice low and deep. "I am so sorry."

Helen Randolph looked up at her cousin, her face white and her eyes brimming with tears. "Hilda, I...."

Hilda Annersley crossed the intervening space quickly, sitting beside Helen she held her arms out. Helen moved into her cousin's embrace, sobbing, her head resting on Hilda's shoulder. Hilda Annersley stroked Helen's brown hair, murmuring soft words of support.

Helen lay there for some minutes, drawing support from her cousin, eventually she sat up. Making an effort she stopped crying and faced Hilda. "Thank you Hilda," she said, a little shakily, "but I cannot stay here crying, I have things to do."

"What things?" Hilda Annersley looked a little surprised at Helen's determination.

Helen swallowed and used her handkerchief to clear up some of the ravages of her outburst. "I must go to the school, tell Nell about her father." Helen's brown eyes darkened at the thought. "Then we must go to Andrew."

Miss Annersley looked puzzled. "But I thought your husband's unit was in Italy?" she said quickly.

Helen shook her head. "His unit was transferred back to Britain just after Christmas," she said quickly. "They are stationed somewhere on the Kent coast." She smiled very slightly at her cousin. "I'm not supposed to know that," she confessed, "but Edgar found out for me." She stopped and bit her lip; "I'll have to let Edgar know, he and Andrew are such good friends."

"Don't worry about that now, Helen," Hilda replied quickly. "We must go and fetch Nell, we'll also need to discover where they will have taken Andrew. If it's somewhere in Kent we'll need to arrange transport."

Helen nodded. "Of course," she said, a little faintly. There was a discreet knock at the door and Mrs Sutton entered carrying a small tray. On the tray was a small decanter of brandy and two glasses.

"I thought maybe you'd want a glass, Mrs Randolph," the Housekeeper said softly, "for your health and the shock, like."

Helen Randolph smiled slightly, "That's very kind of you,

Mrs Sutton, thank you."

The cousins sat for a short while, sipping the spirit, Miss Annersley thought deeply, it was unlikely that, with the build up for the invasion occurring along the entire Southern coast of England, that Helen would just be able to blithely travel to the hospital. She would need to obtain some form of pass or warrant to allow her to go to Andrew. Hilda could think of only two possibilities, one of whom, Edgar Mordaunt, was in Canada and therefore too far away, she turned to Helen.

"We'll need permission to travel to Kent, Helen," she said softly, "I'll get in touch with Jem Russell, he has the contacts to be able to arrange something, I'm sure. I'll come with you, at least to collect Nell."

"Thank you Hilda, I'd appreciate that."

The next few hours seemed to pass extremely quickly; Hilda was able to speak to Madge Russell, as Jem was travelling back from a conference in London. Madge promised that the doctor would arrange things as quickly as possible.

"Although he may only be able to arrange for Helen and her daughter to travel, Hilda," Lady Russell's warm tones continued over the wire, "I'm not sure if the Air Ministry would consider a cousin had need to be at the bedside."

"That's not a problem, Madge," Hilda returned promptly, "I don't need to be there, Helen does!"

A car arrived to take the two women to the station, Helen deciding that the news was too devastating for Nell to learn on the telephone. They reserved a First Class Compartment for themselves and settled down for the three-hour journey. On the train the two women sat in silence, Helen, dry eyed and drawn, staring out of the window for a while. Hilda kept a close watch upon her, concerned. When she saw a solitary tear start to fall, she reached across and placed an arm around her cousin's shoulders.

"Helen," she said softly, "You are allowed to be upset."

Helen shook her head, "No Hilda, I must be strong for Nell's sake, and Andrew's." She tried to shrug off the comforting arm.

"Yes, you must be strong for both of them," Hilda agreed, and her voice pierced through the other woman's defensive shell, "But they are not here, I am. And I can be strong for you."

There was a short pause before Helen nodded slightly then allowed herself to cry in her cousin's comforting arms...

By the time they reached Nell's boarding school it was starting to get dark; the drive from the station was made in silence, Helen preparing herself for her daughter's pain. Hilda Annersley looked with some interest at the first views of the school. She saw a building that had obviously once been a stately home, surrounded by trees, and with copious grounds at the rear and to the sides. If anything the house was larger than Plas Howells was, but this was only to be expected, the Chalet School had not yet returned to the numbers it had enjoyed just before its exile from Austria. As the two women were shown inside a bell rang out and Hilda estimated it to be the beginning of Evening Prep.

The two women were shown into a small sitting room and asked to wait, a short time later the door opened and another woman appeared.

"Good evening, ladies, I am Miss Glover, I am the Senior Mistress. I understand that you asked to see the Headmistress, Miss Dawson, on an urgent matter? I'm very sorry but she is away at the moment, I do not expect her back until tomorrow night at the earliest." The Senior Mistress was a sharply dressed young woman, she had a slight impatient frown on her face.

Helen stood up, "My name is Mrs Randolph," she began quietly, "I have come to take my daughter Nell out of school. I received word today that my husband has been seriously injured. We must go to him."

Miss Glover nodded, sympathetically, "I'm sorry for your news, Mrs Randolph, however I'm afraid I cannot allow any of the students to leave the school without Miss Dawson's permission. She will be back tomorrow night."

Helen looked somewhat shocked, "Miss Glover, my husband has been seriously hurt, time is of the essence. I cannot afford to wait another twenty-four hours."

"Nevertheless, Mrs Randolph, that is the situation," Miss Glover's voice was implacable. "These girls are placed in the school's care, I do not have the authority to allow one to leave in term time, regardless of the reason!"

Helen looked dumbfounded and was unable to speak, on seeing this Miss Annersley decided to intervene. "Helen, take a seat, you're exhausted," she said softly but commandingly. "I will speak to Miss Glover."

Miss Annersley saw her cousin seated with a cup of tea before moving across to face the Senior Mistress. "I should like to speak to you in private, Miss Glover."

Miss Glover looked across and gulped slightly, she nodded and indicated that Miss Annersley follow her outside. She led the way across to a somewhat smaller room; it was obviously the Head's Study. Miss Glover sat behind the desk and indicated that Miss Annersley sit in one of the chairs opposite.

Miss Annersley sat as directed and looked across at the Senior Mistress, she did not see a vindictive or petty-minded woman, rather she saw someone rather unsure of their role but also someone that was basically an honest person. She smiled to herself. "Miss Glover, as I'm sure you have already considered, there may be only a very small amount of time left for Squadron Leader Randolph, his wife and daughter need to move fast if they are to reach him in time to say goodbye."

"I'm sorry, I cannot change my decision..." Miss Glover's response was cut off.

"Miss Glover, you have made no decision here, depending instead on the authority of your Headmistress. Do you think you were given the title of Senior Mistress purely so that you could make no decisions but instead refer everything back to the Head?"

Miss Glover looked angry. "What do you know of my role?" she demanded quickly.

"My name is Hilda Annersley," Hilda responded promptly. "I am Headmistress of a privately owned boarding school, and I have, in the past, also filled the post of Senior Mistress. I therefore am well qualified to speak of your role."

The younger woman looked somewhat taken aback at this information, eventually she managed to ask, "What school?"

"The Chalet School," Miss Annersley replied. "We are currently in Armiford."

"I've heard of it," Miss Glover responded. "I thought it was a foreign school."

Hilda smiled. "No, we were, until the Anschluss, situated in Austria, however it has always been an English school." She paused for a short time, then continued. "I am currently convalescing after a serious road accident, Miss Glover. My Senior Mistress has, for the past ten months, been Headmistress in my stead. She is well able to take decisions and make policies without having to refer to anyone else, myself included. Indeed, if she were not able to do that, she would never have been made my Senior Mistress in the first place."

Miss Glover swallowed slightly. "Perhaps you are different to the normal Headmistress then, Miss Annersley."

"I very much doubt it," Hilda Annersley replied. "Any Head needs to have a Senior Mistress upon whom they can rely to continue their work. Only those with no confidence in themselves, or their Staff, would insist on holding all authority. If your Headmistress were lacking in confidence it would be reflected in the school, and I have heard nothing but good reports about this school." Hilda paused again, looking across at the other woman, "Forgive me, Miss Glover, but I think, in fact, that the one lacking in confidence is not your Headmistress, it is you."

There was silence in the study for a time; Miss Glover's face had flushed slightly with anger at Miss Annersley's words, however Hilda's assessment of her character was correct and her basically honest nature reasserted itself.

"Perhaps you are correct, Miss Annersley," the Senior Mistress admitted very quietly. "I have only held this role for a few months, my predecessor in the post left to become Headmistress at another school. Ever since being told of my promotion I have felt somewhat inadequate, comparing myself to her."

Miss Annersley nodded understandingly. "It is always difficult taking over a post that was previously filled so capably by another. I felt similarly when I was first offered the post of Headmistress. The things that helped me included a Staff Room that fully supported me, a Senior Mistress about whom I had no doubts and a belief in myself." She smiled slightly before continuing. "I'm sure that your Headmistress has faith in you, Miss Glover, she is probably just waiting for you to have faith in yourself."

Another silence, however before it could become oppressive the Senior Mistress lifted her head. "Thank you, Miss Annersley," she said quietly, "with reference to Mrs Randolph's request, I have reconsidered. I will send someone to fetch Nell now, she may leave with her mother immediately."

"Thank you Miss Glover."

The Senior Mistress spoke to someone on the telephone and, after only a short time, there was a knock on the study door and a young girl appeared.

"You wanted to see me, Miss Glover?" the girl asked.

"I did, Nell, there is someone here to see you," Miss Glover indicated Miss Annersley.

Miss Annersley looked across at Nell Randolph with interest; she saw a girl of eleven or twelve, tall for her age and slim. She had the same warm brown eyes as Helen. The girl was looking at Miss Annersley with polite incomprehension.

"I'm Hilda," Miss Annersley said softly. "I've been staying with your mother for the past six months, but we haven't managed to see each other," she smiled warmly at the girl.

Nell smiled back, "Mummy's cousin?" she asked. "I remember, is mummy all right?"

Miss Annersley stood and walked over to Nell, she placed an arm around her shoulders. "Mummy is here to see you, Nell," she began. "She has something she wants to tell you, it's very important." She guided the girl out of the study and across to the room where Helen Randolph waited. Opening the door she gently pushed Nell in while speaking to Helen. "Nell's here Helen."

As she closed the door on the mother and daughter, Hilda saw that Helen had moved across to take Nell into her arms before tenderly pulling her over to the sofa.

The journey back to the Randolph house in Chepstow was taken almost in silence, Nell Randolph, crying piteously, clung to her mother the entire time. Helen spent the whole journey trying to sooth her daughter, holding her close. It was left to Hilda to arrange transport to and from the station and onto the train. In the midst of the tragedy she did feel a very minor sense of triumph that she was able to do this without difficulty; aware that only a month ago it would have been impossible, and aware that this was further evidence of her return to good health.

Back at the house, Nell was given a light meal before Helen helped her to bed, sitting beside her for a long time to ensure that she slept. There was a telephone message for Hilda Annersley and she rang up the Round House to speak to Jem.

"Squadron Leader Randolph is being looked after in Farnborough Hospital, that's Farnborough, Kent, Hilda," Sir James began. "I have managed to arrange for two warrants for travel, for your cousin and her daughter, they will be delivered first thing tomorrow. I'm sorry, the authorities would not countenance a third for you."

"That's not a problem, Jem, Helen and Nell are the important ones," Miss Annersley responded. "Thank you so much for arranging things."

"You're welcome, Hilda, must look after our staff!" Jem Russell's voice was mildly amused. "I did take the liberty of asking after the Squadron Leader, although I know you will not approve!"

"In this case, Jem, I think I can accept the need!" Hilda's eyes reflected her amusement at the doctor's obvious discomfiture about the incidence of patient confidentiality affecting Hilda the previous year. "Please tell me of Andrew Randolph's prognosis."

Jem Russell sighed. "I couldn't find out much, Hilda, but what news there was," he paused for a moment before continuing. "It wasn't good. It may take a few months Hilda, but you should tell your cousin she needs to prepare herself and her daughter for the worst."

Hilda swallowed slightly, "I'll do that, Jem, and thank you again." She rang off. Taking a deep breath she rose to join Helen in the sitting room.

The following morning, after the delivery of the travel warrants, Hilda helped Helen by arranging transport to and accommodation in Farnborough. She also helped them to pack cases for a short stay. Initially Helen had wanted to pack more but, on discussion, the cousins felt that it was more sensible to pack and leave quickly, so as to reach Andrew, rather than take time to pack more belongings. Hilda assured Helen that she was perfectly capable of arranging for a trunk to be packed and sent on. Nell was still very tearful and clingy and Helen felt that the sooner they began their journey the better.

Just before Helen and Nell left, Hilda had an opportunity to speak to her cousin. "Helen, I'll not keep you, I know you have a train to catch. Two things, firstly, don't worry about anything here; I'm more than fit enough to deal with the household. Let me know, when you're able, about your plans and I'll make arrangements accordingly." Hilda looked across at Helen before pulling her closer, speaking very quietly and intensely she continued. "And secondly, and far more importantly, whatever the situation when you reach Andrew, however bad the news, remember that you are not alone. God will be there for you; He will help you and guide you. Even if it is the worst news imaginable, He can help. Just don't forget to ask Him, and use His support." Hilda Annersley's voice reflected her own deep faith as she spoke.

Helen smiled slightly. "Thank you Hilda, I know I can call on God, and I know He will send help. After all, He ensured that you were here." She shrugged slightly. "If Andrew is to be taken from me well, I can only think it's because God wants him. Not a great deal of comfort for either myself or Nell, but perhaps it will help a little." She hugged her cousin for a short time before sadly making her way to the car.

Hilda watched until the car was out of sight, before returning to the house.

CHAPTER SIXTEEN

CO-HEADS

Dear Hilda,

Well we have been in to see Andrew at last. I couldn't believe the time it took to be allowed access. The hospital itself seems fairly Victorian but it has all the most modern accoutrements. Andrew is in a small ward attached to the orthopaedic ward. He is badly injured and in some pain, however he was well enough that Nell and I could visit. Luckily he was able to recognise us and speak to both of us intelligibly—I understand that is not always the case with those suffering such extensive injuries.

Oh Hilda, I had such high hopes, when I first entered the hospital. But on seeing poor Andrew's broken body, I can only hope for a quick release. I have spoken to his doctors, they try to give me hope but I'm afraid there is little chance. I will remain with Andrew until the end. I will keep Nell here until Easter, but then will send her back to school—the Senior Mistress, Miss Glover, has written and said she will be more than happy to provide Nell with an escort—apparently she has family in Kent. I'm glad Nell has had the chance to see her father, and glad for Andrew—he was so moved at seeing Nell. However I do not want her last memories of her father to be those of him dying, so she will return for the summer term.

I've been in contact with Edgar; he'll be flying over in June and, if Andrew has passed on, plans to take us back with him to Canada for the summer. I'll write later about my plans for the house, but please continue to stay there until you return to your School—I know that you do not have a home of your own, so please use mine.

Thank you so much for your last letter and for all the kindness and support, it really means a lot to me. I'll contact you as soon as I have news.

Love Helen.

Miss Annersley sighed after reading the letter from her cousin, she knew that Helen had prayed for a miracle, and, she had to confess, she had as well, despite the information from Jem Russell as to Andrew Randolph's condition. It was almost two weeks since the news had first reached Helen of her husband's fate and she had been in Kent nearly all that time. Hilda placed the letter to one side, intending to write back later that day, turning to the next letter she suffered a minor shock when she noted that it was from the War Office, however she quickly repressed the feeling whilst using a paper knife to open the envelope.

Dear Miss Annersley.

I refer to our conversations of January this year, in which you had consented to appear as a witness in the event of the capture and trial of Rudi Bhaer. I beg to inform you that we have received evidence confirming that Sturmbahnfuhrer Bhaer was killed by the French Resistance in February 1944. This was as a direct response to atrocities carried out by his order earlier in the year.

My thanks for your time and willingness to stand as witness, however it appears that though Rudi Bhaer will be facing a Judge, it will not be an Earthly one.

May God have mercy on his soul.

Yours sincerely
 Arthur Jackson (Colonel)

War Crimes Commission

"It's likely He is the only one that will!" Miss Annersley thought grimly, she looked up as Mrs Sutton entered the dining room.

"I've finished here, Mrs Sutton," she said, smiling. "Annie may clear the breakfast things."

"Very well, Miss Annersley," the Housekeeper smiled. "Oh and I thought you should know that Annie has received her call-up papers. She'll be off the middle of May."

Miss Annersley considered. "Will that leave you very short handed, Mrs Sutton?" she asked.

"It will, somewhat," Mrs Sutton hesitated. "Miss Annersley, Mrs Randolph wrote to me, she plans to stay with Squadron Leader Randolph, doesn't she?"

"She does, Andrew Randolph is very ill." Hilda wondered exactly how much information Helen had given Mrs Sutton.

The Housekeeper nodded. "She said the Master was dying, Miss Annersley," Mrs Sutton said softly, "but that it might be a couple of months. If I may ask, how long will you be staying here?"

Miss Annersley thought for a moment. "I hope to return to the School for the beginning of next term, that's April 24th, a month from now, although that does rather depend on my receiving the 'All Clear' from my consultant!"

Mrs Sutton nodded. "Well ma'am, if Mrs Randolph has not returned by then, it may be as well to shut the place up—the Cook is talking of retiring soon anyway, and I've been thinking of moving in with my daughter in Winchester."

"I'm writing to Mrs Randolph today, I'll mention your proposal, Mrs Sutton."

* * *

"This is the Chalet School, Miss Wilson, Headmistress, speaking."

"Hello Miss Wilson, Headmistress!"

"Hilda! How good to hear from you again, I was just wondering why I'd not received a reply to my last letter." Miss

Wilson spoke warmly.

"I thought it would be quicker to call, Nell," Hilda Annersley replied. "You're not too busy to talk are you?"

"Never too busy when it's you, Hilda." Miss Wilson turned her back resolutely on the many letters and essays requiring her attention. "How are you, my dear?"

"I'm well, the only thing I'm waiting for now is an appointment with my consultant to give me permission to return to work. I should hear from his secretary any day."

"Excellent, so you'll be returning next term? We'll have to get together so I can hand over properly."

"That's part of the reason I rang, Nell," Hilda replied. "I wondered if you'd like to spend part of the Easter break here? I'm going to ask Madge and Joey if they'd like to come down, probably on the Monday, but thought you might like to spend a few days."

Nell Wilson thought for a moment. "I'd love to, Hilda, I'll come down Maundy Thursday and stay the entire weekend, if I may. It'll give me a chance to update you on everything that's been happening at the school."

"Excellent, I'll look forward to it." Hilda Annersley hesitated before continuing. "Confidentially, Nell, I must admit to some feelings of concern about my return. After all, I will have been away from the post for more than a year, and, apart from some one-to-one tutoring, have not taught during that period. I do wonder if my injury has affected my abilities and have no way of knowing until I actually stand in front of a class." Her voice became even quieter as she continued, "On occasion I also wonder if the girls will even remember me—a year is a long time for that age group!" She finished with a slight laugh, however this did not fool her friend who responded immediately.

"Hilda Annersley, what do you mean having worries about teaching and the girls? Teaching is ingrained in you, my dear, you could no more stop teaching, than Canute could stop the waves! And as for the girls forgetting you—I fancy that your reception the day you return will convince you otherwise—have you forgotten how they mobbed you before Christmas?" Nell

Wilson ended with a smile in her voice.

"True, but it will be a further four months since then..."

"Means nothing, my dear, only yesterday I heard one of the little lambs, Bride I think, explaining to Tom Gay that the School had two Heads. They've not forgotten you!"

* * *

Easter was spent quietly, Miss Wilson arriving early in the afternoon of Maundy Thursday. The two women were alone, Helen deciding to remain in Kent to be close to Andrew. She did ring and speak to Hilda on the Saturday before, Andrew had appeared to stabilise and it was thought that he would remain fairly well over Easter. Helen told Hilda that, once the holiday was over, Nell would be returning to school while she, Helen, would be able to devote more time to nursing her husband.

Madge and Joey were arriving on the Easter Monday; neither of them were bringing any children with them, both their youngest was able to be left in the capable hands respectively of Rosa and Anna. They would both stay overnight.

During lunch on the Sunday the two friends were discussing some of the administrative changes that had occurred over the last year. Miss Wilson detailing any changes she felt Miss Annersley needed to know.

"It'll really be easier for me to show you when you return Hilda, that way you'll be able to make an informed decision on whether you want to keep the changes or revert back to the way you are used to doing things." Nell Wilson smiled. "After all, everyone works differently, you may not like the changes!"

Hilda Annersley did not smile, instead thinking deeply, she stared into space.

"Hilda? Are you all right?" Nell Wilson sounded a little worried.

Hilda shook herself slightly and smiled. "I'm fine," she said quickly. "Though I am rather concerned about the effect my return will have on you, my dear. I know that Madge has made you Headmistress during my absence, effectively making us Co-Heads as, to my knowledge, she has not revoked my title! I believe though that she intends that you revert to Senior Mistress once I return and that seems to me to be very unfair." Hilda stopped to look across at her friend before continuing, "Nell, have you thought of applying elsewhere as Headmistress? You would qualify easily and, though I would hate to see you go it would at least ensure that you receive proper acknowledgement for your hard work and seniority."

Nell Wilson looked across in astonishment. "Are you trying to get rid of me? Now really my dear, I'm not planning on leaving the Chalet School even if they reduce me to the most junior mistress!" Nell smiled fondly across at her friend. "Hilda, my love, I only ever took the post of Headmistress on a temporary basis — I always knew that, once you returned, I would be handing it back. And I'd far rather be your Senior Mistress than the Head at Roedean itself!"

* * *

Madge Russell and Joey Maynard arrived on Easter Monday a little before lunch and the four spent an enjoyable afternoon and evening, reminiscing and remembering. It was noticed and remarked upon by everyone that Hilda Annersley had obviously fully recovered.

"Was it so obvious before then, that I was not well?" she asked, intrigued.

Joey nodded. "It was, Hilda, when we saw you just before Christmas, you had a definite hesitancy to your speech. It was almost as though you had to think out each word before you said it." She smiled, her black eyes projecting empathy and warmth. "I don't think I appreciated until then, just how ill you had been. The fact that eight months later you were still 'not right' suddenly showed me how you had suffered."

"I see," Hilda said thoughtfully. "I had no idea that I appeared so unwell even then." She turned to Nell Wilson. "I can understand your concerns at Christmas now," she smiled. "What about now?"

Joey laughed, "Now, Hilda, I am somewhat concerned at how much you resemble your earlier self, during your first term at the Chalet School. I find myself reverting to the sickening Middle of almost eleven years ago!"

Everyone laughed, then Madge turned to Hilda. "Have you heard from the hospital yet, Hilda? I understand you are awaiting a final appointment with your Consultant."

Hilda walked over to the desk and retrieved a letter, she passed it across to her employer.

> *Dear Miss Annersley*
>
> *With reference to your request for a consultation with Mr Roberts, Neurosurgical Consultant, I beg to inform you that it will not be possible to book an appointment until early May. Mr Roberts will be on leave for Easter and does not return until the 10th. I can book you an appointment for first thing that day if you wish.*
>
> *Yours sincerely*
>
> *Phyllis Hunter*
> *Mr Roberts' Secretary*

Madge looked across. "You'll miss the beginning of term then." She sounded apologetic.

Hilda smiled. "After more than a year away, what are a few more days?" She walked over to resume her seat next to Nell on the sofa. "I will admit, though, that my imminent return, was the main reason I asked if all of you could visit."

"You mean it wasn't just delight in our company?" Nell smiled, "Then what was your reason?"

"You!" returned her friend. "After all, Nell, you have been running the school for the past year. I know you have no problems with me returning, but I cannot help feeling that expecting you to revert to Senior Mistress is scant thanks for your hard work for the last twelve months."

"Yes, I've been running the school, Hilda." Nell's reply was swift. "And, though I say so myself, I think I've done well. But it's not something I'd choose to do. I can understand now why you were overworking that term before the accident—the amount of administration necessary is almost overpowering. I wonder how you managed to keep teaching so many classes; because I've found I've had to reduce the number I take."

Hilda nodded. "I know, it was something I'd been meaning to speak to Madge about." She smiled ruefully before continuing, "In fact I'd planned to do so during the Easter Holidays." She paused, before adding, "Easter last year that is! Unfortunately something else came up."

Madge, Joey and Nell all laughed at her allusion to the accident.

"What I'd wanted to discuss, Madge, was that it might have been necessary for me to reduce the amount of actual teaching I did, because of the administrative side of being Head."

"Is that what you want, Hilda?" Madge Russell sounded surprised.

Hilda shook her head. "No, the last thing I want to do is give up teaching. But until the accident I could see no other solution. I can now." She smiled across at Nell. "If Madge agrees, Nell, how would you like us to be joint Heads?"

"Joint Heads? You mean we'd share the duties?" Nell Wilson sounded intrigued.

"Something like that," replied her friend. "We can arrange details later, but it would mean dividing the administrative tasks between us, everything from interviewing staff, both teaching and domestic, to being responsible for payment of bills and services. In short, the school would have two Heads, either of whom could perform any of the duties of Headmistress."

"Wouldn't that be the same as having a Senior Mistress, though?" This from Joey, the only one of the quartet that had not ever run the school.

All three of the others shook their heads, Nell Wilson answered, "No, Joey, as Senior Mistress your main focus is on the teaching staff, oh you may deputise for the Head for short absences, but you rarely run into the sheer weight of the administrative work until you have to fill in for weeks on end. As I discovered last year once we'd disposed of, I mean, said goodbye to Miss Bubb."

"And as I discovered, all those years ago, when Therese became ill at half term. The first term you helped teach, Joey," Hilda put in gently. She glanced across at her friend, sure there was something odd about the departure of the temporary headmistress, Miss Bubb, however Madge was speaking and she turned to listen.

"In a way, it's a return to the situation when I was Head," Madge said thoughtfully. "Therese Lepattre, as a partner in the School, was never Senior Mistress, that was Mollie Maynard, Therese shared the administrative load," Madge laughed slightly. "Yet both she, and you, Hilda, had to manage alone." The owner of the Chalet School looked across at the two women sat on the sofa, noting that both Hilda and Nell seemed extremely keen on the idea. "I've no objection," she smiled. "I think it's an excellent idea, quite apart from anything else it will mean that should either of you have to take time off we will not be left in a similar situation to last year. One of you will have to be senior though, in case of any disagreement."

"No problem there," Nell Wilson returned. "Hilda should have the final say," she smiled at her friend. "After all, as far as the girls are concerned, 'The Abbess' has always been senior to 'Bill'!"

Later that evening, in an effort to ensure that Hilda had all pertinent knowledge about the school, her three friends took it in turns to relate different stories of things that had happened during the last term. Madge had already spoken of her niece, Daisy Venables' adventures in a sudden blizzard, while Joey had spoken of the Sale itself. Then Nell elected to tell Hilda of a rather less well-known incident, involving herself, Madge, Matron Lloyd, Jeanne de Lachenais and a new girl Tom Gay.

Nell had related how young Tom, believing she was catching burglars, had contrived to imprison her Headmistress, the owner of the school, the Senior Languages Mistress and Matron, in a very cold, draughty store room.

"Where, let me tell you, we would have stayed all night, had it not been for Hilary Burn and a loose catch on her door!" Nell ended indignantly. She stopped and looked across at her friend, Hilda was laughing so hard that tears were running down her cheeks, while Madge and Joey were trying, feebly, to support each other. Nell Wilson affected to be insulted by this.

"Will you stop that infernal giggling Hilda Annersley? It could have happened to anyone. It's not my fault one of our girls decides to search for burglars. If you'd not injured yourself then you would have been a prisoner too!"

Miss Annersley stopped laughing long enough to retort, "Oh no, never! That sort of thing never happens to me. As far as the Chalet School is concerned, I'm the one that has to deal with the aftermath of any alarms and excursions! You attract these things—like Joey abusing you at camp and then leaping on top of you during the sale!"

"Slander!" Joey cried. "I did not know it was Bill when I was down that pit! Why doesn't anyone ever believe me?" she added plaintively.

"Probably because it's just the sort of thing you would have done, Joey," laughed Madge Russell. "By the way, Nell, I thought you were adamant that Joey not be told about this episode? I seem to remember you saying something of the sort to Hilary Burn."

"I was," replied Miss Wilson, "but I thought Hilda needed to know what had been going on in her school."

"Not my school Nell," Hilda pointed out, "Madge's."

"Oh, I think it's your school as well," Madge replied. "You may not have been there right at the beginning but both of you," her gaze swept both Hilda and Nell, "are an integral part of the school now. I can't even envisage the Chalet School without the pair of you."

Hilda and Nell glanced at one another quickly, "Thanks for that Madge," Nell said gruffly, Hilda said nothing but her eyes glowed.

CHAPTER SEVENTEEN

THE RETURN

At the window of the Round House, the Russell's family home, Joey Maynard waited impatiently, eventually her watch was rewarded as a taxi cab appeared and drew up outside the house. She turned to the other inhabitant of the room. "She's here, you'd better contact Nell."

Madge Russell nodded and moved to the telephone, Joey, tired of waiting, went to open the door before Rosa could get there. "Hilda, finally! What an age you've been. I thought you'd never get here!" Joey's beautiful voice rang out as Hilda Annersley stepped from the car.

Hilda looked up, laughing. "Joey, it's not my fault if the trains were delayed from Exeter."

"No but you could at least have called and warned us. Now, spill, what did your doctor say?"

"Let the poor woman get indoors first Joey," Madge laughed. "Hilda, I'm sure you could do with a coffee, come on in, travelling can be very tiring, especially if you have had delays."

A little later the three women were sitting in Madge Russell's drawing room, drinking coffee. Joey drained her cup. "Enough of this, I've been patient, now, Hilda please tell!"

Miss Annersley made to reply but was interrupted by a knock at the door, seconds later Nell Wilson erupted into the room.

"I'll have you know I've just left the Fourth on their own, not for Science of course, but even so they are not the safest of ages to leave! It's a good thing that my leg has healed so well; otherwise I'd never have been able to cycle here so quickly.

I have two minutes, no more." She turned to her friend, "Well? Have you been given the 'all clear'?"

Hilda smiled around at her three friends before taking pity on them. "I saw Mr Roberts for only a few minutes today, he has discharged me totally from his care." She paused and then added, "And I have his permission to return to full time work effective immediately!"

She laughed as the other three women cheered.

"Wonderful, now I must fly!" Nell began, "You'll be back today, won't you? Can I tell the rest of the staff?"

Miss Annersley looked at her friend with dancing eyes. "I'm sure you 'can' tell the staff, Nell, but if you're asking if you may..." She stopped there and her face split into a wide grin.

Nell Wilson looked around at the two sisters, both Madge and Joey were quietly convulsing with laughter. "Now I know she's back," she said to them both, her face deadpan. "I've really missed having my English corrected by you, Hilda Annersley! I'll see you later," she added darkly, "and I'll tell the staff!" She grinned and headed for the door.

"Don't let the girls know, Bill." Joey managed to gasp between waves of laughing, "I've had a beautiful idea on how to re-introduce their Headmistress to them!"

Bill nodded and swept out.

"What's this idea Joey?" Hilda Annersley looked with suspicion on her ex-pupil. "I hope it's not too outlandish—after all, it's been over a year since I was last at the school officially, I'm not even sure if they'll welcome me!"

"That's rubbish, Hilda, and you know it!" returned Joey.

Madge looked across at her younger sister. "Nothing too drastic, Joey," she warned, laughingly.

"Trust me! Now you'll excuse me for a minute, Jack and Jem wanted to know as soon as we had news. I'll contact them if I may?" she asked of Madge. Madge nodded permission and Joey disappeared to the telephone.

Hilda looked across at her employer; Lady Russell had barely changed from the first time they had met, more than eleven years ago.

"What are you thinking, Hilda?" Madge asked gently.

Hilda smiled. "Remembering the first time we met, Madge, when you interviewed me for the post of English Mistress. Had I known then just how lucky I would be." She paused for a moment, then, "I owe you a great deal, Madge," she said softly. "There are not many employers that would not only hold a post open for more than a year, but continue to forward my salary for all of that time. I am very grateful."

Madge Russell smiled and reached across to clasp one of Hilda's hands. "Do you have no idea of your worth, Hilda? I would have held your post and continued paying you for twice as long, if it meant that, eventually, you would return to us."

Hilda flushed slightly with pleasure at the words and Madge smiled again. "Now, come along, we must find out all that Joey has planned. She is too close to her own schooldays—I don't trust her!"

Joey Maynard, when cornered by both her sister and Hilda Annersley, had proposed only that Hilda should not be seen by the girls until Evening Prayers.

"Quite apart from anything else, Hilda, they'll not be able to work once they know that you're back," she said, her black eyes twinkling. "They are all sure to want to speak to you."

Hilda laughed and agreed that, if their reaction was anything like the one after the Christmas Play, it might be as well for her to return after the normal lessons for the day. She stayed with Madge and Joey for lunch and then, during the afternoon, while the girls were all resting, was taken back to the School and into the Staff Room.

When Miss Wilson had led her friend into the Staff Room, Miss Annersley had, for a moment, felt unaccountably shy. Although she had seen the majority of the Staff for visits during her year recuperating, and had corresponded with many of them, this was the first time she had seen all the Staff together since the last day of the Easter term 1943, more than 13 months before. Obviously, during her time away, the Staff had given their loyalty to Nell Wilson and, just for a split second, Hilda Annersley had doubts about her own abilities. As she reached the door though she shook herself slightly and presented her normal, calm demeanour. Nell Wilson looked across and smiled as she opened the door.

Inside the staff had been vociferous in welcoming back their chief. Seated in the most comfortable chair in the centre of the room, with a cup of Jeanne de Lachennais' coffee and some biscuits by her side, Miss Annersley laughed as all the staff tried to speak at once, drowning each other out in their enthusiasm.

"Ladies, one at a time!" she protested, at her words the noise abated. Miss Annersley looked round with twinkling eyes. "I don't know," she began, a look of dismay upon her face, "when I was last here I understood that all the staff were gentlewomen, what influence has caused this change in behaviour?"

There was silence for a time as all turned to view Miss Wilson, she, in her turn burst out laughing; the rest of the Staff Room joined her.

During that afternoon, the girls attending school could have been forgiven for wondering what had suddenly caused almost all the Mistresses to become inattentive. Indeed some of them passed over behaviour that, on another day, would have brought serious trouble down on the perpetrators. It was also amazing just how many classes were given work for the lesson because their mistress has business to attend to in the Staff Room! Had they been able to see into the Staff Room all would have been explained.

Later that afternoon Beth Chester, the Head Girl, had a visitor. "Oh Beth?" Beth looked up to see Miss Dene, the School Secretary, at the door of the Prefects' Room.

"Yes Miss Dene."

"Please ensure that the entire school is collected together in Hall before Evening Prayers, Catholics too. The Head has an announcement." Miss Dene disappeared before any questions could be asked.

The Head Girl quickly rounded up her Prefects and informed them of her instructions.

"Can't see what it is that Bill's got to say that couldn't wait until after Prayers," grumbled Gwensi Howells. She turned to the third member of the Triumvirate. "Daisy you were at home lunch time, did Jo say anything?"

Daisy shook her head. "She wasn't in, she'd been called over to Auntie Madge's, left the Trips with Anna and just taken Stephen with her."

"It's very unusual," Jacynth Hardy said in her soft voice, "if Bill wanted to speak to us why couldn't it wait until after Prayers? We always join up again for any notices."

"Most strange, but we'll not find out just sitting here. We'd better get going," Beth continued. "Come on!"

The hall was full; all the girls were in their places being watched over by the Prefects. Strangely not a single member of staff was available and the girls were taking advantage of this fact to chatter softly to each other. Daisy frowned at some Middles to hush them and then caught movement from the stage at the front of the hall.

To the Chalet girls' surprise all the staff appeared on the dais including Miss Wilson, who, instead of making her way to the lectern, stood to one side. It was clear that the staff were excited about something and the girls watched eagerly. A further two figures appeared and the noise from the girls rose as they recognised both Lady Russell and Joey Maynard.

Then a final figure appeared, tall and slim, with brown, wavy hair and blue-grey eyes, dressed in her MA gown and hood. At sight of her the entire hall was suddenly, eerily, quiet, and then in a shout that (her friends were quick to remind her about later) took her back to her days as a Middle. Beth Chester leapt to her feet crying, "Oh, it's the Abbess! She's back! How simply smashing!"

Her words suddenly released everyone else in the hall and the entire school rose to its feet clapping and cheering. Far from attempting to stop the noise the Prefects as one body were adding to it. Everyone in the hall was up welcoming their Headmistress.

For her part Miss Annersley was trying, without success, to quell the noise, while simultaneously both blushing and laughing at her welcome. Turning to look behind her, she saw that all the Staff, Mrs Maynard and Lady Russell were standing and adding their own applause.

Miss Wilson stepped up to call into her ear. "I don't think your poor head could have coped with this last term!"

Miss Annersley laughed and called back, "Not even last week!"

Eventually, taking pity on the Head, Rosalie Dene slipped out of the Hall and, minutes later; the sound of the School bell rang out. The School slowly fell silent.

Miss Annersley looked around, still laughing, with shining eyes, "Thank you all," she said, her rich low voice carrying to the back of the hall. "As you can see, I have returned," she laughed as again a wave of cheering started then raised her hand and the room fell silent.

"For those of you who are new girls my name is Miss Annersley and I am Headmistress of the Chalet School; I have been away for the past year recovering from a bad road accident. I'm pleased to say I am now fully recovered. I hope to meet all of you in the next few days, either for the first time or to renew old acquaintances.

"There are no notices today so we will continue with Prayers. If those of you who are Catholic will file out to the inner drawing room, my Co-Head, Miss Wilson, will join you. Before you go I should like to thank all of you for your Prayers when I was lying seriously injured."

The Catholics filed out quietly, as they did Madge Russell joined Miss Annersley in the centre. "Well Hilda," she said softly, "I don't think you can have any doubts now about your welcome, can you?"

The Headmistress of the Chalet School smiled.

POSTSCRIPT

Later that evening Miss Dene, School Secretary, appeared at the Heads' Study holding a telegram.

"This has just been delivered," she began. "There's no name on it, just a title."

Both Miss Annersley, standing looking out of the window, and Miss Wilson, currently on her knees in front of a filing cabinet, looked up.

"Give it here Rosalie, we'll sort it out," ordered Bill. She swiftly read through the telegram then got to her feet. Walking over to her friend, she passed it over saying, "This is most definitely for you, Hilda."

Hilda Annersley read the telegram....

TO THE HEADMISTRESS OF THE CHALET SCHOOL **STOP**.
CONGRATULATIONS AND THANKS **STOP**.
SISTER JAN WETHERALL **STOP**

THE END